I opened ⌐____ ⌐_____ ___ ____ _____ I loved
ask for forgive____ _____
her. Before I could speak, she looked at me. She leaned
close, and I could smell her skin, fresh and clean like the
smell of a just-bathed baby. She kissed me. It was all smell
and touch. The mint of her mouth against mine. Her
hands running over the back of my neck. My fingertips
against the small scar on her left side. Our eyelashes
brushing. Our legs entwining. A sweet odor. Strong,
aggressive. Honeysuckle, I thought. I was delirious.
There on the banks of the pond, where anyone could see.
I whispered, "I love you."

SAVE ME

AFRICA FINE

Genesis Press, Inc.

INDIGO LOVE STORIES

An imprint of Genesis Press, Inc.
Publishing Company

Genesis Press, Inc.
P.O. Box 101
Columbus, MS 39703

ISBN: 13 DIGIT : 978-1-58571-340-0
ISBN: 10 DIGIT : 1-58571-340-6
Manufactured in the United States of America

First Edition

Visit us at www.genesis-press.com
or call at 1-888-Indigo-1-4-0

DEDICATION

For my Grammy, a.k.a. Odessa Osley (1929–1997), for showing me so much love from the moment I was born and truly believing I could do anything I put my mind to.

ACKNOWLEDGMENTS

Thanks to all those who helped make this book into something I can be proud of, including:

Healing the Mind: A History of Psychiatry from Antiquity to the Present by Michael H. Stone helped Ellison decide to specialize in child psychiatry.

Harvard Med: The Story Behind America's Premier Medical School and the Makings of America's Doctors by John Langone for help with details on what Ellison's first year of medical school would have been like.

Lisa Sander's "Diagnosis" column in the New York Times Sunday Magazine for help with problems Ellison faced in his Problem-Based Learning class.

Despite the sources I consulted, this is a work of fiction and as such, there are bound to be differences between what my characters experience and the realities of medical school. The characters, places and events in my novel come from my imagination and are not meant to reflect real people, places and events. I would like also to thank:

Duke University and my friends there, who made my college experience a much happier one than what Ellison found in Durham.

All the musicians and bands mentioned in the book, whose music I listened to and fondly remembered during the writing of the novel. Every song mentioned reminds me of a special time in my life.

My boys (Jeff, Owen, and Parker), for giving me the time, space and encouragement to write.

PROLOGUE

"Go get a switch."

Pop's voice was flat, angry. I wasn't sure what I had done wrong. There were so many indiscretions I could not keep them straight. Don't talk back. Don't leave toys on the floor. Close the screen door. Keep your voice down. Speak up. Be perfect. Don't be a child.

I was eight. I didn't know how to be anything else.

"Go get a switch."

Choose the instrument of your own beating.

It was an art, picking the switch. Come back with a short stick, one without girth or heft, and the length and severity of the punishment would double. Take too long in the choosing, dare to dawdle, and I would be sorry.

There were different bushes to choose from. Avoid the ones with the stinging thorns that rubbed raw the skin of my back. Avoid the ones with too many tiny offshoots that dug into the flesh like fingernails. The ones that were too stiff turned a simple beating into a caning. The ones with too much give lingered over the skin and left welts.

"Go get a switch."

What if I come back with nothing at all? What will Pop do? Will he go get his own switch? Will he use his hands, the handle of a boar-bristle brush, a belt? Is there anything worse? What if I refuse to be beaten? Can he do it if I refuse to sit still? What if I say I haven't done anything wrong? Will he listen to reason?

Once, before my sister left home, I watched Pop whoop her with the end of a brown extension cord. Not the end that goes into the wall, the other one, the side with six holes in a rectangular block. That rectangle left lopsided bruises on her thighs. I don't remember what that beating was for. My sister was sixteen. Maybe she talked to a boy, got a bad grade, wasn't perfect. Maybe she acted like a teenager. I'll bet she didn't know how to be anything else. It seems like she left soon after, leaving me alone with Pop.

I wish I was old enough to leave. I'd join the Marines, or become a singer and start a band. I'd go be something else besides a boy living alone with his Pop. I'd be someone who looked forward to something better than what he has. I'd be someone.

"Go get a switch."

I found one. Not too long. Not too short. No thorns. I pulled the leaves off one by one. I tested the bend. I drew it through the air to hear the whirring sound it would make every time he raised his hand and brought it down again. That was the worst part. The swift buzz of the switch as it neared the skin. The anticipation of pain was just as bad as the pain itself.

There was no choice.

I picked out my switch and took it to Pop.

Years later, when I became a father, I vowed I would never use a switch on my own son. I was going to be a different kind of man. I was going to be a good father. But the baby, Ellison, cried all night and slept just minutes at a time. Nothing I did helped him relax. When it got to the point where he wouldn't eat, we took him to the doctor. Play music, he told us. My wife, she put on Hall and Oates. I was always trying to get her to listen to what I thought of as real music, real soul music, like James Brown, Otis Redding. But she liked her soul blue-eyed.

I was holding Ellison in one arm and I moved to change the record.

"You think this is going to calm him down?"

She just tilted her head, and put a finger over her lips. That's when I heard it. The absence of screeching. By the end of the first song, the baby was asleep on my shoulder.

" 'Sara Smile.' See, he likes Hall and Oates."

I looked down at Ellison. He blew out through his mouth, hiccupped and burrowed deeper into my shoulder.

"I guess I'm the one who's wrong," I whispered. "Play it again."

She reset the record and walked over to me. Up on her toes, she kissed me on the chin. While I held the baby, she swayed around the room and sang along.

—From *Save Me: A Memoir* by Calvin Emory

CHAPTER 1

March 1999

I expected to feel something as I watched the man being cut open. It was an autopsy, and I stood close to the glass separating us from the room. I watched the rough touch of the medical examiner as she prodded and removed, marked and noted. I thought I should feel something for the loss of a human life, though I had not known him. This man was old, and looked like he hadn't cared much for himself while living. He had been found dead in an alley, probably dead of a simple heart attack, but the job here was to make sure. Maybe he had a family. Kids who still mourned him. A wife left alone, too old to date, too young to give up. His face was empty of emotion, his brow smoother than it must have been in life, his eyes closed. I imagined he hadn't time to resist before death sunk in its claws.

The tart odor of disinfectant combined with the musky smell of sweat in the viewing room. I put my nose to my own shoulder to see if the musk came from me, but my body was dry. The dark-haired woman standing next to me wiped beads of sweat from her upper lip. Her bangs stuck to her forehead in damp strips. She blinked at the open chest cavity, then looked right at me as I watched her. I might have been embarrassed to be caught staring, but her gaze went through me. I hoped she would turn the other way when she threw up.

The room itself was ordinary. It looked like a large, open office. There were closed cabinets and shelves filled with books, videos and DVD cases. The walls were white and featured large dry-erase boards that had been wiped clean. Only a flash of stainless steel table here and a curtained-off section there belied the room's purpose. This was where the dead were dissected.

I could not assign any theatrical romance to the process. I suspected some of my classmates wanted to become doctors based solely on television shows they'd seen. There were rumors about a new one in the works, something about crime scene investigators. It all seemed silly to me. The basic reason for an autopsy was to find out how people died in order to aid the living. It was that simple, not romantic. Not dramatic.

I knew something was wrong when I lost my sense of taste. A cheeseburger felt mealy in my mouth, like chewing congealed potting soil. I couldn't feel the carbonation of Coke on my tongue. Jalapeños were like rubber bands in my jaw. Just before the autopsy class, my classmates fasted for fear of vomiting chili dogs onto the examination room floor. I devoured a turkey club with Thousand Island dressing, large fries and a vanilla milkshake. It all congealed on my tongue like wet cotton balls.

My own mother died almost five years ago. She was on a table just like this man after her car was totaled by a drunk driver. Standing there in my advanced anatomy class, I watched a man become nothing more than a collection of parts. I felt nothing. Too many people believe that the worst thing in life is to be hurt. There's so much talk of unbearable pain, whining about physical and emotional hurt as if it could break one's will. We spend so much time and energy trying to avoid getting hurt, or at least, doing what we *think* will help us avoid being hurt. Most of the time, we just end up in a different kind of pain than we had anticipated. The problem is, *feeling* is a part of the human condition, and feeling isn't always a good thing. But we do feel, and that's what reminds us that we are still alive. You might be suffering, but you're still here, and that counts for something.

Pain is what actually pushes us forward. We have to do something to stop the pain—take the drugs, get a divorce, move away. Forward might not be in the right direction, but it's better than doing nothing at all. What worth does life have if there is no motivation, even is that motivation is negative? What's the point?

Having experienced some of the worst emotional pain in the world when my mother died, I know how motivating hurt can be. It reconnected me and my sister Maren with our father, it pushed me to go to Duke so I could be near Maren, it made me want to try as hard as I could to succeed, to honor my mother in some small way. I'm not saying all that is good—by choice, I haven't seen my father in years. I wanted to go to Berkeley, but couldn't leave my sister. I sometimes wonder what it might be like to do something totally unexpected for a career, but my mother wanted me to be a doctor, so I'm going to be a doctor. The main thing is, the pain kept me alive, kept me moving.

Now, numbness is a different thing altogether, a far worse thing. If you can't feel, how do you know you're still alive, and who cares if you're not? When I realized that the pain I'd lived with for years had been replaced by numbness, I knew something was terribly wrong.

When did I become so numb? I used to feel everything, and, now, nothing. Death is an old friend; first my mother, then a few years later, my grandmother. I knew death. Grief is familiar. Maybe this familiarity with death meant that my life no longer meant much.

But there was a person lying there on the table, and that fact deserved at least a small bit of emotion. If not compassion or pity, then perhaps disgust, even anger. More than nothing. The circular saw buzzed on. Time to look at the brain. The sweating, dark-haired girl clapped a hand over her mouth and rushed from the room. The sounds of her vomiting echoed from the hallway.

"Ellison, are you going to be next?" whispered a classmate who was always competing with me to get the best exam grades. He thought of us at rivals. I didn't think of him at all. But he'd just given me a good excuse to leave—I didn't care if he and everyone else believed I couldn't handle the gore.

I excused myself, and made some vague exculpatory motions with my hands. Maybe the professor, who knew me well enough to know that nothing in anatomy class ever made me queasy, would think I was going to help the girl whose name I couldn't remember, or had never known. I walked out of class and got into my BMW, the same one my mother bought me before she died. I drove, expecting to end up on the highway, escaping. That's what I did. When I needed to think, I drove. When I needed to escape, I drove. My car was a refuge, the place where I could turn up the music and feel the world rushing by. Driving was what I did right after I found out my mother died. Since then, driving was the way I felt closest to her.

Our mother died instantly in the crash, and in that moment, my life, as well as my sister Maren's, changed in ways we were still discovering. We moved from our upper middle-class neighborhood in Evanston to live with our father, Calvin, in Durham. We were no longer privileged kids attending an expensive and exclusive private school. We were reunited with a father we hadn't seen in years, a man we didn't know, a man I discovered I didn't even like. Maren's troubles were worse than mine, although I had my share that first year.

Since then, I'd done fine. I was going to one of the best universities in the country. I was poised to get into any medical school I wanted. I would be a success. Not having a mother since I was seventeen wouldn't hold me back. Not on paper, anyway. But I always looked good on paper. It was only recently that I began to think that I wasn't okay at all, that my accomplishments were hollow. It wasn't until I fell in love with Angela, then lost her, that I realized I had nothing, felt nothing.

The thought of it made me want to sleep, all day, all night. But I didn't, because Ellison Emory was an A student. I would graduate with honors. The world expected me to be okay. I gave the world what it wanted.

But as I drove, I thought that maybe I should stop worrying about what the world wanted and try to figure out what it was that I wanted. So I got in my car and drove. But instead of ending up far away from Duke, I found myself just a few miles away from school, sitting in front of what was my grandmother's house before she died. It was where I lived after my mother died. It was where my father now lived alone.

I used my old key. I would not consider the question of why it was still on my key chain. I hadn't set foot in this house in nearly four years, not since I left for college. Maren, before she left for the University of Florida, always came to campus to see me. I would not, could not, share space with my father. When Grandma Esther died, I skipped the wake.

What brought me back today of all days? I suspected that the numbness had begun in this house. Before then, I felt. After I moved here, feeling became a burden I could not bear.

I could hear the keys clacking on his father's typewriter. His office was upstairs, in the back of the house. I suppressed my annoyance that my father used a typewriter. It was 1999. My father was one of maybe five people left in the world who thought it was romantic to use an actual typewriter instead of a computer.

I took the stairs one at a time and knocked on the office door. Just as my knuckles brushed the surface of the door, it occurred to me that this might not be a good idea.

But my father heard the soft sound. The clacking stopped and the door opened.

"Ellison."

I nodded at him. "Calvin."

Calling my father by his first name had begun as a way to show my contempt. Now it was necessary. I didn't think of the man as a real father. We had only known each other during the years since my mother died. Before that, my father was a stranger. Now, I was twenty-two years old, and believed I no longer needed a father. Calvin.

We made our way down to the kitchen. It felt like neutral ground.

Calvin glanced at his watch. I looked at mine, too, a reflex. Maybe our watches would tell us what to do next, how to talk to each other. I didn't think there was any way to bridge the chasm between us. It was too old, too deep. I wasn't even sure if I wanted to be closer to my father. I was just here.

"Want a drink?"

My watch read three-thirty in the afternoon, but I hoped Calvin meant something stronger than iced tea.

Calvin puttered around the kitchen and sat down after he set two mugs of Heineken on the table in front of us.

I nodded at my father and looked around the room. The kitchen had been redone: new appliances, shining white and black floors and white walls, one of which was covered with gleaming copper pots. Plantation shutters on the windows. Expensive. Tasteful. I turned back to Calvin.

"You've made some changes around here."

"Mama would never let me do anything for so many years. It was always *her* house. It never really felt like mine. Not until she was gone." Calvin paused. "That sounds mean, doesn't it? Like I'm glad she's dead."

I shook my head. "It sounds real." In fact, it was the most genuine thing I could remember him ever saying to me.

We sat back, sipping. I appreciated that Calvin didn't ask me why I was here, didn't bring up the past, didn't do anything except sit.

"I walked out of class today. Anatomy."

"Too gross?"

I leaned back and took a long drink to finish the beer.

"No. That was the problem. We watched an autopsy, right there in the viewing room. It wasn't gross. It wasn't hard to watch. I didn't feel a thing."

Calvin paused before responding. "Maybe we watch too much TV. Crime shows, all that. It makes us casual about death. Or . . ."

I looked away.

"Or."

The word hung in the air. It was the closest we came to talking about the numbness that covered me, a clammy, filmy substance that wouldn't rub away.

Calvin nodded as though something had been decided. He pointed at my glass.

"More?" Before I could answer, he was up and pouring.

We sat that way, drinking, saying nothing, listening and watching the afternoon grow into evening. It was companionable, and I tried to remember the last time I sat with my father without arguing. Perhaps never.

"I've got a new book out. The tour starts next week." Calvin's voice was matter-of-fact, but I knew this was important to him. Maren kept me informed of our father's movements whether I wanted to be informed or not. She'd told me about the book, Calvin's third, his first with a major publisher. It would be his first tour, the first time he'd been paid any real money. I looked around the kitchen again and wondered how much longer my father would live here.

"Where are you going?"

Calvin ticked off cities on his fingers: Atlanta, D.C., Baltimore, down to Florida. West Palm Beach, Jacksonville.

"I'm going to stop in Gainesville to see Maren."

I swirled the foamy remains of my beer.

Calvin cleared his throat. "Maybe you should take some time off. Come with me. I could use an assistant."

I looked up at Calvin's mischievous smile. It was March, and I was expecting letters from medical schools. I applied only to the best ones. It did not seem like a good idea to skip out on the second semester of my senior year to follow my father around on a second-rate book tour. I should be studying, preparing, planning. It was just like my father to suggest this. Irresponsible.

Foolish. I stood up, ready to lash out at Calvin, accuse of him of not understanding what it meant to pursue a goal, to get an education, to be where you were supposed to be. But standing over my father, I felt only the numbness. Even righteous indignation escaped me.

"When do we leave?"

I didn't pack much for the trip, just a couple of pairs of jeans, a few T-shirts and one nicer outfit for the actual book signings. I didn't prepare much at all, because preparing would mean thinking, and thinking might cause me to second-guess the most irresponsible thing I'd ever agreed to in my life. Thinking might mean actually talking to someone at Duke, maybe applying for an actual leave. But I reasoned that we would only be gone a couple of weeks. Lots of students were absent from classes a lot longer than that without setting off major alarms. Maybe I would make up something about an illness when I returned.

Calvin, on the other hand, stuffed three bags into the trunk of my BMW. He made a halfhearted offer to drive, but I wanted to feel in control of something. I liked to drive, and I knew my father did not. I made a point of not commenting on his luggage. I stuffed my own duffle bag into the backseat.

About thirty minutes into the trip, I started to think I'd made a mistake.

"So maybe we should talk, you know, get everything out there," Calvin began.

I groaned. "Come on. We haven't seen each other in four years. Let's just leave the past behind us."

Calvin looked over at me. I pretended that I-85 needed my constant visual attention.

"Do you really believe that's possible?"

No. "Yes."

"Dr. Michaels thinks our family spends too much time covering up our emotions," Calvin said. "We need to open up in order to move forward."

I snorted. "I take it Dr. Michaels is your shrink. He doesn't even know us—who made him the expert?"

I had survived my mother's death and the aftermath only by keeping things inside. It was the only way I could function. If I let my emotions loose, I might never regain control. So no analysis for me. I was strong, not weak. I didn't need to talk to a stranger about my feelings.

I told this to Calvin, who frowned. "Maren saw Dr. Michaels after . . . well, you know. It helped her."

I kept my face from showing my surprise. My sister had never told me anything about therapy. I just figured that her relationship with our half-uncle Chris had served as a wake-up call. I frowned, remembering how I caught them in the middle of having sex. I remembered the anger, the guilt I felt for not seeing what was going on right in front of me. That was when I knew I would stay in Durham, go to Duke instead a college far away from my father. It turned out I hadn't needed to go across the country to avoid Calvin. All I needed was to go to a college that was a few miles away but was its own insulated, self-contained world.

I realized my father was waiting for a reply.

"I'm not like you and Maren."

This sounded mean, although I didn't mean it that way. It was the simple truth. They both tried to make everything okay, tried to smooth over life's bumps as if they weren't there.

These days, I couldn't even be bothered to complain about the little things that bothered me. Right before Christmas, a girl I was seeing, barely an acquaintance, really, accused me of being cold before she flounced out of my dorm room. I never had a chance to tell her that what I felt was more like anesthesia than ice.

Calvin sighed. "Look, I don't want to argue with you. But I do think you need to deal with your issues."

How very enlightened of you, I thought.

"Let me worry about *my* issues."

Calvin shook his head. "I worry about you. I'll always worry about you. I'm your father."

I looked at him. "Drop it. Calvin."

Calvin pursed his lips and looked out the window. We didn't speak again until we were halfway through South Carolina.

Calvin on Ellison as a child:

Ellison was always a difficult little boy. He didn't misbehave much, and he always did what he was told. It was more that he had a way of interrogating me about the littlest things. You know how adults give kids an answer just to stop the questions, to shut the kid up? That never worked with Ellison. Any answer I gave inspired follow-up questions. It was like I was always on trial, being cross-examined by a trial lawyer who had never lost a case and had no intention of starting now.

I once tried to slip out the door on a Saturday. I don't know where Vanessa and Maren were, but Ellison appeared in front of me just as I was about to open the door.

"Where are you going?"

I was going to visit the woman I was seeing behind my wife's back, but I couldn't very well admit it to my seven-year-old son.

"I'm going out, Ellison. I'll see you a little later."

He shifted to stand in front of the doorknob just as I reached for it.

"Out where?"

"I have a meeting."

"Why do you have a meeting?"

"It's for work."

"It's Saturday. Nobody works on Saturdays."

"Yes, Ellison, some people do work on Saturdays. What about the people who work at the library and the bookstore? We go there on Saturday sometimes, and people are always working there."

He knitted his eyebrows together. "You don't work at the library or the bookstore."

I sighed. "Ellison, I'll play with you later when I get back. We'll play checkers."

"I don't want to play checkers. Who are you meeting with?"

I was about to make up an answer when Vanessa walked into the room. I suppose she had been playing with Maren, because she held a doll in her hand. She looked at me with the same frown Ellison was giving me.

"Aren't you going to answer the question?" Vanessa asked, her voice deceptively mild.

I looked away. She knew. No matter how hard I tried to hide my dalliances, Vanessa always knew. She waited a moment, then spoke to Ellison.

"Come on, honey. Your father is going to a meeting. I'm sure it's very important to him."

Ellison narrowed his eyes at Vanessa, then at me. He knew I was up to something, too. He just didn't know what. As I left, relief flooded through me. I'd survived the interrogation once again. Sometimes, I dreaded being around my son. He could see through my cheerful act, and I resented him for it.

—From *Save Me: A Memoir* by Calvin Emory

CHAPTER 2

August 1995

When I arrived at Duke, there were decisions to be made. Not about dorm rooms, roommates, or even food—all that was taken care of already. The decisions that I faced were more subtle, choices that I knew from experience would shape my social life for the near, and possibly distant, future. Back when I lived in Evanston, I'd been one of the popular guys. I'd slept with any girl I wanted at my private school. I'd been invited to all the parties given by white kids who felt liberal and rebellious counting a honey-colored black guy among their best friends. But not *too* liberal. I was familiar with the line of thinking that I was not a *real* black person. I was an exception to the rule they saw played out on the eleven o'clock news. I did not live on the south side of Chicago. I did not curse, carry a gun, kill. I was not threatening. In fact, I was whiter in spirit than many of my whitest friends, if white meant straightlaced, responsible and wealthy. My mother was the star anchor of the hottest gossip show in Chicago. When she died, people were whispering rumors about her being the second coming of Oprah. This conveyed a certain social status to me, and with my looks, I managed to glide through most of high school without any of the adolescent scars my sister seemed to collect like stamps.

So I knew about cliques, and I knew what it took to find the right one. The problem was that I no longer cared about social standing, cliques, or popularity. I knew that college would be different than high school, but I suspected that the social habits lasted long past the time when adults should know better. I was soured on the idea of popularity and its value once I moved to Durham. There, I attended a mostly black high school and I'd been an outcast, an Oreo. Not black enough.

At Duke, I just wanted to study and succeed. I wanted to be left alone. But I soon realized that this university—perhaps all universities—was designed to force interaction. The setting denied the loner what he wanted most. It demanded that I play the game.

The first decision to be made involved my roommate. The college assigned freshman roommates based on common interests and backgrounds. Race was not a factor, but I doubted that it was coincidence that my roommate was black, smart and middle-class.

"Ralph, right?"

These were the first words Jason Davis uttered to me. I had arrived at school early to escape my father, but not early enough to beat my roommate to the bed near the window. The room was larger than I expected, and I would soon learn that it was part of a coveted suite. Our room was connected to the one next door by a private bathroom, and the suite featured a small sitting room as well. There were only a few of these suites in my freshman dorm, and they were doled out carefully.

I was startled. "No, I'm Ellison. Am I in the right room?"

The roommate smiled. "No, I know. You're named after Ralph, right? Ralph Ellison."

I nodded. I never knew what to say to people who brought up the source of my name. My name was just a part of me, not a connection to a writer whose work I'd never read.

"I loved *Invisible Man*," he said, sticking out his hand. "I'm Jason."

I nodded. I was not about to reveal my ignorance. "Nice to meet you."

Jason Davis was several inches taller than me, and I topped six feet. He wore his hair shaved close to his head, and his dark skin was just a bit pockmarked on his jaw, perhaps evidence of a battle with acne. Jason wore the kind of clothes that I could never pull off: baggy pants, oversized T-shirts, sweatshirts, football jerseys. The latest sneakers, dark sunglasses, a single diamond earring in his ear. Jason looked like hip-hop. I wore sport shirts with Ralph Laurent logos, shirts I'd had for years, since I couldn't afford them anymore, with khakis and loafers. Jason looked like he was going to a club or a party. Somewhere cool. I looked like I was going to a recital. I wore the uniform of white, Midwestern suburbia, not because I thought it was stylish, but because it was the only thing I knew. I envied Jason upon sight. He wasn't good-looking, not in a conventional sense, but his eyes were intelligent.

We sat down on the beds. Jason offered me the one near the window, which I refused.

"So we got the suite. Surprise, surprise," Jason said.

"What do you mean?"

Jason explained about the suites and showed me around.

"Yeah, it's nice, but why is it a surprise that we got the suite? Don't they just hand them out randomly?"

Jason laughed. "Are you serious?"

I shrugged. "I guess I am."

"Wait, you don't know who I am, do you?"

"Are you famous?" I couldn't keep a tinge of sarcasm from creeping into my voice. Jason either didn't catch it or chose to ignore it.

"No, but my dad is. He's Grant Davis. NBA basketball coach. Baltimore Bombers." Jason was incredulous. "Got to the second round last year?"

My face remained blank. "The second round of what?"

I liked sports okay, most sports. Except basketball. I didn't get basketball and knew nothing about NBA coach Grant Davis and his son Jason.

"This is one of the biggest basketball schools in the country," Jason added, watching my face. "Wow, you really didn't know."

I smiled. "I thought you were just being an egomaniac."

Jason held up his hands. "I'm not like that, seriously. It's just that, growing up as Grant Davis's son, you get used to people knowing who you are. It comes with the territory."

There was something in Jason's tone that made me suspect that being Grant Davis's son was not altogether a good thing. I was curious, but didn't want to pry.

"So, son of Grant Davis, I guess I got lucky in drawing you as a roommate."

Jason spread his arms wide and laughed. "I guess so, Ralph. I guess so."

Jason took me to my first college party the Friday night after classes began. He already seemed to know lots of people, judging by how many greetings he gave and received as we walked the quad.

"Maybe you really are famous," I joked.

Jason shook his head. "My dad's been coaching in the NBA for ten years. All the players make sure he knows who they are. Recruiting."

Jason also knew where the best parties were.

"Chris and Bryan are having a party tonight at their apartment. That's the one to go to."

I had already decided that the best way to appear less ignorant was to stay quiet. I was uncomfortable about the idea of the party. My social life had pretty much ended when my mother died. I'd forgotten how to have small talk, how to look casual standing around listening to music, how to flirt. The popular Ellison who was invited to every party in high school seemed like another person together, a stranger whose mannerisms and emotions were foreign to me.

I liked Jason, so I agreed to the party.

"Who are Chris and Bryan?"

Jason laughed. "I keep forgetting you're not a fan. They're players on the team."

I cleared my throat, trying to think of something to say that would make me seem cooler.

"Are all of your teammates close? I mean, do you guys hang out?"

Jason smiled again, but his lips were pressed tight and he averted his eyes. "You got it wrong, man. I'm not on the team. I don't even play basketball."

I wondered why an NBA coach's son didn't play, but I could tell from the tightness of Jason's shoulders that I shouldn't ask. I watched as he rummaged around for his wallet and keys. Jason had the door open and was a step down the hall before he spoke again.

"You ready?" he called back.

No. I stood. "Let's go."

Someone once told me that the on-campus apartment village was originally low-income housing that Duke bought cheap and then used to house some of its students. This theory was supported by the fact that most of the inhabitants of the little campus village were black students. The implication, I realized, was that Duke was steering its black students toward the university's version of the projects, a fact which I doubted. Why would the administration even bother? A ghetto isn't just about the buildings, it's about the attitudes bred throughout generations. If you think you're low-class, you will be, no matter where you live.

At that first party with Jason, I didn't know Central Campus was a black neighborhood, but I did notice that most of the faces at the party were my color or darker. The most conspicuous white face was that of Chris, the team power forward and co-host of the party. I stood to the side while Jason greeted Chris as soon as they stepped onto the tiny front lawn of the ground-floor apartment. I looked around while Jason and Chris engaged in a long, complicated handshake involving a partial hug and mumbled words I couldn't hear. Taking in the massive group of people swarming in and out of the apartment, I was struck by the smell of beer and sweat, the core-rattling thump of the bass coming from speakers, the haze of smoke that wafted from cigarettes. I watched as couples danced, some pressed against each other, others standing separate and dancing alone. The only clues they were couples were occasional eye contact and nodding. I looked at the girls; there were twice as many girls as guys, I thought. I knew it was probably just the thrill of being at my first college party, but I could swear that I'd never seen girls this lovely. Girls I knew must be smart, girls who probably studied chemistry or literature during the day, then came out at night in tight baby T-shirts and low-slung jeans, showing their bellies while they danced with their arms in the air.

For the rest of my life, I would remember that smell, that bass thump, that haze. It would always remind me of this first party, the first time in a long time I had felt hope and a sense of simple pleasure shared with other people. I closed my eyes and tried to make out the song that played, but the words were indistinguishable from the beat.

"Ellison, this is Chris." Chris gave me a small nod and we slapped hands. I was relieved that I wasn't expected to participate in the full handshake-hug thing.

"Welcome to the party." Chris smiled and spread his arms wide, as if to take in the entire scene.

I nodded. "Hey." I was trying to think of something else to say when a girl walked up to us.

The girl was tiny. The top of her head came up to my shoulder, and her head was covered with a cap of twists and curls that added another few inches to her height. Her features were doll-like: pouty, full lips colored with dark pink lip gloss, a round, upturned nose, prominent cheekbones. Her eyes were sharp hazel beacons shining out of a dark chocolate face. I bet that every man she met commented on her eyes. They were impossible to ignore. But it wasn't just the color or the shape, like perfect almonds. Her eyes spoke for her, told what she was thinking even in her silence. There was laughter there, something knowing and sharp. She saw through me with those eyes. I could never lie to this girl. Those eyes would know. The eyes, they were the eyes of a woman, even though she had the narrow shoulders and thin arms of a girl.

She raised an eyebrow and smiled at me. I didn't realize I'd been staring until I noticed Chris's broad grin and Jason elbowed me in the side.

Chris raised one eyebrow at me before turning to the girl.

"What's up, Angela?" I might have described Chris' look as a leer. I wasn't sure whether it was ironic or not.

"Whatever, Chris. Don't start with me. You were a dog last year, and I hear you haven't changed." She sniffed and turned her back to him.

Chris put on a look of faux innocence, and Jason laughed.

"Damn, man. Classes just started and you've already started in on the girls?" Jason said.

Chris shrugged. "I'm a senior. There's no time to waste."

I was silent. I felt like I needed to study people as carefully as I studied my biology textbook. There was so much I needed to know before I could feel as comfortable in my own skin as Jason seemed to be.

Angela rolled her eyes at Jason and looked at me. "I hope you're not going to let these *gentlemen* be a bad influence on you."

"Hey, hey, now. Don't put me in with Chris—I'm just standing here, minding my own business," Jason protested. "I am, in fact, a perfect gentleman."

She stared at Jason but said nothing to refute his claim. I thought she was teasing, but she looked so serious.

"I'm incorruptible. Plus, I hardly know them." I waved at Jason and Chris as if to dismiss them. They both hooted, accusing me of being a traitor before they wandered off to get beer. I met Angela's gaze. What did those eyes see in me?

"Incorruptible, huh?" Finally, she smiled.

I felt something shift inside my chest. I knew I was a romantic, though I would deny it if ever accused. I knew I had a way of seeing things in terms of what I thought they should be instead of what they were. It was impractical, and had led to trouble all my life.

But when I met Angela, there was this connection, like a thin line of gossamer silk leading from my chest to hers. It was so light as to be invisible to others, and I was sure Angela didn't know it was there. But I felt it, and I saw it.

At that moment, I didn't want to spend another day without her. If I could have, I would have followed her home and simply watched her from morning until night. What did she eat, how did she sleep, what did she dream? I wanted to know. I needed to know. The need felt desperate—it would not be ignored. This wasn't something I'd ever felt before.

Angela might never talk to me again, might not even remember we'd met. But I knew right then that I would love her.

"Absolutely." I smiled, although I knew my own grin was no match for hers.

She nodded. "We'll see."

That party was a start. The start of my social life, the start of my being accepted, not as a token dark face or a light-skinned oddity, but as myself. At least, the self I created for Duke. The new Ellison was quiet but not morose. I was funny but did not strive to be beloved. I studied hard, went to some parties (but not all—being at *every* social event would make me an altogether different type of person), and I was commonly thought to be Jason Davis's best friend.

I wasn't sure that was totally accurate, although it served my social purposes to be associated with Jason. Jason was the consummate diplomat, friendly enough so that no one had a bad word to say about him. Sometimes, I wanted to ask Jason about this. How had he mastered this persona by his eighteenth birthday? And, more importantly, was it real?

Jason and I shared our living space and talked about the parts of our lives we could risk sharing. Neither of us mentioned our fathers, or family in general, except to give basic information. This was just fine with me. I wasn't sure what Jason was keeping to himself, but I knew my own secrets, and I'd just as soon keep them as such.

Instead, we talked about classes and parties and girls. There was no shortage of attractive girls who seemed willing as soon as I was ready to make a move. Jason and I discussed these prospects at length, more for the conversation than to make any real plans. We agreed that freshman year was no time to hook up with a serious girl-friend. But I was lying. I did want to be with one girl. Angela. She was perfect and out of my league, which only made me want her more. But I was embarrassed to tell Jason, so she was the only one I never talked about.

And so, choices were made. I began to carve out my place in the Duke social structure. I should have felt relieved to finally find my place after more than a year of feeling displaced. But all I felt was worry.

Calvin on becoming a writer:

Where I'm from, being a writer isn't an actual career choice. I remember telling my fifth-grade teacher that I liked to write stories. She patted me on the head and told me that I should enjoy it now, because when I was older I'd have to choose a real job.

The way they taught reflected this thinking. English class was about diagramming sentences and learning correct grammar. We rarely read books, and when we did, it was some old boring story from a textbook that had been used by hundreds of black kids over the last twenty years.

I complained. "Can't we read something more interesting? They have lots of books in the library downtown in Raleigh."

The teacher was a young woman, certainly not older than twenty-five. She wasn't what people in rural North Carolina thought of as pretty. She had dark, ashy skin, wore thick, round glasses and had the kind of narrow figure that inspired people to say she was built like a broomstick.

She had left our little town to go to college, and God knows what brought her back. Now, I imagine that she came home to take care of a sick parent and never quite made it back out. Or maybe she had a bad relationship, came home to her people to heal and was afraid to leave again.

Whatever her reasons for teaching school in our rural Southern town, that day when I asked about reading books, she was worn out from a day of trying to educate thirty country kids, most of whom wouldn't make it past the tenth grade. Strong young men got jobs when they were old enough. School was viewed as a luxury that we couldn't afford.

The teacher had two choices. One, she could encourage me to keep learning, feed my lust for knowledge, smile at my enthusiasm. Or, she could shut me up—asking too many questions made her job harder. She was putting in her time—wasn't that enough?

"Calvin Emory, you went all the way to Raleigh and back to tell me how to do my job?" she drawled. She stretched her lips back over her teeth as the rest of the class laughed. It wasn't like any real smile I'd ever seen.

The other kids teased me.

"Calvin's a nerd!"

"Why are you trying to make more work for us?"

"He must think he's white."

"High yella, more like it!"

I waited for the teacher to reprimand them, but she .lidn't. She just gave me that same lips-stretched-over-teeth thing that she was pretending was a smile.

That was the moment I decided to become a writer.

—From *Save Me: A Memoir* by Calvin Emory

CHAPTER 3

March 1999

Atlanta was in the grip of a warm March day when my father and I arrived for his first book signing. As we drove along the congested highways to the hotel, I opened the car windows and shrugged off my jacket. Calvin was asleep in the passenger seat, and had been for some time. This was a relief. I did not want to talk anymore.

The hotel was the type of place that maintains a careful balance between luxury and purpose. This was a place that catered to business travelers, but only those who could recognize the cut of a Black Label suit at a glance. The lobby was an expanse of plush carpeting and cut glass, and workers lingered in unobtrusive silence, watching the faces of guests, providing what was needed before the guests even knew what they wanted. Classical music emanated from hidden speakers, and I could hear the far-off clink of drinks being poured into heavy glasses from the hotel bar. It was midday, but business travelers who spent more time in Town Cars than in their own vehicles were entitled to a Grey Goose or two to take the edge off between meetings.

Walking through the hotel, I marveled at how different Atlanta was from any place I'd been before. There were so many black people of all different types. Black women cleaned the bathrooms and checked into the hotel with full sets of Louis Vuitton luggage and diamonds covering their fingers. The bellboys were black; and the bartenders, too, were black. While I waited with Calvin to check in, I noticed that the man in front of me looked familiar, and it took me a few moments to realize that the man was a regular in television commercials.

It was the first place I had been where I wasn't both middle class and a minority. Growing up in Evanston, we were the only black family in our neighborhood, and Maren and I were among the few black students at our private school. After we moved to Durham, black faces were more commonplace, but so many of them worked only in service jobs, and they only lived in certain parts of the city. The nicer hotels there were filled with white parents coming to visit their kids at Duke, or white people visiting the area for Research Triangle jobs.

Being in Atlanta and seeing so many people who were like me—educated, middle class and black—both pleased and depressed me. There was a place for a black middle class, but there weren't enough places like it.

Because I joined the trip at the last minute, I had to share a room with Calvin. As we unpacked, I wondered at how quiet he was.

"Are you nervous?" I had decided to make an effort to be nice. After all, I was here for a reason. I wasn't sure what that reason was, but I didn't want the trip to be a rerun of all my other interactions with my father: arguments that escalated until neither of us could hear the other over the din of hurt feelings and misunderstanding.

Calvin nodded. "This is my first real book tour. Just that the publisher sent me out here says a lot. Sometimes . . ." Calvin stopped and looked down. I waited. After a long moment, he cleared his throat.

"Sometimes I'm not sure I can do it."

I didn't respond. Calvin had never expressed any doubt about his writing before; or, at least, not to me. I had always disdained my father's talent as frivolous. His first book was published a few months before I left for college. There had been a large party at our house, and I still cringed at the memory. I was not proud of the person I was that night. I mocked the book and refused to read even a sentence of it. I slept with my father's girlfriend out of spite. I embarrassed Calvin by drawing him into a fight in front of the guests. Then, I tried to justify my actions. The book was called *Jesus Wore Khakis*. The girlfriend, Arnetta, was a willing participant. The fight was inevitable after my father disappointed me again and again. I was only seventeen. My mother was dead. The excuses went on, but they didn't change a thing. They didn't relieve the guilt and the shame.

The worst thing was that I never apologized to Calvin. I couldn't take any of it back, but I could have apologized.

The problem now was that I didn't know how to say I was sorry in a way that would mean something. Too much time had passed. And I wasn't sure whether I was sorry for Calvin or for myself.

I sat down in the bed, a pair of jeans folded on my lap. I looked up at my father, who still looked down at the floor.

"The publishers think you can do it. They wouldn't spend money on a tour, even a small one, if they didn't think you were good enough." I offered this to make him feel better, to make that look disappear from his face. I wasn't quite ready to take on the burden of Calvin's insecurities. I had enough of my own.

"I think you can do it, too."

Calvin looked up and offered me a small smile. I nodded, stood up and went back to unpacking my duffle bag.

The book signing was at an independent bookstore, Reeds, in Buckhead. The store stood alone on a corner in a building that looked like it might have housed a restaurant in some previous incarnation. The brick looked aged and settled, and the large plate-glass windows revealed the brightness of the store and its cozy furnishings in the disappearing dusk. It was the kind of bookstore I liked, small and easy to move around in, the kind of store that I knew would soon be swallowed up by Barnes and Noble or Borders. There were still a couple of stores like Reeds near Duke, because the campus community could support quaint anachronisms around its immediate borders. But Reeds had no Duke, and I felt an anticipatory nostalgia as I approached the doors.

Calvin's signing was set for seven o'clock. We had arrived thirty minutes early. He spent the ride over chattering about trivialities (sports, television shows, books he'd read) while I tried to keep up by uttering reactions and nodding when necessary. I knew he was nervous about reading from his novel. When we pulled into the parking lot, I realized that my own stomach was in knots.

Posters in front of the store's glass doors featured a photo I had never seen. In the picture, my father looked like a stranger. He wore a goatee and a dark jacket over an open-collared dress shirt. He wore glasses, the same ones he wore now, but they were perched at the end of his nose in a way that was not conducive to actually seeing through them. The Calvin on the poster looked serious and thoughtful, as if he were a real writer. I shook my head. My father, with a book deal and this mini-tour, *was* a real writer.

Calvin beamed at me as we entered the front of the store.

"That photo came out great. I had a professional shoot it."

I thought the photo was somewhat contrived. "You looked different in it. Good," I added.

We went to the back of the store, where piles of Calvin's book were presented in artful stacks and twenty chairs were arranged in a semi-circle. Looking at the title of the book, I realized that Calvin had never told me what the book was about. Of course, I'd never asked. While he chatted with the woman in charge of events for the store, I slipped one of the books out of a pile and looked closely at the cover.

It was called *Save Me*. On the cover was a picture that I recognized. A little boy, about four years old, stood in front of a church. He wore overalls and a sweet smile full of adoration for whomever stood behind the camera. His hair was shorn close to his head and he wore thick glasses that looked comically large for his plump face. The photo was in black and white, and part of the boy's face was lost in the shadows. Still, there was optimism in the smile, the optimism of a four-year-old who still believes in magic.

The photo had been one of my grandmother's favorites. It had held the place of honor on her bedroom dresser. She'd once told me that it was her favorite photo of her little boy. Of Calvin. She'd called him her little boy, even though Calvin was in his thirties and a father at the time, even though he no longer believed in magic. She'd told me this while she was in the hospital after her first stroke. I had wondered if she were losing track of time. Months later, she was dead of yet another, more serious stroke, and I didn't go to her funeral.

Now, looking at the picture, I realized how much I had never asked her, mostly because I didn't want to admit I was interested in what Calvin was like as a boy, before he failed me as a father.

I looked up to make sure Calvin was still engaged, then turned my back and read the inside cover. I shivered as I read the book's description. It was a memoir. The story begins with Calvin's childhood in rural North Carolina, where he is raised by his mother and never gets to know his father. The story moves to Chicago, where Calvin marries and has two children, Ellison and a girl named Maren. But the marriage doesn't work, and the memoir details the pain of the divorce and his efforts to make a new life for himself.

I slammed the book shut, my cheeks burning. There was more to the cover description, but I did not want to see the description of how his ex-wife died in a car accident. I did not want to see how Calvin struggled to connect with his estranged children. I did not want this book to exist.

The memoir is a cruel medium. It requires complete revelation and abandon, something I was never comfortable with. It doesn't allow for privacy, for secrets. And what family doesn't have secrets it wants to keep hidden? I supposed it would be fine if Calvin chose to reveal all about his own life, but our lives are inevitably tied to the lives of others. What about our desires? Do we have a say? Are we not as important as my father's desire to lay his soul bare to the world?

An autobiography is something different, because it's about influential, important, famous or infamous people whose lives have somehow impacted the culture. We want to know about those people so we can understand how our culture has been changed. How did this person come to be a part of all of our lives to some degree? And what does this person's fame or influence say about the rest of us?

But who cares about Calvin Emory, besides, of course, Calvin himself? Has he impacted the culture? I know the memoir is meant to be more personal and intimate, but that's exactly the problem. There's no such thing as intimacy between one person and the world of readers, and even if there were, one should have the right to choose that intimacy. I didn't have a choice. Maren didn't have a choice. Only Calvin chose, apparently without regard to how we might feel about it.

The least he could have done is ask. Undoubtedly, I would have said no and he would have done it anyway. But the right thing to do would be to ask before revealing our family to the world. It wasn't a family to be particularly proud of, in my opinion, and I'd just as soon not have everyone know all about the way my father abandoned Maren and me, my mother's death, my conflicts with Calvin. Among other things. In fact, I couldn't think of one thing about our family worth sharing, not one thing I wouldn't feel ashamed for a stranger to know about us.

Being a father meant sometimes sacrificing your own desires for your children. Didn't it? Why couldn't he do that, just once? And why couldn't I stop expecting it from him, when he'd made it clear that he was never going to be the kind of father I wanted him to be?

Calvin had wandered off and I stuck the book back into the pile. I slumped into a chair, my foot tapping, my teeth clenched. I averted my eyes from the stacks of my father's books. Calvin had used our lives, without asking, for his book. He got to tell *his* side of the story. And seeing it on paper would mean reliving it all again.

I made a sudden move out of my chair. I thought I heard my father calling me as I walked out of the store.

"It's not fair."

I sat on the bed closest to the window. I had not turned on any lights when I got back to the hotel room. I watched the darkness take control of the skyline for a brief moment before the city of Atlanta realized what was happening and began to flick on lights. In offices, houses, other hotel rooms, no one was willing to let the darkness be. I wore a watch, but I didn't look at it when Calvin walked in.

"Ellison? Why are you sitting in the dark?"

I could hear him shuffle into the room and feel along the wall for the switch. He found it. The yellow bulbs burned the dark away, but I didn't turn from the window. Now all I saw was my own reflection, and my father behind me. He stood with his arms folded. I couldn't read the expression on my own face.

"It's not fair. It's not yours."

I hated the whine in my voice. I knew I sounded like a child. But I couldn't help what I felt. It wasn't fair. He needed to know. He needed to admit it.

"What's not fair? What's not mine?" There was annoyance in his voice. How dare he be annoyed?

"The story. It's our life. It's my life. Not yours." My words clipped short.

I turned then. His face was wan in the cheap glow. His arms were still folded, defiant against my questions.

"The book? The one you never asked me about, the one you haven't even read? Who are you to tell me what to write?"

Calvin stepped toward me as he spoke, his forearms tight. I almost wished he would hit me. Then I could hate him.

I stood. He was close enough for me to smell his breath. Apples and alcohol, probably some kind of designer martini. I glanced at the clock and his eyes followed mine. It was 2:17 A.M. A sheepish look floated across his face, then disappeared. I gave him a nasty smile.

"Tell me, does Calvin finally find true love in the end? Does he reunite with his children? Do they all live happily ever after?"

He backed away and slumped down onto the nearest bed. I stood over him, my fists clenched.

"Ours lives are stories, Ellison. And it's my story, too. I don't have to apologize for that." He lay back on the bed, his hands covering his face. "It's too late to have this conversation. Can we talk about it tomorrow?"

I watched him for a few moments. His breathing grew deep and regular. I wanted to feel angry enough to put my fists to his face. I wanted to feel enough rage to put a pillow over his face and feel him squirm under my grip. I wanted him to hurt. I wanted him to care.

I grabbed my duffle and stuffed in my things. Our lives are stories. That was the problem. It wasn't just a story, not to me. It was my life.

Calvin on Ellison's birthright:

My son, Ellison, has always been hostile about my writing. Like everyone I grew up with, he seems skeptical of the idea that writing could be a career. Or maybe he's just skeptical of me.

I don't think he knows that I'm not the only writer in the family. His mother, Vanessa, was also a writer at one time. I think she turned to television because people always told her how articulate and beautiful she was, so it seemed like a natural fit. But I always thought she was a good writer, too. No one else ever said anything about her stories, though, so I can't blame her for going into television instead of writing. Hell, maybe I was wrong—I'm not an expert. But she wrote these small, self-contained stories that told me so much about her, the way she thought, what she feared.

She stopped writing long before we broke up, and she put all her stories in a box in a closet. When I moved out, I had an impulse to take them with me. A little piece of her would always stay with me, and she would never even know. My favorite story was called "R.S.V.P." I don't think she would mind that I'm including it here.

R.S.V.P.
By Vanessa Emory
The invitation to Tate's engagement party was just like her: sophisticated, elegant, perfect. Her perfect parents requested my presence at their perfect party thrown at a perfect hotel in Palm Beach. The thick cream paper, the embossed lettering, the smooth script—it all rose up from my

coffee table, accusing me. You are not good enough, it said. You will never be good enough.

After ten years of being Tate's friend, I was tired of coming in second, tired of sitting back while Tate and everyone else assumed that she was more important than me. I loved Tate. I hated Tate.

Now, she was getting married to Paul Newcomb, senior aide to Senator Michael Miles, a man who would have been voted Most Likely to Launch a Successful Political Career if people voted on such things. Tate's parents loved him. Tate loved him. The sight of his self-satisfied smile made me nauseous.

I filled out the response card. The words I wrote looked as if I had written them with my left hand. I felt as if I were going to a funeral. I wanted to be the type of person who would put everything aside and just be happy for Tate. I was the type of person who checked the boxes, licked the envelope and sealed it.

I pretended to love Tate. I was too much of a coward to admit I hated her. I walked to the mailbox, set the envelope inside. I raised the red flag on the side of the mailbox and went back inside.

This character was so much like Vanessa. She hated coming in second to anyone, probably because it so seldom happened. She always wanted to be the smartest, the most beautiful, the most successful woman around, and she would go to great lengths to get what she wanted. This char-

acter is consumed by what she thinks is her failure to be better than her best friend, and I have always suspected that feelings like those motivated Vanessa to succeed.

I see this in my son as well. Ellison has all these ideas about how life should go, how his family should be, how he should be. He can't face coming in second, just like his mother—that's not how things are supposed to be. When Vanessa died, it was the worst kind of blow a perfectionist like Ellison could endure. How can you have a perfect family without a mother?

—From *Save Me: A Memoir* by Calvin Emory

CHAPTER 4

October 1995

Angela worked at a coffee shop just off campus on Ninth Street. In the fall of 1995, there wasn't a Starbucks on every corner, and actually, coffee hadn't yet become the drink of choice for everyone over the age of twelve. The shop was called the Coffee Bean and it was a bright, open space with spotless white walls and stainless-steel light fixtures. The round tables sat no more than four people and were made of polished teak, and the smell of coffee brewing mixed with the fragrances of homemade pastries baking in the kitchen.

What I liked best about the Coffee Bean was that it was never crowded. I sometimes liked to study there instead of the library, which could be almost too quiet. Without some ambient noise, I tended to distract myself enough to spend hours doodling in the margins of note-books instead of studying in the library's carrels. The coffee shop provided something like white noise—the gurgling of industrial pots, the light from floor-to-ceiling windows facing the street, the murmured laughter of the few other regulars.

I walked in one early Thursday in October and placed my order without really looking up at the person taking my order.

"So you're not even going to say hi?" Angela handed me the paper cup and smiled.

I'd thought about Angela a lot since we met at the party, but I didn't have much opportunity to talk to her on campus. My schedule was different than most people I knew because I liked early-morning classes that left most of my day free. Jason, and nearly everyone else I knew, only took eight or nine o'clock classes under duress, and I rarely saw familiar faces as I walked to my biology and calculus classes on weekday mornings. I always searched the sleepy faces looking for Angela's, but I hadn't seen her since the night we met.

Now, I took my coffee and tried to think of something clever to say.

"I didn't see you."

"I'm standing right here," she teased.

"Uh."

I only managed the one syllable and stood there with a dumb smile on my face. A girl with pink-framed glasses standing behind me finally cleared her throat. Angela shook her head at me in mock disappointment and took the girl's order while I went to find my regular seat by the window.

I spent an hour that day pretending to work on a paper for my English class and sneaking glances at Angela when I thought she wasn't looking. She was small, but she had an air of authority behind the counter, as if she was born to be in charge of this coffee shop at this moment. I watched as she mixed complicated drinks I'd never tasted—cappuccinos and lattes, with skim milk or two percent, with whipped cream or without. In between customers, she sipped from her own cup and read a paperback book. I strained to see the title: *The Bridges of Madison County*.

After an hour, I decided to stop the charade and try the library instead. The assignment was to write about a popular culture myth, and I still hadn't picked a topic, even though the ten-page paper was due in a few days. I loved my math and science classes, but I was bored by English, and I didn't need much to distract me from writing the paper. I needed to get away from Angela if I wanted to avoid staying up all night writing the night before it was due.

"What are you working on?" Angela appeared at my table, holding her place in her book with a finger, as I gathered up my things.

I thought maybe she was just being nice, talking to me because I was Jason's roommate, or because I clearly hadn't accomplished much in the time I sat in the shop. I didn't care. I was happy to talk to her, even if she was motivated by pity.

"English." I made a face, and she laughed.

"Come on, it can't be that bad."

I shrugged. "It's so inexact, so much about interpretation. In calculus, there's one right answer, and if you use logic, you can find it. In biology, the hypothesis leads to the theory, which leads to the law. Use logic, and you'll find the answers eventually. In writing, there are no right answers. I hate it."

I hadn't meant to go on a rant, and I worried that she'd think I was a freak. But she just laughed again.

"I'm an English major, you know."

I felt my cheeks heat up, and I knew she could see me blushing. It was one thing I hated about having pale skin. Most black people didn't visibly blush, but it happened to me all the time.

"No offense," I said weakly, then laughed at myself. "I'm sure that makes it better that I just ridiculed your major."

She gave me a crooked grin. "Maybe I can help. What's the assignment?" She sat down and I settled back into my chair. I explained the assignment.

"I mean, how can I narrow that down? I don't really think about stuff like that," I complained.

She held up the book she'd been reading. "Did you read this?"

I tried not to show my distaste. "Umm, that's not exactly my kind of book. It's a romance novel, right? They made a movie of it, Clint Eastwood is in it."

"Not a romance novel in the sense that it's a genre book," she corrected me. "But it is a love story. It's about a middle-aged woman who is remembering a hot fling she had with a photographer years ago. It was this singular moment of romance and sensuality in her life and the book is really all about the road not taken, missed chances, the ideal of romance. You know?"

I didn't know, but I nodded anyway because she was so excited as she talked about the book.

"So you like it?"

When Angela really laughed with abandon, she had a way of throwing her head back, her mouth completely open, to let out a sharp cackle that made me laugh, even though I didn't know what was so funny.

"No, I think it's sentimental mush. This is what you should write about—the way popular culture portrays romance, the myth of finding your romantic or sexual match just through the workings of God, or fate. That's the myth—love takes work, and it's messy and it's not always a handsome stranger who comes to the house and turns your world upside down."

She took a deep breath, and, again, I was at a loss.

"So you don't like it, then?" I smiled at her. She smacked me on the head with the closed book.

"Do you want to borrow the book or not?"

That night, I resisted the temptation to just go see the movie at the mall instead of reading the book. Usually, schoolwork came easy to me and I would never consider cheating. I even came up with a rationale to justify seeing the film: the assignment specified pop culture, and, clearly, movies are a part of popular culture.

But then I thought of Angela. She was reading the book, and I got the feeling that she wouldn't take me as seriously if I watched the movie instead. She seemed like the kind of person who would always choose the book over the movie when given the chance. It was Thursday night and Jason was at yet another party, so I ordered a pizza and opened Angela's copy of *The Bridges of Madison County*.

I expected to hate it, to feel as outraged as Angela did about the sexist implications of the romantic plot. But from the first pages, I found myself engrossed in the thin novel, which was written as if the narrator was telling a true story. I was a sucker for truth, since I felt that was one thing I had not gotten enough of from my father, and to be honest, my mother, either. In the first chapter, the narrator described himself as a mere vessel of a great story. He was giving voice to what would otherwise be silent, and that appealed to me. There had been so many times in my family where the truth was hidden, either deliberately or incidentally. My sister, Maren, would rather everyone get along, and I knew that my desire to confront our father had hurt her. But here, in this novel, was a man who saw what I saw.

And then there was Robert Kincaid, who sounded like just the kind of man I wished I could be. A traveling photographer, always on the move, his own boss, his own man. He was a man completely comfortable with himself, not at all self-conscious or filled with self-doubt. He knew his place in the world, and he embraced it with quiet dignity and rugged charm. I wanted to be Robert Kincaid.

The book was short, not even 200 pages, and when I looked up from the last page, four hours had passed and I had eaten the entire pizza. My mind drifted, and I could see myself as Robert Kincaid with Angela as my Francesca. We had a connection, at least from my perspective, but instead of spending just hours together, we would find a way to be together. We wouldn't spend our lives regretting missed opportunities, imagining what might have been.

But my realistic side didn't remain silent for long. I could barely talk to her, let alone ask her out. I wasn't her type. I wasn't like Jason, Mr. Popularity, who was always surrounded by people. I hardly knew anyone Jason hadn't introduced me to, and when I had met Angela at that first party, she seemed just as comfortable in the crowd as he did. Here I was, Mr. Romantic, imagining something that wasn't even remotely possible. The ringing of the telephone interrupted my reverie.

"How's your paper coming?" It was Angela. I hadn't even thought about the paper since I started reading the book, and now I felt dread come over me. The assignment was to demonstrate how popular culture perpetuates a myth. But I thought the romance between Robert and Francesca seemed real—they hadn't ended up together. She stayed married to her husband, he went on with his career. They were in love, but love couldn't change the reality of their lives.

I told all of this to Angela, and when I finished, there was a long silence. While I waited for her to respond, I regretted everything I had said. First of all, what kind of a guy likes this kind of novel? Second, I knew Angela hated the book, and I wanted her to like me. I was going over what I *should* have said when she finally spoke.

"You make a good argument, I guess, but don't you think it's old-fashioned? The wife finds passion and excitement, but gives it up to stay married to a boring guy? Her whole life was ruined."

"Not ruined. She was a mother, remember, and she cared for her husband, too. So she made what seemed like the right choice. What's old-fashioned about trying to do the right thing?"

"Okay. But what about the letter to her kids, the one at the end where she tells them all about Robert? Who does that?"

I was quiet for a moment, thinking about mothers and children.

"I wish I had a letter from my mother like that after she died. It wouldn't matter what it said, as long as it was honest and from the heart."

I hadn't meant to get so serious. I fought back the debilitating sadness that always threatened to take over whenever I spent too much time thinking about my mother. I wouldn't let myself do it. I couldn't afford to let it take over, and I didn't want pity, not even from Angela.

But all she said was, "Wow. I'm going to have to read it again. You've made me think of it in a whole new way. Are you sure you don't want to be an English major?"

I laughed. "Please—I can't even finish this one assignment, because now that I loved the book, I can't figure out what to write about."

"Maybe I can help. It's the least I can do, since you seem to be worse off than you were this morning. Let's meet for breakfast. Bring the book." I could hear the smile in her voice. I wondered if she could tell that a large, goofy grin had just spread across mine.

After that night, Angela helped me with all my English papers. Once I got through the first one, I didn't really need much help, which I think she knew. But I liked talking about books with her, developing paper ideas, arguing over writing styles. Sometimes I went to the Coffee Bean to work and Angela spent her breaks reading over my shoulder or offering suggestions on books I should read. Other times, we went to the library or sat on the quad when the weather was nice. We developed a true friendship, not based on the coincidence of rooming together, as it was with me and Jason. I liked him, but I always felt I had my guard up with him, although I couldn't quite pinpoint why. But with Angela, I could be honest—at least, about books and writing. She was the only person who knew I'd never read *Invisible Man*, even though I was named after Ralph Ellison. She understood when I told her I couldn't get through the first five pages of *Beloved*. She didn't laugh when I admitted that Stephen King and John Grisham were more to my literary tastes.

I learned more about her as well. Angela Michaels wrote poetry and wanted to be a journalist. She was the editor of her high-school paper and she was from Chicago, like me. She wanted to pledge Delta and she played intramural tennis. She was funny, and even when her humor was biting, her smile took off the edge. I liked everything I knew about Angela, and if I could have, I would have spent every free moment with her.

But there were limits. Angela never invited me to her dorm room and I didn't invite her to mine. I figured she only saw me as a friend and having me in her bedroom would just be weird. Jason was hardly ever in our suite, but I still never brought Angela there. I didn't want her to think I was trying to pressure her into something more than our burgeoning friendship. I kept my crush under control, hidden and safe. Angela liked me, and that was enough.

Calvin on meeting his ex-wife:

When I met Vanessa, I couldn't believe my luck. She was everything I had always wanted in a woman: smart, pretty, fun. I didn't really think of her as a real person, a person with gifts and flaws just like anyone else. If I'm being honest, I didn't even know women were real people—I was young, and women were still like alien beings to me. Growing up so sheltered by my mother and living in a town where all the women were either wives and mothers, or they were preparing to be wives and mothers, I had no idea that a woman could have facets that had nothing to do with me. Women were supposed to take care of men, I thought, and when I met Vanessa, I thought she was the perfect wife for me and mother for my future children.

I was young, you know, and I felt cooped up in Durham. It was the same people doing the same thing all the time, and I felt that if I didn't get out, I'd end up just like everyone else. I took a bus to Chicago. I'd never been there, but I'd heard there were a lot of black writers there and I thought I could learn something. Most people were running off to New York back then, but something about Chicago called me.

It was late summer, so the weather was still nice. But as soon as I stepped off the bus, I noticed there were police cars everywhere and news cameras filming. There had been a murder near the station, and it was big news.

I'd never seen anything like this back in Durham, so I hung around the edges of the scene, watching the cameramen squat to get just the right angle, listening to the police bark orders at each other.

And then I noticed a pretty girl who was holding a pad and pen and pushing her way through the throngs of people to talk to the main cop. She was so petite and beautiful, I couldn't believe the way she forced the cop to talk to her as she scribbled on her pad.

Something clicked inside me, and I suddenly had to know this lovely, tough, determined woman. I snuck underneath the police tape, went up to her and asked her out. Vanessa went out with me, but she didn't like me at first. I had to wear her down slowly, but it wasn't long before she fell in love, too.

Putting someone on a pedestal never works. Looking back, I can see that I was desperate to be loved. There was a hole in my life, and it threatened to suck me down into it. Vanessa, with her beauty and poise, would save me.

It was too much to ask of another person, and it's a wonder we lasted long enough to have our two children, long enough to regret all the mistakes we made. The mistakes I made. I wish I had known then what I know now. The only person who could save me was me.

—From *Save Me: A Memoir* by Calvin Emory

CHAPTER 5

December 1995

In December 1995, I had my first Christmas as a college student. While everyone else was putting wreaths up on their doors and lights around their rooms, I was avoiding the truth. The truth was that I had no intentions of going home. I would not drive the five miles to my grandmother's house. I would not endure another Christmas like the last one, where I'd missed my mother so badly it felt like I had lost a limb. This would be my second Christmas without her, and I'd just as soon spend it alone.

Not even my sister, Maren, could change my mind.

"El, you have to come home." She called just as I was returning from my last exam, biology. I already knew I aced it.

"I'm not coming. I can't be around him."

I'd made a pledge to myself never to talk to my father again. It wasn't practical, but the thought of it—freedom from a man I believed I hated—was satisfying.

"It's not just Dad. Grandma Esther isn't doing all that well."

My stomach lurched, but I said nothing. I knew my grandmother was ailing. She hadn't been well since the first stroke. But my self-preservation instinct was stronger than my compassion for a woman I'd known only a year. To stay sane, I had to stay away from my father.

"I know. I'm sorry about Grandma Esther."

I remembered last Christmas. My first without snow, without piles of gifts under the tree. I'd spent the days leading up to Christmas looking for a part-time job, dreading the actual day that would be spent trying not to fall asleep or be saved at my grandmother's church. I'd felt utterly alone, more so than if I actually had been alone. I had no intention of repeating *that* experience.

"What about me?" Maren's voice sounded small and young, as if she were six instead of sixteen. I thought about all she'd been through during the past year; we had shared some of the same experiences, but she'd also been subjected to different, worse things. The guilt of leaving her behind in the house was mitigated only by the fact that she seemed to be able to forgive our father his short-comings. I would not. Could not.

I told myself Maren would be okay. But it wasn't a case of believing what was most convenient. I knew she would be all right, not because of anything I could do, but because she was stronger than me. I envied her way of looking at the world through a veil of optimism. The veil would protect her. My emotions, on the other hand, were raw and exposed. She could spend Christmas making the best of things, hoping that someday we wouldn't need to pretend everything was fine. In my darkest moments, I didn't think anything would ever be fine ever again.

"I love you, Mare. But I can't."

I knew she would understand. She always did.

She sighed. "We'll miss you."

I said nothing. We both knew this wasn't altogether true.

"*I'll* miss you."

"Me, too. But you'll visit me after Christmas. Come stay with me for a few days. See what college life is like."

Maren laughed. "I've stayed with you before. I know what college life is like."

I smiled. "Not in January. You don't know what college life is like in January."

❧

"Come home with me," Jason said. He was packing his duffle bag with the few items he would need to spend two weeks at his parents' home in Baltimore.

I shook my head. "I'm not a charity case—I could go home. I just don't want to."

I could tell Jason wanted to ask why, but he didn't. It was one of the things I liked about him.

Jason punched me in the shoulder.

"I don't care about you, idiot. I need someone there with me."

"Ouch." I rubbed my arm.

"I'm serious, you big baby."

"Isn't the rest of your family going to be there?"

Jason shrugged. "That's the problem. My family." He gave me a pleading look. "So?"

I wondered if it was wise to get in the middle of another family's drama. But anything was better than the alternative.

"I'll go, but you have to promise not to hit me again."

"Okay, deal. Now pack up and let's go."

Jason's father had been the coach of the Baltimore Bombers for nine years, and there were already elaborate plans in the works to celebrate his tenth anniversary. In those ten years, he'd taken the Bombers from mediocre to one of the premier teams in the NBA. He won three championships there and was the sports world's version of royalty. Some people loved him, more people hated him, but everyone agreed that he was a winner. It was, after all, part of the title of his recent autobiography: *Winner Take All: My Life on the Sidelines.*

Jason told me all of this as we approached Washington, D.C., during the five-hour drive from Durham to Baltimore. We rode in Jason's car, a brand-new Lexus SUV with black-tinted windows. I felt like I was riding in a spacecraft, hovering over the other cars.

"You sound like a press release."

Jason laughed. It was a hollow, forced sound. "What I sound like is my dad. There's nothing he likes better than talking about himself. So be prepared to hear it all again."

I looked out the window as we crawled through Washington traffic. The man in the next car had a strained look on his face, as if the traffic caused him physical pain.

"Anything else you want to warn me about?" I glanced at Jason, who wore the same pained look as the man in the silver Volkswagen.

Jason shrugged. "My father is embarrassed that I don't play basketball. He's mad that I chose to go to Duke because he hates the coach. He's mad because my mother won't give him a divorce no matter how much he cheats on her. He wishes I were someone else's son, and he wishes he had more children, but I'm an only child and he can't deny that I'm his. Is that enough?"

We were at a standstill, so Jason took his hands off the wheel and sat back. We looked at each other for a long moment. I wasn't sure who laughed first, but it didn't take long for our cackling to fill and shake the car. We only recovered from doubled-up hilarity when the car behind us produced a long honk.

Jason shook his head, and I wiped my eyes.

"Well, this'll be fun."

Jason's house, or, as he referred to it, his father's house, was the largest, most sterile home I had ever been in. It was in a posh neighborhood called Mount Washington, full of modest homes, condos, bungalows and huge Victorian and Georgian mansions like Coach Grant Davis's home. It sat at the top of a hill, looking down on the other homes that were not so fortunate. The Davis home was a two-story Georgian made of pale yellow brick with pillars accentuating the front entrance and either end of the home. The windows were all framed with dark green shutters, and chimneys indicated multiple fireplaces throughout. A vast expanse of emerald lawn carpeted the land in front of the house. I marveled that there wasn't a hint of brown in the grass, even though it was December, and I considered how much money it must cost to fight nature. I might have mistaken it for a typical New England home except it was three times the size.

Jason used his key to open the door, and he led me into a foyer with eighteen-foot ceilings and a crystal chandelier that reflected the setting sun like a prism. I was disoriented as I watched my shadow play on the creamy wall nearest me. The wall was bare floor to ceiling, except for a framed drawing that seemed dwarfed by the space. I didn't understand why the drawing was all alone until I stepped closer. It was black and white, a group of musicians drawn with child-like broad strokes: large heads, prominent noses, instruments clutched in hands and against torsos. The style reminded me of ancient Egyptians pictured on the walls of caves, of Picasso, of tight, smoky rooms filled with music. A discrete rectangle underneath gave information: *Le Jazz*, c. 1967. I recognized the name. Romare Bearden. I had seen other works by the artist in the Chicago Museum of Art.

"Do you like Bearden?" The voice, not Jason's, startled me from my reverie. I whirled around to face Grant Davis.

He towered over me. I only registered the man in segments. Enormous, manicured hands. Expensive charcoal-colored suit with a white shirt open at the collar, no tie. Black loafers that reflected light from the chandelier. Trimmed beard flecked with gray. A wide smile that did not reach his light-brown eyes. He was standing about six inches closer than I would have preferred.

"He's amazing." I put my hand out, trying not to glance around to see whether Jason was still in the vicinity. "I'm Ellison Emory. Jason's roommate."

Grant Davis's handshake was too firm. I tried not to wince.

"Jason says good things about you." His eyes searched mine, as if Jason's word could not be trusted.

I met his gaze. As the moments ticked by, I felt a bit of nostalgia for my own hapless, non-threatening father.

"Thank you for having me in your home. I really appreciate the invitation."

Grant Davis raised an eyebrow. "Were you invited?"

I couldn't stop my eyes from flicking around the foyer. Where was Jason?

"Well—"

Grant Davis broke into a hearty laugh. I didn't trust the laugh. "I'm just kidding, son. Any friend of Jason's is always welcome here." He led me through the foyer by the arm. I worried I would have a bruise later.

"Let me give you the grand tour."

Jason's mother had immaculate hands. They were hands with manicured nails that were painted by little

Korean ladies at least twice a week, hands that had never been soaked in harsh dishwater. Hands that shook just a bit when she dragged a tumbler full of vodka to her mouth. She smiled at me over her glass as she took a gulp. I sat across from her and I could smell the stench of hours of drinking on her breath. It was a little after seven-thirty on Christmas Eve.

"I'd like to say Jason has told me all about you." She glanced over at her son. I did, too. Jason wouldn't meet our eyes, instead cutting his thick steak as if every slice was a matter of life and death.

"But, of course, my son doesn't talk to me." She smiled at me.

"We talk all the time. You're just too drunk to remember," Jason said drily. Mrs. Davis took a long look at her glass. She wasn't ruffled by her son's comment. "Oh? Well, I hope I enjoy these talks we have."

Jason shook his head, and his mother let out a low chuckle. I began treating my own steak as if I was performing a triple bypass.

We sat at a long mahogany rectangle. It was far too large for the three of us. We were being served our dinner by actual waiters, and the food had been prepared by a chef who was permanently on the Davis payroll. Jason's mother did not cook.

Coach Davis wasn't there. He was at the arena, preparing for the Christmas Day game against the Knicks. It was one of Jason's complaints about his father: He was always either playing or planning to play basketball on holidays.

Mrs. Davis rotated her glass in a circle, making the two cubes of ice clink against the sides. I wished my family was a neat little package that could be easily presented to strangers, like scented candles or a bottle of wine. Then again, at least my mother had never been as disconnected as Mrs. Davis. My mother spent a lot of time at work and she wasn't perfect (at least, not my idea of the perfect mother), but when we together, she was engaged and interested in me and Maren. Every year, we went on a trip together for Christmas, and we always laughed, even when life didn't seem very funny.

Even the blowout arguments between me and Mom were better than what Jason had with his mother, which was more like guerilla warfare, with Jason and his mother as snipers hiding behind sarcasm and alcohol. Jason's father wasn't here, but that was less surprising to me. I was used to fathers who disappeared when you needed them most.

Catching this glimpse of Jason's home life actually made me feel bad for him. On the surface, he seemed to have everything—good looks, expensive clothes, popularity, self-confidence. But if all those things were important, he wouldn't have needed me to come home with him as a buffer between him and his parents. When I met Jason, I thought he had everything figured out, but seeing his family made me realize that maybe he was as lonely as me.

I cleared my throat. "Well, Mrs. Davis, I'm from Chicago. Or I was. Now my family lives in Durham."

She raised an eyebrow and looked over at Jason, who had turned his attention to the fingerling potatoes laced with butter and chives. She looked back at me. Her sad eyes were the color of grass. I waited for her to ask me why I wasn't spending the holidays with my own family.

"I grew up in Chicago, too. My brother still lives there, as do my parents. I never go back." She winked at me, then she gulped the remainder of her drink. As if by magic, a waiter appeared with a fresh drink. "And please, call me Lila. If we're going to spend Christmas together, we should at least be on a first-name basis."

"Okay, Lila."

She nodded and took another long drink. Jason watched her, looking like he might just cry. I looked away from both of them. We spent the rest of the meal in silence.

꧁

Later, Jason and I slouched on leather sofas in his basement, which was more like a luxury apartment than any basement I'd ever seen. We watched Chris Rock perform stand-up on the wide-screen TV. Jason poured beer into chilled glasses.

"So, how are you enjoying life at Grant and Lila's house?" Jason tried to smirk, but it came off more like a pout.

I shrugged. "Everyone's family is fucked up, right? I'd rather be with yours than with mine, believe me." What I didn't say is that I'd take a drunken mother over a dead mother any day.

Jason looked at me. "Tonight was nothing. Things are even worse when my dad is here. He tries to be some kind of paternal figure. Big Daddy. But he's like a bad actor playing an even worse role."

I sipped and nodded. "My father is the opposite. I'm not even sure he's aware that he is supposed to be someone's father. I mean, we hadn't seen him in years before we moved to Durham. He never even called."

This was the most I'd told anyone about my father. Jason held up his glass.

"I propose a toast. To families that suck. Merry Christmas."

We touched our glasses together and drank. I heard a car start somewhere outside, then loud voices.

I looked at Jason. "Who's that?"

"My mom goes to midnight mass every year."

This made me smile. "She doesn't drive, I hope?"

Jason laughed. "She pays a waiter extra to drive her there and back. Last year she passed out in a pew and they called my dad to come get her. She didn't wake up until ten o'clock on Christmas night."

I held up my glass. "Merry fucking Christmas."

We went back to Duke on New Year's Day.

"You don't mind going back early, do you? There's someone I want to see," Jason asked me the morning we left.

I shrugged. "I'm easy. Who are you meeting?"

He smiled. It was the first genuine smile I'd seen since we got to Baltimore.

"Remember that girl, from Chris's party? The little cute one?"

My neck stiffened, but I managed to nod. Not Angela. She's mine.

"I have been asking her out all semester but she's been turning me down. She was with some guy from back home. But they broke up, and she finally gave me a yes. We're going to a movie Friday night."

When did all this happen? Jason knew that Angela and I were friends, but I'd made it sound casual and incidental. I couldn't risk letting anyone know how important Angela was to me. Vulnerability was not my strong suit. Still, it felt as if Jason had treaded on my territory. In my mind, Angela was *mine*.

But I hadn't asked her out. She was too perfect. She might say no. Jason had no such concerns.

It occurred to me that I had not been the only one deliberately not talking about Angela. Jason hadn't ever mentioned that he was calling her. My stomach tightened.

"That's great. She seemed really . . . nice."

Jason jumped up and grabbed his keys. "Everybody has been trying to get with her. But I'm in there. You know?"

I knew. I picked up my bag and followed Jason out the door.

I knew.

Calvin on his half-brother:

I have a half-brother named Chris. He was born the year we moved to Durham. I never knew who his father was—Momma wouldn't say. I couldn't even venture a guess, because I was working long hours at the local department store trying to save up enough money to move away and go to college. As far as I knew, all Momma did was go to work and church, so it was hard to imagine when she had the time or opportunity to get pregnant.

She never really talked to me about being pregnant. I just noticed that she was gaining weight, then her belly started to get larger and larger until it was obvious what was going on. Then one day she announced that I would have to take her to the hospital when it was time, so I should give her the phone number to the department store in case I was at work when the baby came.

And so my brother Chris was born. He was dark where I was light, with hazel eyes and a dimpled smile. I was eighteen years old, and the last thing I wanted in my life was a baby. I had always been my mother's focus, so it was hard to adjust to the idea that she now had another son. A son that she doted on, spoiling him with presents and constantly carrying him in her arms.

I am ashamed to admit I hated him. He was just a baby. But he changed everything in our family, and he grew into an insufferable brat. When I moved to Chicago, I missed Momma. But she had Chris now, and I always thought she had a little less love for me after he was born.

Years later, when Chris almost destroyed my little girl, I wanted to kill him. I might have done so if it wasn't for

Momma. I never told her about how Chris molested Maren. She was old and I was afraid it might kill her. All my life, she sacrificed for me. I wanted Chris to rot in jail for what he did to Maren. But staying quiet was the sacrifice I made for Momma.

—From *Save Me: A Memoir* by Calvin Emory

CHAPTER 6

March 1999

There was something comforting about being back on the interstate. Although I had never driven this far south, I-75 looked like any other interstate I'd ever been on. Periodic rest stops, construction lane closures in the wee hours, a certain tranquility at three, four and five in the morning. I hadn't stopped for food or gas before leaving Atlanta. There was no time to waste in putting distance between me and Calvin. When both my car and I needed a break, I chose a rest stop outside of Valdosta, not far from the Florida state border. I was headed to Gainesville to see my sister, Maren, a sophomore at the University of Florida.

It was ingenious how every interstate rest stop had been standardized for travelers. You didn't have to worry about eating strange food in strange part of the country. Every rest stop had Burger King or McDonald's. Cinnabon. Starbucks. Dozens of bathroom stalls and countless vending machines. Grubby people exiting their cars, blinking at the bright lights and trying to decide whether to drink Coke or coffee. You might not like it, but it was familiar, and familiarity trumped quality every time. I wondered if I looked as bleary-eyed and disoriented as the people around me. No one gave me a second glance, so I probably did.

I chose Starbucks and Cinnabon. I pumped my gas, then headed back toward my sister. It was after six and the sun peeked out, as if it were not sure it would show itself. I thought about Calvin, passed out in his hotel room. I willed my shoulders to unclench and I took a deep breath. I would call Maren when I got to Gainesville.

Since my sister went away to college, we didn't see each other often. During holiday breaks, she came back to Durham but she stayed with Calvin. It was a reminder that she could move on and I could not; extraordinary, because she had much more to forgive than I did. It was, after all, Calvin's half-brother who had been both her molester and, she thought, her first love. But four years had passed, and she seemed to have healed much better than I had.

She visited me on campus, but they were brief times spent trying to make up for all the time we missed. It was a relief to see her. She was my connection, the only person who loved me, I thought, no matter what. After our mother died, I appointed myself her protector in all things. I failed. She survived anyway.

I think I gasped when my sister opened the door to her dorm. She wore frayed jeans and a grey hooded sweatshirt with "UF" emblazoned on the front in orange.

It was still early on a Friday morning, and she still wore black-rimmed granny glasses on the tip of her nose. Her hair, grown longer than I'd ever seen it, brushed her shoulders in a mess of tangles. She smiled at me, and I wanted to cry. She looked so much like Mom.

This was nothing new. Maren had always resembled our mother, even at fifteen when she felt ugly and boyish. She could never see what I saw, what the world saw.

Back then, Maren's beauty lurked around the edges of her eyes, waiting for its chance to escape her insecurities and fears. Now, she was twenty years old, and I knew without being told that she drew second and third glances. There were differences, of course. Our mother had been fair-skinned. Maren was brown. Maren's eyes were dark and her hair was kinky, not straight. But those were superficial things that didn't matter. Standing there, an escapee from college, my father, my life, I saw Maren with fresh eyes. What I saw was our mother.

"Why are you staring at me?" Maren frowned at me and looked pointedly at her watch. I had called her on my way onto campus. It wasn't even eight o'clock yet. "I have an exam at three, you know. I was up studying all night."

I grinned and grabbed her into a bear hug. "I'm happy to see you, Mare. I missed you."

She thumped me on the back and mumbled into my chest, "I missed you, too."

Her roommate was away for the weekend, so I slept in Maren's dorm room all day. We met up after her test that afternoon.

"How did it go?" I handed her a jacket I'd grabbed from her room. She wore only a shirt-sleeved T-shirt and jeans. It was technically spring, but the cold breeze and cloudy skies told a different story.

Maren made a face. "Biology. I hate it."

I couldn't relate. I'd always loved biology, any kind of science. It made sense to me. There was uncertainty, but science promised a logical way to find the truth. All you needed was perseverance.

But Maren had always hated science classes, math, anything with a right answer.

"Why are you taking bio?"

She shrugged. "I'm taking calculus, too." She wouldn't meet my eyes. We continued walking toward my car. She wanted to go to the mall, then dinner. I hated the mall, but I loved Maren.

We stopped at the passenger door. I grabbed her arm before she opened the door.

"Mare. Don't waste your time trying to make other people happy."

She stared at the door handle, willing it to open.

"What do you mean?"

I squeezed her arm, then let go. "Look at me."

Several long moments passed before she did. She was trying not to cry.

"You think because I like science that you have to? You think that will make me proud of you?"

A tear rolled from one of her eyes and she swiped at it, angry at its escape. She folded her arms over her chest.

"I could be a doctor. We'll both be doctors."

And then everything will be okay. I knew that's what she was thinking. My sister spent too much energy trying to make everything okay. She'd been a mediator since she was small—between our mother and me, between our father and me, between anyone who seemed the least bit unhappy and whatever caused their pain. But mostly me. She was always trying to make sure I was okay. And I always thought I was protecting her.

I shook my head.

"We are who we are. You could be the best doctor in the world. And still, we are who we are."

She watched my eyes as I spoke. I didn't know if I was making sense.

"I guess what I mean is, nothing will ever be okay if you keep pretending that it is. You know?"

She nodded. "But if I stop pretending . . ."

I put my arms around her shoulders and drew my sister close to my chest.

"If you stop pretending, then everything will be okay."

The tears came then. When she was finished crying, I felt as if she'd released something in both of us. We pulled apart, and I smiled at her.

"Now dry up. There's no crying at the Gap."

Maren had been here for two years, but this was the first time I had visited Gainesville. I had intended to drive her down from Durham, to set her up in her freshman dorm, to make sure she would be safe. But of course, Calvin had insisted that this was *his* job. I would not do the drive with our father. Maren had cried, but even my sister the mediator had to agree it was best for Calvin and me to avoid the close quarters of a road trip.

I wished I had remembered that wise decision before I agreed to go on the book-signing tour with Calvin. Well, that didn't last long. Anyway, I don't know what I was thinking. Why would I look to Calvin, of all people, for some kind of solace? He didn't have answers. I didn't even know what the question was.

I sat on an upholstered bench in the mall that looked liked every other mall in the world. The bends and curves of Gainesville's streets were strange to me, but the people were familiar. It reminded me of Durham: a place known by outsiders and students only for the university the city hosted. But also a place where regular people, people with jobs that didn't require a Ph.D. or even an A.A., lived, worked, laughed, mourned and resented the presumptuous intrusion of professors and students.

Academics swooped in and out of the city with the seasons, bringing both their money and their derision. Or perhaps derision wasn't the right word. Indifference was more like it. The people in this mall were invisible to the students, unless they needed a refill on their Coke or a price check on a pair of one-hundred-dollar shoes. The differences weren't necessarily economic, and I was a perfect example of this. I had no money at all, really, although I hid it well behind my aging BMW and my designer clothes, leftovers from another era. It was more about class, and the knowledge that Gainesville, or Durham, or any other college town, was a mere rest stop on the way to somewhere better. Or, if one lived here, it was a means to an end that had nothing to do with caring about the city itself.

From the corner of my eye I saw a young woman with pockmarked skin and brassy blonde hair that hung limp around her face. She wore a cheap nylon jacket and jeans that were too tight. She dragged a grubby toddler behind her. His face was covered in some kind of sticky dirt, and it looked like he'd drawn on his bare arms in brown marker. I was trying to make out what he'd written when I realized the woman, who wasn't any older than me, was glaring.

She recognized it immediately, the difference between us. We might both be at the mall, but we were different. I was just like those UF students who used up Gainesville and then left as soon as they could. She was stuck here with her dirty kid and no father in sight. To make matters worse, I was black and wearing a cashmere sweater that probably cost twice as much as her week's grocery budget.

I caught myself feeling sorry for her. She seemed to know it, because she hissed as she passed me.

"What are you looking at, nigger?"

I put on my biggest, most ingratiating smile and waved to her. She stomped off, madder than ever. I sighed and sat back. I couldn't work up the energy to be offended. I couldn't really blame her for hating someone. That it happened to be me was beyond both of our control.

Maren flitted in and out of nearby stores, holding up bags as a kind of plea for my patience. I shook off the memory of the young woman and smiled at Maren, a real smile, this time. I would sit there all night for Maren. She was buoyed by our earlier conversation. She thought I had granted her permission to do what she wanted, take the classes she wanted, to be whatever she desired. The thing was, she had never needed my permission. All I did was tell her the truth. I didn't feel like I'd learned much in my twenty-two years of living. But I'd told her one of the things I was sure of.

Watching Maren spend money neither of us had, watching her try on clothes that made her look impossibly pretty, imagining her free of the crippling burden of our family history, the numbness was all but gone.

"Are you okay?"

This was the first reference Maren made to my sudden appearance at her doorstep on a random Friday morning. She was good that way, knowing when not to ask questions. Sometimes I thought it got her in trouble, this reluctance to question motives. It was certainly part of the reason why our uncle Chris was able to convince her they were in love. He helped her forget what she'd always known—that no matter how close in age they were (he was twenty-one when she was fifteen), no matter how tenuous the DNA connection (he was technically only our half-uncle), no matter how good he made her feel, it was wrong. Of course, it was his fault, not hers. The only thing was, this lack of questioning made her an easier target, if there was anything easier than a motherless fifteen-year-old with self-esteem issues.

We were sitting at dinner in the restaurant Maren had chosen. It was one of the chains, something with an Italian name that was two steps above the Olive Garden but not nearly as good as real Italian food. Our mother would have hated this place, with the hokey opera music playing in the background, the cheery wait staff and the cheap table wine. She had loved Italian food, but only if it was expensive and authentic. Also, since she was a locally famous television personality on her way to being a nationally famous one, she liked a place where it meant something to be seen.

I pushed my menu aside and fiddled with my paper napkin.

"Have you talked to Calvin?"

Maren frowned. "No. Please tell me nothing happened."

I weighed this. What had happened, exactly? I went to him for some kind of solace, enveloped in a misguided (delusional?) father-son fantasy, and he did what? Proved to me yet again that all he cared about was himself? Was that news?

"Have you read his new book?"

She raised her eyebrows. "Have you?"

I was happy that the cheery waiter, Brett, came by to take our orders. I couldn't talk about the book without going off onto a rant, and I didn't want to spoil our dinner together. The other alternative was to pretend that

I didn't care about *Save Me*. But I had promised my sister that I'd never lie to her.

Maren ordered some kind of pasta with vegetables. I got the veal parmesan. It didn't matter. I knew I wouldn't be able to taste it anyway. I decided not to get into the whole Atlanta thing. She'd find out one way or another, and I didn't have answers for the inevitable first question: Why did I ever agree to go with him in the first place?

"Did you know it's a memoir?"

Maren nodded. She looked off to the side of the large dining room, where a family, parents and two small kids, had been stashed. It was late for dinner—nine o'clock—and the little boy showed some signs of tiredness. The main sign was that he dripping ketchup from the dispenser on the floor around his chair in a bright red semicircle. His parents seemed not to notice, as they were shoving lasagna into their mouths and gulping the cheap table wine. The little girl, perhaps four years old, was slumped in her chair, asleep with a piece of garlic bread clutched in one hand.

Maren watched this with a slight smile. I wondered what she was thinking. Then she turned back to me.

"You didn't answer my question. Are you okay?"

Our dinner arrived then, giving me a few minutes to consider my answer while our meals were covered in fresh ground pepper and freshly grated parmesan cheese.

I wished I could lie to Maren, tell her something that would make her feel good, make her feel safe. But we promised each other we wouldn't lie.

"I walked out of class earlier this week because I watched a dead man being cut open and I didn't feel a

75

thing. I went, of all places, to see Calvin. He and I went to Atlanta together, where I left him alone in a hotel room last night. I came here without calling, or without any reason, really, except that I missed you. I just ordered a plate of something I can't even taste. I haven't tasted food in months."

I took a dramatic bite of my dinner and chewed the amalgam of Playdoh, cotton and grass.

"So no," I said, my mouth full, "I'm not okay."

Maren set down her fork and looked at me.

"Is it Angela?"

I tried to swallow, but the wad caught in my throat, stretching and pulling. Finally, my mouth and throat were clear, but the mass sat in my stomach, heavy and threatening.

"I gave you the list. I never said anything about Angela."

Just to say her name made my stomach tighten around the undigested lump.

Maren stared. I shrugged and took another bite. Angela hadn't been in that classroom. She didn't drive me to my father's house. She wasn't in Atlanta, and she definitely hadn't written a book about my family.

But of course, Maren was right. It was Angela. It was always Angela.

Calvin on careers and relationships:

When Vanessa's career began to take off, I was overcome with a crippling sense of jealousy. She was a natural in front of the camera; when I first saw her doing the news on a small cable station, I couldn't imagine her more comfortable anywhere else. She was meant to be on television, and I mean that in the best way possible. Vanessa was everything we want from the people who deliver news—sincere, intelligent, beautiful, articulate.

And I hated her for it. Even though she was still working freelance when we broke up, I knew that she was headed in the right direction. And where was I headed? Nowhere, really. I studying a variety of subjects in college, none with overwhelming success. I must have changed my major four times before I settled on English, and that's only because it was the subject in which I had the most credits. I had no intention of being an English major when I first went to college. I had read all the beat poets in high school, and I had this romanticized notion of a writer as someone who wasn't created in the classroom, but in the world. College was a way for me to get out of Durham and into the rest of the world, so I wasn't too concerned about what I studied.

The problem was, I didn't write a decent word while I was in college, and afterward, when Vanessa and I got married and had the kids, I used them as an excuse for why I wasn't writing. The excuse didn't hold up to scrutiny, because being a wife and a mother didn't stop Vanessa from actually pursuing her goals in a realistic way. I just worked as a substitute teacher and other odd jobs, not wanting to be too tied down when the muse finally visited. I was certain that a career would block any creative inspiration, and I'd read enough Hemingway and Faulkner to convince myself that drinking to excess was also part of the necessary creative process.

Instead of hating myself, I tried to diminish each of Vanessa's successes, trying to convince her that she wasn't doing nearly as well as she thought. Every step forward, I reminded her of someone who was three steps ahead. The drunker I got, the meaner I became. I was certain that she simply didn't believe in me, and if only she supported me, I could have written freely. I can't blame Vanessa for finally tiring of me.

—From *Save Me: A Memoir* by Calvin Emory

CHAPTER 7

Spring 1996

I watched Jason and Angela fall in love. I didn't want to. But it was there, every moment of the day, even when I wasn't with them. I couldn't look away. It wasn't like watching something horrible happen and being drawn to the morbidity of it all. It was more like watching a movie, something I never would have chosen, maybe a romantic comedy. I started watching convinced I would hate it, convinced that I could not be touched by the sentiment. But it wasn't long before I was swept away by the sweetness. But the sweetness had an aftertaste that lingered long after the pleasurable part was gone. Watching Jason and Angela fall in love made my own loneliness, and my desire for Angela, all the more unbearable.

Yet I watched. It was the closest thing I had to love. I couldn't look away.

I also couldn't help thinking of it as some kind of logical process. I outlined it in my head as it happened. Every event seemed to follow another as if it were inevitable. Each new step was unsurprising, predictable. It never occurred to me to try to interfere. Before this, I had considered myself a realist, perhaps fatalistic in my world view. Shit happened and there was nothing you could do about it. Your mother died, your father was a jerk, you followed the path set before you whether you wanted to or not.

But as I watched Angela and Jason become Angelaandjason, I realized that my view of life wasn't quite so negative. I hadn't thought much about God. But this thing between them somehow seemed right, in a good way. It was not my place to try to keep them apart. They were meant to be, and it wasn't just shit happening. At the beginning, what they had was pure. It was good. And so I simply watched.

Step 1: The First Date

The campus was still deserted when we got back to Duke, save for a few souls who would rather putter around an empty dorm than endure the post-holiday let-down at home.

I lay back on my bed, my arms folded, with the back of my head resting on my hands. I had propped a book up on my bended knees, and I turned a page every once in a while to make it look like I was studying.

Jason whirled around our suite with more energy than I'd ever seen from him. He splashed on expensive cologne, changed pants three times and tried to choose between two ties.

"Which one?" he asked, holding them both up to his throat.

"Umm, does this place require a tie?" They were going to a restaurant in Chapel Hill. I'd heard of it because it was a big date night spot, but I'd never been there. In any case, I thought a tie was overkill. "You don't want to seem too eager."

He nodded. "Good point." Jason tossed aside the ties and rummaged through his closet for a sport coat.

"What are you reading, anyway? Classes haven't even started yet."

I looked down at my book. It was my calculus text-book from first semester.

"I'm just reviewing." I figured the vaguer, the better. Plus, he was an English major who was allergic to math. He wouldn't know any better.

"Blue or black?" He held up two jackets. It was starting to feel like a fashion show.

"Blue."

Jason slipped on the sport coat and smiled at me. "You know a lot about date clothes."

For someone who never dates, I finished for him in my head. He was still smiling, so I knew he didn't mean to make me feel like a sharp stick had just stabbed into my chest.

I laughed and hoped it sounded genuine. "I'm an expert from way back. I'm just laying low, actually *studying*."

Jason made a face. "No one studies over Christmas break."

Including me. I tossed the book aside and stood up.

"I'm going to find something to eat. Have fun." I called this back over my shoulder as I left. I tried not to wonder whether Angela was spending this much time worried about her clothes, too.

Step 2: The Courtship

By late spring, I was devoting more time than was needed to organic chemistry, and Angela was a regular in our suite. In fact, she was there more often than I was. I made it a point to see her as little as possible. I felt transparent. I was convinced that if we spent enough time together, she would know that I was falling in love with her right along with Jason. Worse, maybe, I feared Jason would see it.

It was the end of spring break when she made her first appearance in our suite. Jason had gone home to Baltimore (without me this time) and I spent the week reading and thinking of Angela. Mostly thinking of Angela. She consumed my daydreams in the purest way. I thought of her skin, her smile, the way she held her own the night of that first party. I imagined myself in Jason's place, taking her out to dinner, using my family's money to buy her gifts that were expensive but not presumptuous. In my mind, she and I were never far apart, and she found my imagined combination of charm and introspection impossible to resist.

This was as far as I let it go. In my mind, Angela was not a sexual object. I saved those thoughts for other women on campus, those mortals who could not approach Angela's stature. I would not sully her image with mere sex.

But at the end of spring, it seemed Jason had no such qualms. It was the Saturday before classes and was warm, so I decided to go out for once and get some fresh air. I knew moping around the dorm wasn't a good idea, but that day was the first all week that I was motivated to do anything else. I drove over to Chapel Hill and looked through used CD shops on Franklin Street. I was in the mood for something depressing. I flipped through the CD singles for something that wouldn't remind me of Angela. Live's "I Alone." "Can't Stop Lovin' You" by some dubious incarnation of Van Halen. Madonna: "I Want You." Even "Fantasy" by Mariah Carey. Wasn't there even one song that didn't somehow remind me that not only did I ache for Angela, but that I was utterly alone?

I abandoned the record store empty-handed, got a large coffee from a shop down the street and headed back to the dorm. I wasn't expecting Jason back until the next day, so that's why I was paralyzed by the sight of him and Angela entwined on the bed, naked.

I stood in the doorway long enough for the outlines of Angela's soft curves to imprint themselves on my brain. That image of her, sleek and brown, on top of my best friend, has never left me.

I backed out, silent and ashamed. I made no noise as I shut the door, surprised by the anger I felt. I have never decided with whom I was angry, or why. Me, for watching longer than I had to? Jason, for taking her away from me? Angela, for not seeing me? The worst part of my voyeurism was the fact that by necessity, I would always be an outsider. Jason and Angela each had something I wanted. Jason had Angela, and Angela had love.

Thou shall not covet. I knew I was wrong, but I had no idea how to stop watching, how to shift my focus so I wasn't reminded of what I didn't have at every turn. I coveted. There is no commandment that told me how to get rid of the envy I felt for Jason and the desire I felt for Angela. Just say no? Just do it? How?

I spent the rest of the day in the library. When it closed, I sat in my car. I planned to stay up all night but, at some point, I slept, and when I woke up, the sun shone through my front window. I had slept sitting up in the driver's seat. I had dreamt of Angela.

Step 3. In Love

In the romance of Jason and Angela, I took on the role of confidante to both of them without the other one knowing.

"Can I tell you something? I mean, I know Jason is your friend, but I need to talk to a guy about this. You're the sweetest guy I know."

We had both emerged from the Social Sciences building at the same time. I had given her an awkward wave and she came up and hugged me. Now, we walked toward the Bryan Center to grab something to eat. Finals were almost over and I was both relieved and anxious at the thought of the coming summer. Jason would be spending the summer in Europe with his mother. All I had planned was a short trip back to Chicago with Maren to visit our mother's grave. Not exactly a fun vacation.

Angela and I had become friendly over the past months. How we could not—she spent nearly every free moment in our suite, and, of course, I liked her. It was impossible for me to hold her relationship with Jason against her, not when she told me her favorite books were mysteries about some Scotland Yard cop named Jury. How could we not be friends, when she agreed with me that there was nothing better than Taco Bell in the middle of the night? She was the only other black person I knew who would admit to preferring Weezer over Nas.

These things made me want her even more. These things seemed to make her see me as some kind of asexual boyfriend, one to whom she could spill her secrets without risk. She called me "sweet." I hated it. I loved it.

I promised to seal my lips with Super Glue. She went on.

"I think I'm in love with your boy."

She seemed to think this was a shocking revelation. I looked down at her.

"And?"

She sighed. "And, what if I tell him I love him and he doesn't say anything? Or he gets scared? I want to tell him before he goes away for the summer."

I had some time to think as we entered the front doors of the Bryan Center, walked downstairs to order sandwiches and settled into one of the TV rooms. On a regular day during the semester, this room would have been packed with people getting their daily *Young and the Restless* fix. But during exams, even the hardest partiers shut themselves into carrels at Perkins Library. We had the large room to ourselves. I turned on the television for background noise. It was three o'clock. *Oprah* time.

"To be honest, I think you should tell him how you feel. Not only is it obvious that he's into you, but you don't want to pretend you don't care. Not with something this important."

I meant what I said. I couldn't lie or try to get in the way of Jason and Angela. Thou shall not bear false witness. After nearly six months of watching them together, I was convinced they loved each other.

She took a bite of her turkey club and smiled at me.

"You're right. I'll tell him tonight."

She spoke before she'd finished chewing and a bit of lettuce stuck between her teeth. It was adorable.

That image of her body flashed through my mind, as it did about a thousand times a day. I banished it and turned up the volume on the television.

"Good. Now can you shut up? Oprah's revealing the secrets of housewives today."

Angela punched me in the arm and took another bite. I settled into the worn sofa.

"I'll bet you dessert that one of them is smoking crack while her kids are at school."

"Cheesecake?" Angela's tone was childish and hopeful. It was another adorable thing about her—she ate like a guy, especially desserts.

"Of course."

"I say she's turning tricks after PTA meetings. Bet's on."

The next week, I sat on the bed, watching Jason pack up his things for the summer. We'd already taken down all of the posters from the walls. Our bookshelves were empty. My own clothes were packed, but I was only moving across campus to another dorm room, where I would spend the summer taking extra classes. Jason had talked me into renting an apartment off campus with him next year. His parents would pay for his half. I had found a part-time job with one of the biology professors to pay for mine. Angela was going home to Chicago.

Jason tried to jam one final pair of jeans into his stuffed suitcase.

"Can I tell you something? Promise you won't laugh."

"I'm not laughing."

He cleared his throat. "I think I'm in love with Angela."

Oh really? Did he think I didn't have eyes? Ears? A heart?

"That's cool, man. Why would you think I'd laugh about that?"

He grinned. "Well, we spent all that time talking about how we weren't going to get tied down. And now, I'm ready to get tied down, you know what I mean?"

I tried to smile back. "Yeah. I know what you mean."

The bare walls of the room felt as if they were closing in on me. None of this was news. I knew he loved Angela. And she loved him. But a tiny part of me, the part I wasn't proud of, had hoped that she was fooling herself, that he didn't feel the same. That tiny little shameful part wished he would break her heart and leave her for someone like me to save. I was ashamed. I wished I were a better person. I wished this wasn't happening.

Calvin on love:

When I met Vanessa, I couldn't believe my luck. She was everything I had always wanted in a woman: smart, pretty, fun. I didn't really think of her as a real person, a person with gifts and flaws just like anyone else. If I'm being honest, I didn't even know women were real people—I was young and women were still like alien beings to me. Growing up so sheltered by my mother and living in a town where all the women were either wives and mothers, or they were preparing to be wives and mothers, I had no idea that a woman could have facets that had nothing to do with me. Women were supposed to take care of men, I thought, and when I met Vanessa, I thought she was the perfect wife for me and mother for my future children.

Putting someone on a pedestal never works. Looking back, I can see that I was desperate to be loved. There was a hole in my life and it threatened to suck me down into it. Vanessa, with her beauty and poise, would save me.

It was too much to ask of another person, and it's a wonder we lasted long enough to have our two children, long enough to regret all the mistakes we made. The mistakes I made. I wish I had known then what I know now. The only person who could save me was me.

—From *Save Me: A Memoir* by Calvin Emory

CHAPTER 8

March 1999

I sat in my car on the campus of the University of Florida with my last exchange with Maren ringing in my ears.

"You take care, kiddo." I chucked her under the chin and she laughed.

We stood next to my car. I opened my door and climbed in.

"You know, I'm thinking, maybe I should change my major."

I looked up at her. She smiled.

"I'm thinking English."

I nodded. "We don't need too many doctors in the family anyway."

I watched her walk back toward her dorm. So there was that. I felt satisfied that I had accomplished at least one positive thing in the past two days. Now I drove away, uncertain of where I would go next.

There was a gnawing feeling at the back of my head. I drove a few miles away from campus before I realized what it was. Guilt. This was nothing new for me. It seemed like I'd been feeling guilty about one thing or another since the day my mother died. Maybe before. But the time before my mother died, when my family was predictable, imperfect but intact, had become a haze of unreliable memories. In five years, I could no longer remember the contours of my mother's face without staring at a photo. And each time I stared at the photos, I saw Maren in my mother instead of the other way around. My sister was flesh and blood, living, needed, trying. My mother was gone.

Why was I guilty? My mother died before I had a chance to tell her that it was okay that she wasn't home a lot, that she put her career before my desire for a more traditional mother. I never had the chance to stop the bickering, to tell her that I loved her flawed, lovely ways. I was seventeen when she died, and at seventeen I didn't know how to apologize. I didn't know that she could be taken from me without notice. I didn't know how fleeting love truly was. Angela had taught me that.

Why was I guilty? Because while I was busy hating my father after we moved to North Carolina to live with him, my sister found her first love, a love that was muddy gray and destined for failure. I was all she had, and I failed to protect her and instead had worried most about how much I hated our father.

Why was I guilty? Because I left school without letting anyone know. Because I left my father passed out in a hotel room. Because of Angela. Because I promised her I would be strong, and, in the end, I was too weak to do the right thing.

Angela wouldn't speak to me. Chris was gone. And the thing Maren had asked of me before I left was simple.

"Go back and talk to him. Just try. He's our father, and hating him doesn't change that," she said.

I had refused to do it so many times before, but there was something different about the way she asked, as if she was trying to show me something I couldn't see on my own. I didn't know if my sister was right. Was there a chance of a relationship between me and Calvin?

His next book signing was in Jacksonville. I headed east.

There wasn't much to see on the seventy-mile trip from Gainesville to Jacksonville. The weather was balmy, so I kept the windows open. Stray papers blew around the car and some out onto the highway, but I didn't care. They weren't my papers anyway, since I kept my car in pristine condition. Perhaps they were Maren's, or Calvin's. There weren't any particular sights, but the smells were unfamiliar. At one point, I passed by a burning field, and in the distance I could see the orange light of flames. There was the fragrance of yeast as I drove past a bread warehouse. It reminded me of childhood .rips to Milwaukee, driving past Pabst and feeling nearly choked by the smell of hops. And, as I grew closer to Jacksonville, I could taste the salt in the air. The coppery smell of the beach was unmistakable, although I was still miles from the water.

The perfumes kept me company as I considered what to say to my father. How could I make him see how much his indifference hurt me, hurt Maren? Before our mother died, we hadn't seen Calvin in years. Why didn't he care enough to see us before our lives were ripped apart? I wasn't sure I could find the words to explain how angry I had been at seventeen, even before I lived with Calvin. How would I explain the way I avoided him after I went to college, even though we lived just miles apart? How could I explain why, this week, after more than four years, I came to him?

Part of the problem was that I didn't have the answers. I just knew that I had to say something. It occurred to me, as I chewed through another tasteless rest stop meal, that my life depended on it. If I didn't talk to Calvin now, at least try, I feared that I might spend the rest of my life in this bubble, detached and alone. If I didn't settle things with Calvin, I would lose myself for good.

I was struck most by the sound of Calvin's voice. It was deep and smooth, confident. The words, as he spoke them, felt like velvet. Even though I had never read more than the inside jacket of his novel, the words were familiar, like old friends I didn't even know I was missing. I focused not on what he was saying, but each word. It was the only way I could listen.

I sat in the back of a sizeable crowd, all of us in folding chairs in the B. Dalton in the Regency Square Mall. It struck me that I was spending a lot of time in malls since I'd left Durham. Florida was filled with "villes" and massive shopping centers. As I drove into the sprawling city, I wondered why the western suburbs existed. Who would live in Florida and not demand to be close to the water? Without the ocean, Florida was common, nothing special at all.

I had arrived just as he was shuffling through the book, finding his place. Calvin was absorbed in his own impending performance and so he didn't notice when I took a seat and moved it directly behind a wide woman sitting in the back row. I didn't need to see him. I didn't want him to see me. Not yet.

I couldn't tell whether the book was good or not. I didn't want to think about it. I still felt as if he'd stolen from me by deciding to tell his story, which was also my story. But I was also sorry that I couldn't stop running away whenever my father slighted me. He'd been doing it my entire life. During the drive from Gainesville to Jacksonville, I decided that I would not run from him anymore. I was a man. I had to face Calvin.

His voice stopped. There was a moment before the applause erupted. I looked around at smiling faces. The crowd had enjoyed the words, what they meant. They had probably been listening. I slouched down in my seat, shielded by milling customers and a short line of people waiting to have their copies of *Save Me* signed. Soon, the crowd dispersed and Calvin looked up. Our eyes met. His face showed no reaction at first, but I thought I saw his jaw tighten. I stood and approached his table.

"So maybe we should talk." I kept looking in his eyes for some sign, of what, I don't know.

He looked down at the book he still held in his hand and nodded.

"Maybe we should. But Ellison, you have to promise me that you're going to stay and actually talk. You can't leave every time someone says something you don't like."

But you *can* pass out, or pretend to be asleep, when you son asks you a hard question? You *can* write about your family secrets without even a courtesy heads-up? You *can* be a shitty father and seemingly not care?

I thought these things, but I didn't say them. I was a man. He was never going to be anything other than himself. I could spend the rest of my life fighting that, or I could face it. Like a man.

"I came back, didn't I? I didn't have to, but I did." If I wasn't allowed to act like a child, he wasn't allowed to treat me like one. "So maybe we should talk."

He nodded. "You hungry?"

We walked out of the store and toward the rental car Calvin had obtained in Atlanta. That guilt crept up the back of my neck, but I brushed it away. I couldn't let guilt get in the way. I'd made a list in my head of the things I wanted to tell him. I wouldn't be able to speak my mind if I was worried about feeling guilty. I was wrong to leave him in Atlanta. He was wrong, too, in a lot of ways that were worse than leaving someone in a hotel room. So now what?

"How about seafood? Somewhere on the water?"

I shrugged. "Sounds good."

Calvin didn't miss a turn on the way to the restaurant. I was called One Ocean Way. I presumed it was the address. We were sitting and Calvin had ordered a bottle of wine before it occurred to me that he must have been here before. He glanced at the menu before putting it aside to sample the pinot grigio. I felt subdued by the muted crowd surrounding us, by the heavy white table-cloths, by the prices of the entrees. I felt like it was the first time I'd ever been to a nice restaurant, though my mother took me to many, mostly against my will. The menu was a long rectangle weighing heavy in my palms. I chose scallops when the waiter asked, and I ordered a beer to get up my nerve. I told myself I would say every-thing I had to say to Calvin. I told myself to be calm. Be clear. Be honest. Be a man.

Instead, I downed two more beers before the food arrived, and Calvin matched me, finishing his bottle of white wine. He ordered another bottle, and by halfway through the meal, we were drunk and laughing. Calvin told me the story of how he met my mother the first time. I'd heard it before. Mom used to tell it to me, to remind me that I was born from love, even though that love didn't last. But I liked hearing him tell it. I liked that he told it exactly the same this time as he had the first time I heard him tell it, when we'd first moved to Durham. That time, Maren was with us and I watched her relish the story, yearning to get closer to our mother in any way she could. That time, I didn't want to hear it because it just reminded me that my mother was gone. This time, it reminded me that my mother would always be here with me.

"I was young, you know, and I felt cooped up back in Durham. It was the same people doing the same thing all the time, and I felt that if I didn't get out, I'd end up just like everyone else. So I took a bus to Chicago. I'd never been there, but I'd heard there were a lot of black writers there and I figured I could learn something. Most people were running off to New York back then, but I don't know, something about Chicago called me."

He paused to gesture to the waiter for another bottle of wine that we didn't need. I was already feeling woozy. I ate my food without tasting it, hoping it would absorb some of the alcohol. Hoping that this time, it might taste like something instead of nothing.

"So I got there, and it was late summer, so the weather was still nice. But as soon as I stepped off the bus, I noticed there were police cars everywhere and news cameras filming. There had been a murder near the station, and it was big news.

"Well, I'd never seen anything like this back in Durham, so I hung around the edges of the scene, watching the cameramen squat to get just the right angle, listening to the police bark orders at each other. And then I noticed a pretty girl who was holding a pad and pen and pushing her way through the throngs of people to talk to the main cop. She was so petite and beautiful. I couldn't believe the way she forced the cop to talk to her as she scribbled on her pad.

"Something clicked inside me, and I suddenly had to know this lovely, tough, determined woman. So I sneaked underneath the police tape, went up to her and asked her out," Calvin finished, staring off into the air over my head as if he could see that Chicago street corner. I wanted to turn and look too, but I knew she wasn't there.

"It was love at first sight."

Five years ago, I'd found that notion corny and trite. I told him so then, but he told me I'd change my mind one day.

I pushed my plate away and accepted the full glass my father offered me. I gulped down half of it before I realized that the last time he told me that story, we'd also been drinking. Why was it that we could only talk when we were drinking?

I told him about Angela, about how we met, about how we became friends while she dated Jason. I told him that nothing ever happened between us. A lie. I told him I now believed in love at first sight. That was true.

Calvin grinned at me. "So you believe me now. That's how it was with your mother and me. Right from the start. And no matter what happened later, we always had that."

His face got serious. "Does Angela love you?"

I shrugged, wanting to change the subject. "It doesn't matter. It's in the past."

He shook his head. "If she loved you, you'll always have that."

I started to believe him. I wanted to believe him. I was going to ask him more, get him to convince me that things might work out after all with me and Angela, even though she hadn't spoken to me for months, even though she promised never to speak to me again. Even though she had never said "I love you." But Calvin called for the check, and the mood was broken.

I don't know how we made it back to the hotel. I don't remember getting a room or taking off my shoes. The last thoughts I had were thoughts of long ago, when things were not difficult between me and my father. When I was still eight years old, during the time before he went away. I let the tenderness wash over me. I was almost asleep before I remembered that there had never been a time when things weren't difficult between us.

Calvin on fear:

One of my biggest regrets is that I let fear dictate too many of my choices as a young man, and, unfortunately, as a mature adult as well. If I had to give one reason why my marriage failed and my family fell apart, it is fear. Don't misunderstand me: there are always many reasons why a relationship doesn't work, and it's never the fault of just one person. But all the reasons why Vanessa and I couldn't be together were rooted in fear.

After Ellison and Maren were born, things changed between us. We were no longer a couple, but a group of four, and Vanessa and I had barely learned how to be together before we started having babies. She was different; a mother first and a wife second, I thought, and that felt like a betrayal. I was afraid of not coming first in her life. I didn't believe our love would survive it. So I made the possibility of failure a certainty by having affairs with women in such a blatant way that Vanessa couldn't ignore them even if she tried.

I was punishing her for putting my needs below those of the children. I was proving to Vanessa, and myself, that I was still desirable, that there were women who would put me first, even if my wife no longer wanted to. I made sure that I was not the victim in the eventual demise of our life together.

None of the affairs were long-term. None of them were with women particularly beautiful or irresistible. It wasn't really about sex. I was just afraid to try to make things right, because if I failed, it meant that something was wrong with me.

—From *Save Me: A Memoir* by Calvin Emory

CHAPTER 9

Spring 1997

Jason and Angela dated for a little over a year before he started cheating on her. We didn't talk about it, not at first. It started with calls from girls I knew weren't in any of his classes. Girls who hung around with basketball players and football players and sometimes lacrosse players. Girls who, when called by a basketball player or a football player or sometimes a lacrosse player, would appear as if by magic, dressed in short skirts or tight pants and tank tops, even in winter. Girls who were available at two o'clock in the afternoon or two o'clock in the morning. Girls who were not Angela.

It was somewhat unusual that these girls called Jason, since he wasn't a basketball player or a football player or even a lacrosse player. I supposed that being the wealthy son of an NBA coach was good enough.

It started with calls, but it wasn't long before some of the girls started hanging around the apartment we rented near campus. Jason paid his share of the rent with his allowance. I paid my share by working in biology labs and as a research assistant. This kept me out of the apartment most of the time, but when I was there, I watched the girls fawn over Jason. They laughed at everything he said, even when he was being serious. They cooked him dinner and brought it over on nights when he had to study or write a big paper. And they slept in his bed on nights when Angela wasn't around.

They usually traveled in twos, for reasons I could not understand. After a while, they lost their anonymity and I began to recognize distinct pairs. It seemed that every girl had a wingman. I imagined them roaming the campus looking for basketball players and football players and sometimes lacrosse players, one standing guard while the other one cooked or laughed or had sex. Did they trade off? How did they determine which one was lookout for the night? Were they all blonde? Didn't they have studying to do like the rest of us?

I considering asking these questions one night when I ended up sitting in our living room with a girl named Sandra. She was tall and lanky, with a head full of curly blonde hair and a pouty expression. She wore wire-rimmed glasses that she spent a lot of time adjusting for emphasis when she talked. I suspected they were decorative rather than prescription lenses. She wore a white and blue Duke T-shirt and denim shorts even though it was after eight o'clock at night and fifty degrees outside.

It was a rare night that I didn't have homework, so I sat on the couch, flipping channels. Jason had disappeared into his bedroom with her friend just moments before.

"So, what are you watching?" She flopped down next to me and peered over her glasses at the screen. I changed channels even faster and refused to look at her.

"Nothing."

"I'm Sandra."

I looked over at her. She had crossed her long, smooth legs and was kicking the top leg back and forth.

"I'm Ellison."

She beamed at me for no reason, and I looked back at the television. She expected me to make conversation with her, to want to talk to her. I didn't.

"Cynthia really likes Jason." She said this with an air of confidentiality. Now we were best girlfriends sharing a secret.

"Who's Cynthia?"

She threw her head back and laughed. I noticed that all of her reactions were calculated and extreme. It was almost like she thought she was being filmed and wanted her emotions to play big for the audience.

"My friend, silly." She pushed me lightly on the arm. An excuse to touch me. "You're so funny," she giggled.

Maybe the wingman's job included hitting on the roommate. I frowned.

"Are you always like this?"

"Like what?" Eyes wide. Textbook innocence.

"Pretending to be a ditz." Now she frowned.

"You got into Duke, so you can't be that stupid. Why are you hanging around here while *Cynthia* fucks Jason?"

I wasn't just trying to provoke her. I really wanted to know. At that moment, it seemed important for me to understand this antifeminist phenomenon of perfectly intelligent young women acting like groupies, not just for athletes, but for anyone with a perceived edge. Growing up, my mother had drilled into me the idea that women could be anything they wanted, whether that was a housewife or an astrophysicist. It was all a matter of choice, she always said. Mostly, she told me this in her own defense when I was mad because she refused to play June Cleaver to my Beaver. But the lessons had stuck. I expected women my age to be ambitious and interested in ideas that went beyond makeup and short skirts. I expected any woman who got into Duke to be a cut above, to challenge the world, to challenge me. I expected more than this artifice.

So what was the point? To find a husband? Surely these girls were smart enough to know that men don't marry women who give themselves this easily. Men liked the chase, the challenge, the idea that their woman was special, not available to anyone with a bank account or a jump shot. But then, that was an old-fashioned notion, too. I prided myself on being right-minded about women and gender and sex, but I had to acknowledge that most men wanted to spend their college years having wanton sex and then graduate and marry the girl who said no.

There was certainly always a game being played between men and women at Duke, but I feared that these girls, Sandra, Cynthia and the others, were playing the wrong game. Or they were playing the right game but had been given the wrong rules. I knew that when Jason looked back at his college years, he wouldn't even remember their names. Hell, he might not remember their names next week. Looking at Sandra, so deliberate and desperate, I knew that she would regret all of this.

One of my deep disappointments at Duke was the sheer number of girls like this. Some were obvious like Sandra and Cynthia, but others pretended to understand the game yet still made themselves readily available to anyone who was willing to put in a little time and less effort. Sometimes I grew cynical. I believed all the girls were like this. Except Angela.

Sandra reared back at the word "fuck." "You don't have to be so nasty about it. They're just having fun. Jason's cool."

"Jason has a girlfriend."

Sandra shrugged, dropping the act. "So where is she?"

We both turned back to the television. I paused on Channel 4. *Friends* was on.

Sandra bounced in her seat and clapped her hands together. The act was back. "Ooh, I love *Friends*!"

I rolled my eyes and changed the channel.

Later that night, I sat at the kitchen table, flipping through notes for a test I already knew I would ace. I wasn't cocky, just confident in my ability to learn and regurgitate information. I wished my social life went as smoothly as my classwork did. It was nearly two in the morning, and I knew I should get some rest, but I wasn't sleepy. I had just gotten up to scoop out a bowl of ice cream for myself when Jason came trudging in the room.

Cynthia was long gone, and I hadn't seen him since. I assumed he'd fallen asleep in post-coital exhaustion, although even thinking about that made me feel sick. It wasn't the idea of my best friend having sex. Who cared about that? It was the idea that he was throwing Angela away for trash like Cynthia.

He sat down at the table and grinned at me. I pretended to be engrossed in my ice cream.

"So Sandra was cute, right? She told Cynthia she was into you, so I told her to bring her over." Jason nodded at me, still smiling, then stood up to get himself some ice cream. "She's more your type than mine, anyway, so I settled for Cynthia." He threw this last bit back over his shoulder.

He was pretty pleased with himself for someone who was throwing away the best thing he could possibly have. Plus, he essentially gave me Sandra? Her presence was a gift to me? This was a new wrinkle in the whole tawdry scene. Not only was he cheating, but he was giving me the gift of sex? It smacked of some kind of prostitution. I couldn't tell who should be more offended, me or Sandra. Although, if I'm being honest, I was bothered more by the fact that he deemed Sandra my type.

He sat down, looking smug, his mouth full of chocolate chip ice cream. I knew I should let it go. I knew it was none of my business. I knew saying something would just cause problems between us. He was my best friend. He was pretty much my only real friend.

I couldn't let it go.

"What about Angela?"

He shrugged. "What about her?"

"Why are you doing this? I thought you loved her." I hated the sound of my voice. I was whining. I was nagging. I could hear my own feelings for Angela beneath the words.

This wasn't about Jason, not exactly. Yes, he was acting weird, and I was starting to think that I didn't know him as well as I should. But then, our relationship had never been all that deep. He was my entry into Duke's social life, the way in which I masqueraded as normal. Most people knew me through Jason, and his wealth and personality made it easy for people to accept me even though I was generally quiet. If I was being honest, I had to admit that I mostly liked Jason because of what he provided: friendship, connections, a guide through the maze of college society. Now that he was showing me another side of him, it wasn't fair of me to complain.

This wasn't about Jason at all.

He rolled his eyes at me. "I'm only nineteen. I'm not ready to get married."

"Who's talking about marriage?"

He snorted. It was derisive and mean. "She is. I mean, not now. But she's always talking about the future." He squinted his eyes and spoke in a cruel falsetto. " 'Someday, after we're married, maybe we'll go back to Baltimore to live. When can I meet your parents? Shouldn't they meet their future daughter-in-law? Let's name our first son Daniel.' "

He lowered his voice to normal, now waving his spoon in the air. "She pretends like she's joking, but I don't know. It doesn't feel like a joke."

I could think of worse things than naming future children with Angela. I liked the name Daniel. But now

I knew what was bothering Jason. It wasn't the idea of being with Angela, specifically. It was the other stuff. Moving back to Baltimore. Meeting his parents. I knew he wouldn't want her to see what I had seen during that first Christmas break, which Jason said had been pretty low-key for his family. I knew he couldn't imagine settling down under the nearby gaze of Coach Grant Davis.

So this wasn't about Angela, either. Not for Jason.

"I know it's weird when girls talk like that. But Angela, she's special, you know? I know she's just joking. And even if she wasn't, you could do worse than to have someone like her thinking about staying with you for the long haul, you know?"

Jason looked at me for a long moment. He scraped up his last bit of ice cream before he spoke.

"You sound like she's your girlfriend, not mine." He raised his eyebrows at me. I couldn't tell if he was joking. I knew I'd said too much.

I decided to give a hearty laugh. I was going to treat it like a joke.

"I'm just saying, she's a good girl. And these skanks like Cynthia aren't even in her class."

He stood up and smiled down at me. It was a thin smile that hid more than it revealed.

"Don't worry about me and my 'skanks.' I've got it under control." He walked out of the kitchen, and in a few minutes, I heard the front door slam.

I looked at the clock. Three A.M. I wanted to call someone. I needed to talk to someone. My first thought was Angela. But what could I say to her? I'd promised myself that I wouldn't get in between her and Jason, no matter what. I wanted her, but not by default. I wanted her to want *me*, not as a consolation prize. I couldn't talk to Maren about something like this, and, of course, my father was out of the question.

I grabbed the Duke directory and looked up a name She answered on the second ring.

"Sandra? It's Ellison."

If you can't beat 'em, join 'em. The pot calling the kettle black. What goes around comes around. Choose a cliché, any cliché. All of them probably explain why I started sleeping with Sandra. And Cynthia. And a few others. But really, I just needed to put some emotional distance between me and Angela. If I was with other girls, I couldn't spend every moment thinking about Angela. I couldn't love Angela and have sex with Sandra. That was the lie I told myself. And I needed to put some physical distance between me and Jason. I was still furious about what he was doing to Angela, even if I understood it better than even he did. In betraying Angela, he became someone I didn't much like. So I stayed out of the apartment as much as possible, and when we were there together, we were in our separate rooms, sometimes alone but mostly not.

This was the first time in my life I did something for the mere feeling of it, without thought or premeditation. And the thing was, I liked the feel of Sandra's skin under my fingers, the taste of her lips, the smell of her hair. We spent all of our time either naked or preparing to get naked. We had little to say to each other. I don't know why she was with me, even in the casual way in which we defined our relationship. Maybe she thought I had money because of my clothes and car. I never told anyone much about my family, just Jason, who kept my family secrets the way I kept his. I didn't really care why she liked me, if she even did like me. I just liked that she was almost always there when I needed her, and when she wasn't, there was someone else ready to step in and take her place.

The sex was good; it was better than good. But before and after, I loathed myself. Not just for being a hypocrite, not just for what I was doing, but for what I was not doing. Angela deserved to know about Jason, and I was her friend. It was clear that she and I were better friends than Jason and I had ever really been. He and I still went to parties together, we still talked about our fathers every once in a while. But I realized that we didn't really have anything in common besides fucked-up families. And that wasn't enough. I should have told her.

But I didn't.

I hated myself for it.

Calvin on Arnetta:
Arnetta was a woman I dated during my difficult years living with Momma, trying to get my writing career off the

ground, becoming an instant father again after so many years apart from my kids. She was much younger than me, a secretary at the local high school who flirted with every attractive man she saw. She was pretty and vibrant in a way that could not be trusted. Her prettiness depended on makeup and suggestive clothing, on pouted lips and false smiles. Her vibrancy was sometimes manic, as if she was desperately trying to wring every bit of experience out of her life, no matter what the consequences.

She was the type of woman who was fun to be around for short periods of time, especially when I needed someone to remind me that I was still alive, still virile. But after a few intense weeks, I would become exhausted by her energy and she would become suddenly aware of my age. We would then be more off than on until we forgot what we didn't like about each other and were reminded of the good times.

I wasn't surprised that she seduced Ellison when he was seventeen. He came to live with me nearly broken by his mother's death, although he would never admit it. Vulnerable men were Arnetta's specialty. And he hated me, so it wasn't a complete surprise that he would have sex with Arnetta. I'm not claiming that I wasn't angry and hurt by it, especially since there's nothing more difficult for me as a father than trying not to see my son as a competitor. But enough time has passed that I actually feel bad that Arnetta latched on to him the way she did. They were both trying to get back at me, but the one who may have been affected the most was Ellison.

I don't love Arnetta, and I never did. This will come as no surprise to her, for I believe she has even less regard for me. But I do love my son. My mistakes and shortcomings as a father may have hidden this simple fact from Ellison, but it is true. I love him more than he could know.

—From *Save Me: A Memoir* by Calvin Emory

CHAPTER 10

March 1999

South Beach was a riotous mix of color and sound. The sharp angles of the restored art deco buildings screamed in pink, green and coral. It was late when I got there, nearly eleven o'clock at night, but the sidewalks were filled with swarms of people moving in a languid rhythm back and forth, everyone looking for the best party, or at least the next one.

It seemed every other building was a hotel, each with its own expensive restaurant serving creative dishes piled high and skinny on plates. The servers broke a sweat as they raced to serve the diners filling street-side tables made of wrought iron. I glanced at my watch twice, surprised that so many people were eating this late.

I stopped at one of those hotels, an expansive one that was decorated in shades of white. Its name, The Tides, was spelled out over plate-glass doors in lettering that reminded me of that old movie *Where the Boys Are*. It was set in Fort Lauderdale over a spring break, but I remember that all the lettering on buildings was like The Tides in the movie. Rounded, sleek, nostalgic.

I chose The Tides because it had an outdoor eating area right in front of the hotel, but it was set up above the sidewalk where guests could look down on the passing crowds rather than dodge elbows and feet as people squeezed by on the sidewalk. The tables were set with heavy white cloths and real silverware. I ordered a Heineken and sat back in the seat, enjoying the warm ocean breeze. The hotel was right across the street from the water. I felt the weight of the salty air on my skin.

Miami was the final stop on Calvin's book tour. We went our separate ways after Jacksonville. He was meeting up with his old girlfriend Arnetta, who now lived in West Palm Beach. He invited me along, but he was drunk at the time and it seemed he had forgotten that I'd had sex with Arnetta in our backyard at the party celebrating his first book. I was drunk, too, so I spent a few minutes wondering how he could be so forgiving, even getting to the point where I felt quite tender toward him, if only just for a moment.

Arnetta was one of those women who liked the idea of every man wanting her. I'm sure that sleeping with her off-and-on boyfriend's seventeen-year-old son was a coup, especially since her boyfriend was in his thirties and Arnetta was just twenty-two at the time. I no longer had any illusions that she liked me. She worked at my school, and I remember seeing her for the first time. She'd made me feel welcome in what turned out to be a very difficult environment. The first day of my new school in Durham, I'd spent more time thinking about Arnetta and very little time thinking about the fact that I couldn't possibly fit in. People who talk about segregation, integration and all of that always ignore the most important things about being a kid. It's all about fitting in. Whatever the color of your skin, the car you drive (or don't), the house you live in—none of that matters as long as you belong. When I lived in Chicago with my mother and Maren, I went to a mostly white private school. At St. Francis High School, I took honors classes, and even though there were some other black kids in my class, I was almost always the only one in my classes. But the thing is, I fit in there. We were all the children of well-off parents who drove foreign cars and wore designer clothes. I'm not saying that race didn't matter, or that we were all colorblind. That's bullshit—no one is colorblind. No one should even want to be. But however different my skin made me, my house, my car, my clothes were more important, and I was accepted.

In Durham, I went to school with more black kids than I ever had before. For the first time in my life, I was in the majority. So it should have been easy to fit, right? That's what some people think, that it's easier to be around people of the same race. We understand each other in a way that white people never could.

But it's wrong. I was an outsider at McNeil High School. No one dressed like I did. No one else drove a BMW. No one talked the way I did.

"You talk so white," they used to say.

"Bryant Gumbel," they used to call me, behind my back at first, then, as the animosity grew, to my face.

"You think you're so pretty," the guys said. They made fun of my curly hair, light skin and grooming.

Probably if I had been there another year, they would have started calling me gay.

So race isn't the one thing that binds us, or separates us, for that matter. It's also about these other things, money, appearance, perceptions. Race plays into it, when it's convenient, but it's not the most important thing. This is what black people know, in our most secret hearts. We categorize and judge each other. White people do it to us, but we also do it to ourselves.

That was what I learned my last year in high school. I can't say I never learned anything at McNeil. But before it all began, that first day of school, I had Arnetta's smile to keep me company. She was a touchstone that whole year, and it was a long time before I realized that she wasn't just being nice, that there was something more going on if I was willing. I wasn't, not until my anger toward Calvin became unbearable, not until I decided to punish him for everything that was wrong in my life.

After we had sex, I saw that her smile hid a nastiness in her. She had her own reasons for punishing Calvin. But I suppose those reasons weren't enough for her to actually tell him what she'd done. So he was with her in West Palm Beach and I was here in South Beach, eating scallops over angel hair pasta, watching as people who seemed impossibly cool walked by. They seemed to know some secret that someone like me would never understand, and the knowledge gave a sense of purpose to their strides. Another time, this might all have made me feel left out, but I had no illusions about this place. I didn't fit in here, but it was okay. South Beach would let me watch, if only for the night.

The bookstore was in Coral Gables, near the University of Miami. I was sitting next to a 97-year-old woman wearing white stockings under white heeled sandals, a yellow suit that she bought in the late 1960s and enormous sunglasses with lenses dark enough to hide not only her eyes but half her face. She was eating a hard candy, which I know because the wet sound of it clattering against her tongue and dentures was amplified in my ear. *Clink-squish-clack-smush. Clink-smush-clack-squish.* I gave her a pointed look, but she was listening and sucking with rapt attention. It took a while, but she finished off what I suspected, from the odor, was a butterscotch. I glared at the side of her face, which was in part obscured by a white helmet of hair. If she pulled out another piece of candy, I would not be responsible for my actions.

Calvin was in the middle of his reading. He read from Chapter One, then skipped around through the rest of the book. I wasn't listening—again—but this time I had an excuse. Arnetta was sitting on my other side. She, too, was enthralled by Calvin's reading, or at least, she pretended to be. I was unprepared for the flood of memories I experienced when she walked up and said hello.

"Arnetta. Hi." I didn't know what to say. I hadn't expected her to be in Miami for the reading. I hadn't expected to ever see her again, really. I could feel my cheeks redden. I was embarrassed for me and for her. I looked over at Calvin, who was flipping through the book, inserting Post-Its and penciling notes in the margins.

She never took her eyes off me. "Ellison. It's so nice to see you." She enveloped me in a tight hug that went a moment too long. I pulled away.

"You're even more handsome than the last time I saw you, if that's possible." She flashed me a smile. I couldn't decide if she was flirting with me. I mumbled something about finding a seat and went to sit in the back. I hoped she would want to sit in the front near Calvin, but instead, she followed me and sat on my other side. I was glad when the reading began so that we couldn't talk.

But I couldn't concentrate on Calvin's words. I was aware of Arnetta's scent, something exotic and musky, perfume made of spices and the petals of unfamiliar flowers. When she shifted in her chair, her bare arm brushed against mine, making the hairs there stand at attention. Her hair was grown long, and she'd developed a habit of tossing it back off her shoulders in a movement that was all grace and glamour. She wore something simple, dark jeans and a white button-down shirt, but I could see the curves of her body through her tailored clothes.

Someone's cell phone rang behind us, where a few shoppers stood listening. A man answered the call and I listened, happy for the distraction. He spoke through clenched teeth but his voice was loud.

"I just got my wisdom teeth out and they wired my jaw shut again. At first it was excruciating . . . No, you're breaking up. I'm going to take this outside."

He walked away, muttering to himself about cell phones. His jaw was wired shut *again*?

Just then, Arnetta nudged me. I looked at her and she grinned.

"*Again*? How many times has he gotten his jaw wired shut?" she whispered.

I smiled. "I know. Also, impressive that he could carry on such a loud conversation with his jaw wired shut."

Arnetta's laugh tinkled through the air, but only a few people near us heard it and turned around. The rest of the crowd was clapping because Calvin had just finished and was ready to take questions.

She turned her attention back to Calvin. I replayed the sound of her laugh in my head. She was definitely flirting with me.

I scooted my chair a little farther from hers and shook my head as if to clear it. I wasn't that person anymore. I wasn't a boy anymore. I didn't need to get back at Calvin. I didn't need another complicated woman in my life, even if it was just another one-night stand with Arnetta. When the questions ended, Calvin sat at the table signing books and Arnetta stood next to him.

"Good job today." I looked out the window and gestured toward my car. "I've got to get going."

I could feel Arnetta watching me. "Are you sure? Calvin has some business this afternoon, so I thought you and I could hang out until he's done."

I heard the intent behind her words, maybe because of what happened between us. Maybe because she wasn't at all subtle. Her gaze was anything but innocent, and I wondered if she even cared whether Calvin knew what she was up to. I glanced at him. He smiled and seemed to believe this would be a good idea.

In that moment, the strongest memory came to me. It wasn't the night we had sex, but before that, when all there was between us was possibility. I stood there, watching the scene in my mind as if it happened to someone else, not me.

I didn't know whether I should say hello. I saw her in the halls once in a while, and she usually nodded and smiled. But I didn't know if she actually remembered me or just smiled at all the students as some sort of goodwill gesture from the administration.

"I'm sure we have it in your size. Let me go check," I said formally.

Arnetta smiled. "Aren't you even going to say 'hi?'" she teased.

I shrugged. "I wanted to, but I wasn't sure if you knew who I was."

She laughed. "How could I forget you? It's not often that I have a cute new student nearly come to blows with his father right in front of my desk."

Now I laughed. "Yeah, I guess that is kind of memorable."

She just kept looking at me, still smiling, and I didn't know what to say, so I turned the shoe over to look for the sticker number. "I'll go get these for you."

I watched Arnetta as she tried on the sandals. I again noticed how young she looked, and I liked the way she still

119

managed to look sexy in blue jeans and a dark red shirt, wearing little makeup, her braided hair up in a ponytail. When she caught me staring, she raised her eyebrows and smiled.

I averted my eyes, pretending to be busy with something on the counter. She made me feel shy. And she'd called me "cute." I wondered if she was still seeing Calvin.

"So, how do they fit?" I asked casually.

"I love them—ring me up."

As I handed her the receipt, I took a chance. "Can I ask you a question?" I said hesitantly.

Arnetta waited expectantly and I cleared his throat. "Well, I was just wondering, well, are you still dating my father?"

She looked at him for a long moment. "Calvin and I are friends," she said slowly. "Why do you ask?"

I took a deep breath and spoke before I could talk myself out of it. "I just thought that maybe you'd want to go out for coffee or something sometime," I blurted, keeping my voice low so the other customers wouldn't hear. All the reasons for her to say no ran through my mind in the few seconds it took her to respond.

"You don't think I'm too old for you?" she asked, looking at me appraisingly. "I'm twenty-two."

Twenty-two was even younger than I'd first suspected. "I'm almost eighteen," I said hopefully.

She laughed as if I'd told a joke. I smiled, but I didn't think it was all that funny.

"Ellison, I like you, you seem really cool. But I just don't think it would be appropriate, you know?"

I sighed and nodded. If she had said yes it would have almost been too much—my mood couldn't get much better. "Yeah, I know."

I was grateful that she had at least been nice about the whole thing, so I smiled at her to show that there were no hard feelings. "Enjoy those sandals," I said.

She looked me in the eye and held me gaze for just a beat longer than necessary. "I will."

I watched her walk away until another customer came along and blocked my view.

I shook away the memory and tried to look apologetic. "You know what? I've really got to get back to school."

I looked only at Calvin. He nodded. "I'm glad you're going back. You need to finish strong, be ready for graduation, medical school next year."

The fatherly advice sounded unnatural coming from him. There was an awkward silence before I mumbled a goodbye. It seemed that Calvin and I were destined to take two steps forward and one step back, over and over again. Were we headed in the right direction? I didn't know. I wasn't sure that all that had passed between us could be overcome. I wasn't sure I was willing to make the effort. The only thing I was sure of was that our problems weren't only Calvin's fault. Arnetta's come-on at the reading reminded me that I had done my share of things to hurt my father, even if I thought I was punishing him for all the years he was out of contact with me and Maren when we were kids.

I was starting to realize that life didn't work like that— I couldn't make someone pay for old sins, especially not if it meant that I committed new sins in the process. One

thing the trip had taught me was that I was tired of bat-
tling with Calvin, tired of wondering who I would have
become if I'd had my father around when I was younger,
tired of feeling resentful and angry about the past.

Walking away from Calvin and Arnetta, I felt as if I'd
been away for a month instead of a week. I needed to get
back to my classes, but that wasn't all. There was another,
more important thing I needed to do. I needed to talk to
Angela.

On the way out of the store, I bought a copy of *Save
Me*.

Calvin on North Carolina:

*I love summer in North Carolina. I can't speak for
coastal towns that might be spoiled by ocean breezes; I've
only lived in the middle of the state, where the heat hovers
over the flat landscape like a blanket tucked too tight. Every
way you turn, there it is, heat the doesn't move, doesn't
change, won't let go.*

*Some people fight it like an enemy they can't beat. But I
embrace it, let it envelop me. The only strategies involve gallons of sweet iced tea and as little clothing as possible. Sit very
still, or better yet, lie under an open window. Don't try to
work or play or talk. Just lie still and wait for that occasional
breeze to flutter over your damp skin. That breeze is a gift
given only to those who embrace the North Carolina summer.*

—From *Save Me: A Memoir* by Calvin Emory

CHAPTER 11

Summer 1998

The summer after my junior year was hot, hotter than anything I could remember from back in Chicago. There was something different about North Carolina summers. I grew up on the lake, and while East Coasters scoff at the idea of Lake Michigan (as opposed to the more vast Atlantic Ocean), it provided entertainment and a breeze during the summers of my youth. We welcomed summer, even those humid, ninety-degree days, because it was such a change from the gray winters, the snow piled up in the corners of mall parking lots, the endless parade of boots and scarves and single lost mittens. The humidity was bearable because there was the cool water of the lake, festivals and, always, an early evening breeze.

In Durham, summer brought a thickness to the air that was unrelieved by a nearby body of water or a breeze. The days were still, the nights more so, and there was the constant shifting between air-conditioned rooms and the merciless heat outside. Many people in Chicago had no air conditioning, since the summers were so short, and, if you lived close enough to the water as we did, you only needed to open your windows to feel instantly cooler. In North Carolina, air conditioning was a necessity, and those who did not have it suffered during those long months between May and October, sometimes even November.

I always felt sticky during North Carolina summers. I couldn't take enough showers. As soon as I dressed and stepped outside, my clothes began to wilt and dampen. The summer after my junior year at Duke, I wanted to spend all my days lying under a fan in our apartment, which had a window unit that only seemed to work properly when we didn't need it. Instead, I spent the summer as a research assistant for my chemistry professor. My white lab coat was a necessary evil, so I took to wearing shorts and T-shirts underneath while I carted stacks of books back and forth between Perkins and the science building.

But perhaps I was romanticizing Midwestern summers. It may have been sweltering, but the summer of 1998 was the best summer of my life.

In April of that year, Angela caught Jason cheating. Not caught, as in found phone numbers in his pants pocket or heard an incriminating telephone message. Caught, as in walked in on Jason standing in his bedroom with a girl on her knees in front of him. Jason tried to explain. Was it really cheating if she was the one technically doing all the work? Angela picked up a British lit textbook and hurled it at Jason's head.

"It hit the other girl," he told me afterward. It bothered me that he didn't even say her name. "I tried not to laugh." But he laughed when he told me. I didn't bother to laugh with him. He was trying to pretend like it wasn't a big deal, that he didn't care that he'd devastated Angela. I cared.

I watched his face. When did he become so smug? When did he develop that uncompromising set to his shoulders? I didn't know why Jason had changed, and I realized that we never really talked about anything important. We were not friends, not real friends. Neither one of us could let down our guard enough for that to happen. Over the past few months, Jason and I had become strangers. The girls, books and our own reticence created a gulf that I could not bridge. I realized I didn't want to.

I went to her apartment later that day. Her roommate was out and Angela was sitting on the sofa in the dark, wrapped in a blanket. The television was on but the sound was so low that the voices were murmurs. I had never been to her apartment before, but of course, I knew where it was. The first thing I noticed was a framed print on her wall. It was a reproduction of *Le Jazz*. The original hung on Coach Grant Davis's wall in Baltimore. I wondered if she knew that.

"Are you okay?" She arranged herself on the couch after letting me in. Her eyes were vacant as she stared at the television. I saw next to her, the blanket a mountain between us.

"She smiled at me." Her eyes still watched the screen.
"Who?"

"That slut. With Jason. I walked in on them, and she just stood up, as proud as you please. And smiled at me."

I didn't know what to say. I just watched Angela as she watched the screen. After a while, I went into the kitchen and made some soup I found in the cupboard. Angela shook her head when I offered it to her, but she took the bowl and sipped from the spoon. I think she did it to make me happy. The programs changed from day-time game shows to the evening news, and we just sat there. When she started to cry, I held her hand over the blanket mountain.

Angela and I took African-American Literature together that summer. She was an English and African-American studies major, so it made sense for her. For me, I just wanted to do something different, something to break up the long, hazy days. And I wanted to be near Angela.

That summer, I discovered writers and ideas I never knew existed. I learned about slave narratives and the Harlem Renaissance. I finally read Ralph Ellison, and I hated Hurston. I recognized the anger in *Native Son*. The class ended with some contemporary things: Mosley and Wideman and Walker. I wasn't sure I understood Walker, and I went through Mosley's stories and novels so quickly that I was left longing for more. I loved James Baldwin. Angela liked Toni Morrison. We spent hours talking about why. I wished the class, and the summer, would go on forever.

That summer, I discovered that Angela was a real person, with feelings and flaws I had never imagined. Both her parents were closet alcoholics, so she didn't drink. She had an irrational love of romantic comedies, overdone drivel that fed into hopeless Cinderella fantasies. She was studying to be an English teacher, eventually a college professor. But her secret wish was to be a wife and a mom, staying home to care for four, five, even six children. She was old-fashioned and stubborn. I wished the class, and the summer, would go on forever.

We didn't talk about Jason. I tried, once. She was telling me about her high-school boyfriend. He was her first love. She thought they would get married. Their parents had been friends since high school. It had seemed like a perfect match.

"But there's no such thing when you're sixteen," she said. We were sitting outside a coffee shop in Chapel Hill. She drank coffee constantly during the day, said she couldn't study without it. We'd grabbed a sidewalk table. It was cloudy and humid, one of those days where rain would be a relief to the thickness of the air. But all of the tables were filled. Franklin Street was a mix of bars, secondhand record stores, restaurants and small shops selling everything from clothes to incense. College kids came from all the area schools to hang out here, where the vibe was relaxed, a throwback to simpler times. Franklin Street was what made Chapel Hill a quintessential college town. But it wasn't a place just for kids—the atmosphere welcomed people of all ages and races.

During the regular school year, Franklin Street was always vibrating with energy. There were fewer people here for the summer, and a certain laziness hung in the air. Most of the people sitting around us were young men and women, studying during the summer but not taking anything too seriously. Summer was for relaxing, for fun. We were still young enough to feel the pull of irresponsibility when the weather warmed. I looked at the twosomes around us, wondering whether they were real couples, or more like us: man in love, woman oblivious.

"He broke up with me the night before graduation. He was supposed to come to Duke with me, but he told me he'd decided to go to Berkeley instead. Like he wanted to get as far from me as possible. He told me I was too traditional. I wasn't ambitious enough. What's wrong with wanting to be a teacher, a wife, a mom? Why is that wrong?"

She said all this in a rush, as if the words needed to escape before they disappeared. I could see her trying to hold back tears. She sipped her coffee and wouldn't meet my eyes.

"That guy sounds like a jerk. Your dreams are your own—they're not for anyone else to judge. You deserve better than him. And Jason."

It was more than two months since she discovered Jason was cheating. We never really talked about it. When I mentioned his name, she turned sharply toward me.

"He's your roommate."

Was she accusing me of some complicity? Maybe she was right. I knew he was doing it. Maybe I should have told her. But self-preservation had stood in my way. I knew what happened to the messenger.

"I'm not perfect. But I never would have done that to my girlfriend." I paused and swallowed hard. "I never would do that to you."

Our gazes held for a few beats. She was the first to look away. She shrugged and shook her head. She looked down into her empty cup, then smiled up at me. I couldn't read the smile. It was a perfectly friendly, perfectly empty smile, meant to return us to safer territory.

"I need more coffee. You?"

I smiled back and tried not to wonder whether to consider this a rejection. I watched her back as she stood in line to order.

Classes ended in early August. Most of the other summer-school students left campus during the time between the end of summer classes and the beginning of the fall semester. We were going to be seniors. Jason and I had agreed to live together again, although we hadn't spoken all summer. He was in Baltimore, working for his father as an intern in the Bullets' public relations department. I called him once to work out the details of the rent. He spent the entire conversation name dropping, telling me about all the parties he went to, all the basketball players he was friends with. I didn't recognize most of the names and I didn't care about the parties. I think he knew that.

Angela had to be out of her dorm room by the end of the week. She had a ticket to go home to Chicago, but I could tell she didn't want to leave. It was just after nine on a Tuesday morning. We had just turned in our final paper for lit, and the day was sunny and the grass was still damp and cool. We decided to take a walk through the gardens before the steam began to rise.

I liked to walk through the Sarah P. Duke Gardens. It was like a botanical oasis in the middle of the gothic architecture that housed the business of education. There were expanses of lawns, fountains and flowers that I should have known the names of, but didn't. When I needed to think, I wandered the five miles of pathways and trails, sometimes wishing to get lost, sometimes just sitting on a wooden bench trying to separate all the sounds and fragrances. People were always walking through the gardens, either students taking shortcuts to classes or tourists visiting and exploring. But the mass of greenery silenced human noises and created a sense of privacy around each person. I always felt I was alone in the gardens, even when I passed groups of giggling high-school students trying to decide whether Duke was their top choice.

The gardens felt like my place, and that made me happy to walk through them with Angela. Of course she'd been there on her own, but I took her along my favorite little paths, away from the main sections where most people went. As we walked, I told her about all the plants and flowers, making up names to make her laugh.

"I had no idea you were such an expert." We sat on rocks next to a pond in the Asiatic Arboretum.

"That's probably because I'm not."

There was silence as we sat and watched the fish make ripples just underneath the surface of the pond.

"I'll miss this when I go home." She looked at me. "I know it's only for a few weeks, but being with my parents for a few weeks feels more like years. You just don't know."

I raised my eyebrows and thought of my father. "Oh, I can imagine. My family isn't exactly the Cosbys."

She shrugged. "Even the Cosbys aren't the Cosbys, if you know what I mean."

She smiled at me and I blurted it out before I could think.

"You could stay at my place. I mean, until your roommate comes back and you can move into your apartment."

The moment the words left my mouth, I wanted to take them back. I didn't want her to think I was trying to play house. I told myself that my intentions were only honorable. I told myself that I only wanted her if she wanted me, too. I would not use the fact that her roommate was spending the summer in Paris to my advantage. I almost believed me.

She tilted her head and looked out at the water. Maybe she was considering whether she wanted to set foot in the place where Jason lived and had betrayed her. Maybe she wondered about my motives. Maybe she saw through me and was thinking of how to let me down easy.

I opened my mouth to take it back, to apologize, to ask for forgiveness. I opened my mouth to tell her I loved her. Before I could speak, she looked at me. She leaned close, and I could smell her skin, fresh and clean, like the smell of a just-bathed baby. She kissed me.

It was all smell and touch. The mint of her mouth against mine. Her hands running over the back of neck. My fingertips against the small scar on her left side. The musk between her thighs. Our eyelashes brushing. Our legs entwining. My pelvis pressed against hers. A sweet odor. Strong, aggressive. Honeysuckle, I thought. I was delirious. There, on the banks of the pond where anyone could see. I whispered.

"I love you."

She murmured back. We fell asleep for a few moments, lying in each other's arms, our clothes rumpled and tangled. We were the only two.

When I think of the rest of that summer, it comes to me in a series of vignettes, a montage of scenes that show how Angela and I felt about each other. In a romance novel or a film it might seem clichéd, but living through it, it seemed we were the first two people to ever be in love.

After class, we usually went to the Coffee Bean when Angela wasn't working a shift. We sat drinking free coffee, escaping the North Carolina summer sun and making top ten lists. Top ten Chicago restaurants. Top ten celebrities we would want to date. Top ten movies from the 1980s, cheesy pop songs, children's books, episodes of Seinfeld. We argued over Spandau Ballet's "True," whether songs based on dances like "The Macarena" counted, whether Madonna deserved to be in the category of cheesy pop. We agreed on "Say Anything" and the first "Lethal Weapon." I had never told anyone that I loved Hardy Boys mysteries when I was a kid, and secretly, I also read Nancy Drew when I went to the library. I laughed when she was able to recite entire pages from *The Lorax* by heart, and although it was impossible to decide which of the Seinfeld episodes was the best, we made ourselves cry reciting lines from our favorites.

Sometimes, we talked about family. At least, she talked about hers. Her father was serious and stern, and her mother was solidly middle-class but always wishing she was more.

"My mother wanted me to be a debutante," Angela said, wrinkling her nose. When I thought of debutantes, I thought of rich white girls in ball gowns and white gloves, entering the kind of society I knew little about.

"Black people can be debutantes?"

Angela explained the structure of the organizations, which were often affiliated with black fraternities and sororities. High-school kids gathered for service projects, formal socializing, networking for college scholarships and part-time jobs. But there was another side to it all. Angela talked about how the black elite held these balls and tried to encourage pairings between teens of the "right" class. But the pairings couldn't be too close, of course, because teen sex and pregnancy was for the lower classes. Black people couldn't afford those kinds of mistakes, since the Talented Tenth represented black culture to the world.

"It all goes back to slavery, to the Africans being taught that the more like white people they were, the better."

I considered this. Angela was full of theories about the oppressed and racism. She saw the world in very definite terms, and she didn't tend to see the grays. I knew I was like this, too, but about different things; not politics, but family, relationships, love. In terms of race, I'd been on both sides, accepted by whites as a token, shunned by blacks as a sellout, and I thought that these things had less to do with race and more to do with class and human nature.

"So who were you paired with?"

She made a face, sticking out her tongue and rolling her eyes. I laughed.

"His name was Richard Lovell. He went by Dick, and I think that says it all."

I smiled. "I've never understood guys named Richard who go by Dick. Rick, Ricky, Richie, Rich, Ric with no 'k'—there are just so many other options."

"I know!" Angela was still making a face, but giggling at the same time. "It speaks to character, right? He had no sense of humor, didn't get irony at all. I mean, if you call yourself Dick, but with a wink, it's creepy, but at least you're acknowledging some kind of awareness of the culture."

"So was that the main thing, his name? I just want to make sure I have the whole picture."

Angela thought for a moment. "When his parents offered to buy him any car he wanted, he picked a Taurus. We were in *high school*. It was green."

I gave a mock shudder. "Well, no wonder you refused Dick and all the debutante accoutrements."

Angela nodded gravely. "My mother is still mad about it."

"Where do you think old Dick is now?"

She shrugged. "Probably still driving that stupid Taurus like he's fifty instead of twenty-one."

∽⊘

One week, Angela and I challenged ourselves to the task of going to a matinee every day. We would randomly pick a movie each day, and we were required to watch it in its entirety, no matter how bad.

"Let's make it interesting—we each have to finish a tub of popcorn by the end of the movie, or else it's two movies the next day," I told her.

"Two tubs of popcorn the next day, too?"

"Of course."

"You're on."

We began with *I Still Know What You Did Last Summer* on Monday.

"Brandy's not a bad actress, but this movie is ridiculous," Angela whispered, *sotto voce,* in the middle of the movie.

135

"Shhh. You know black people already have a reputation for talking during movies. Don't feed into the stereotype." We giggled until the one other person in the theater shushed us.

Tuesday was *Armageddon*. Angela got teary when Bruce Willis sacrificed his life so that his daughter might live happily ever after with Ben Affleck.

"You're such a sap," I teased. She punched me in the arm with a fist while she wiped her eyes with the other. "Resorting to violence doesn't make you seem any tougher, you know."

We saw *Can't Hardly Wait* on Wednesday, which inspired a catch phrase we repeated to each other whenever the other wasn't expecting it.

"I can't feel my legs. I CAN'T FEEL MY LEGS!"

Thursday: *Dr. Doolittle*. It tested my resolve, and I took a long bathroom break in the middle. Angela threatened me with two tubs of popcorn, claiming that overly long bathroom breaks were cheating.

"By the way," she added, "didn't Eddie Murphy used to be cool?"

On Friday we saw *Lethal Weapon 4* in homage to the original, and agreed that the only good thing about it was Chris Rock.

We saved *Out of Sight* for Saturday because Angela insisted we read the Elmore Leonard book first, and I read much more slowly than she did.

"I think I'm in love," I sighed during one of the movie's early scenes.

Angela looked at me, her eyes big.

I stared at the screen. "With Jennifer Lopez."

She shook her head, and in my peripheral vision I could see her smiling.

"I'm adding George Clooney to my top ten list," she said.

"You're just trying to compete with me. He's not your type."

"Oh yeah? Who's my type?"

I looked at her and slipped my hand into hers.

"Me?" I couldn't help but make it a question. I wasn't quite confident enough to assume anything, despite what was happening between us.

She looked at me for a long moment, and then she nodded.

"You."

On Sunday, we stayed in bed all day.

Calvin on redemption:

I changed a lot during the years I was away from my children, after Vanessa and I divorced and I moved back to North Carolina. When I first went home to my mother, I was still in the throes of my addictions. For me, it wasn't a specific drink, and I never was too interested in drugs. Even the women, if you consider that a type of addiction, weren't that important to me. I suppose it's this way with all addicts: it's the feeling that matters, not the substance. Anything that provides the feeling you're seeking becomes the drug of choice.

I don't much about other people's struggles with this type of thing. I'm not a student of the twelve steps, although they seem reasonsable enough, especially the simple idea of taking one day at a time. I didn't go to rehab (mostly because I couldn't afford it and I was ashamed to ask for help), and I didn't attend meetings. So all I know about it is from inside me, and that is the feeling I was seeking when I cheated on Vanessa, drank too much and pushed her away. All I wanted was to avoid rejection. Acceptance is the other side of that, I suppose, but avoiding rejection goes farther than that. If I don't commit to one person, she can't reject me because I provided an excellent reason for us to break up.

The drinking was a part of the same not-so-clever plan, but it was also a way to isolate myself socially. Alcohol became my friend so I didn't have to cultivate human, adult relationships. No friends, no family, no rejection. Just as I distanced myself from my ex-wife, I did the same with my children. I left them before they could decide I was a terrible father. I decided it for them.

Or at least, that's what I was trying to do. After Vanessa died and the kids came to live with me, Ellison rejected me all over again, and I found myself trying to prove myself not only to him, but also to Maren. Daughters are easier on their fathers; Maren forgave my past, present and future sins, although I had no right to expect her to. Ellison may never do the same. I don't know if I blame him one bit.

—From *Save Me: A Memoir* by Calvin Emory

CHAPTER 12

Summer/Fall 1998

Maren and Angela met only once before that summer. Angela was still dating Jason and I was still pretending that I didn't dream about her every night. It was in January, right before Maren went back to school after Christmas break. She came to the apartment and we all sat around playing cards. Jason drank too much, and at times I thought he might be flirting with my sister. At some point, Jason went out to get more beer, and Angela feel asleep on the sofa. I got a blanket and covered her. Later, Maren seemed quiet and didn't say much as I drove her back to Calvin's house.

"You like her, huh?"

I glanced at her. She was looking out of the window into the quiet darkness.

"Angela? We're friends." I tried to sound casual.

Maren turned and looked at me. I kept my eyes on the road as if I had to pay strict attention, as if I didn't know the way by heart.

"You *like* her."

"She's Jason's girl."

Maren blew air out of her nose. Not quite a sigh.

"Angela's a cool girl," I added.

Maren didn't answer. We were at the house. She leaned over and kissed my cheek.

"Dad wanted me to ask you to come over tomorrow for lunch before he takes me to the airport."

She had said this in a mechanical voice. She was doing her duty as the only person in our family who would still try to mend things. I loved her for it. But it was annoying to have to keep turning her down.

"I'll take you to the airport, and I'll take you out to lunch." But not with Calvin. I didn't have to say it. She knew.

"Good night, Ellison."

"Be safe," I called to her back. She raised her hand in acknowledgement, but she didn't turn back. I watched until she closed the door behind her.

∽◎

Six months later, Maren came to see me just before she left for fall classes in Florida. Normally I would have been circumspect about a relationship—Maren and I were close, but we didn't talk about our love lives. But what I'd told her about my summer and Angela set off Maren's radar.

"I don't feel like I got a chance to really talk to Angela when we met. Remember, you were still pretending nothing was going on between you two?" Maren said one night over dinner. We had chosen a diner near Duke's campus because Maren loved their cheeseburgers, and we were halfway through the meal when she brought up Angela.

"Nothing was going on then."

She blew out air from pursed lips, impatient with me. "Okay. But there certainly is something going on now. Maybe we could all get together before I leave."

During summers when she was home from college, we tried to get together as much as possible. Maren still lived with Calvin during summers and vacations. The fact that I refused to go to our father's house sometimes made it difficult for Maren and I to hang out, and I regretted that I didn't see her often. I would never have admitted it to my sister, but I missed her terribly during the school year. I had stayed in Durham to attend Duke so I could be near her, and although I didn't begrudge her attending whatever college she wanted, I still felt a little lost without Maren always nearby.

If my sister had ever asked to meet another girl I dated, I would have teased her and then refused her request. Then again, Maren had never asked me about a girl before, and I had no desire to hide Angela away. I loved her, and I wanted to shout that to the world.

"She must be something special," Maren continued, smiling. "You never talk about your girlfriends at all."

I felt a little shy. This was a new thing, talking about my feelings, revealing myself to people. But I was happy, that crazy-in-love kind of happiness that spreads across your face before you can stop it.

"She's cute and smart and fun, and seriously, she's just everything I ever wanted. I think I'm in love. No, I know I'm in love."

It was several moments before Maren stopped staring at me. She shook her head as if clearing lint from her brain.

"So tell me about her—not just the adjectives, but what she is really like."

I thought for a moment. "She likes to talk about ideas, and she has really strong opinions. I don't always agree with her, but she always gives me some new perspective on whatever we're talking about. She even convinced me to read *The Bridges of Madison County.*"

My sister nearly choked on a French fry. "You read that book? Read it—not just watched the movie?"

I shrugged, embarrassed.

"Wait, you *liked* the book? Seriously, Ellison, it's like I don't even know you right now. I really need to get to know this girl."

I shifted in my seat, a stupid grin on my face. Usually I was the one who teased my sister, not the other way around. Angela was changing everything in my life, and it didn't bother me a bit.

"Tomorrow. You can meet her tomorrow."

The next day, we met at the Coffee Bean during Angela's shift. When we arrived, Angela was working in the back so we chose pastries to accompany our coffee and sat down.

"Do you have enough milk in there?" I never understood why Maren drank coffee when she put enough milk in it that the liquid was barely even brown.

"What do you care?"

"You're my sister," I said, pouring faux concern into my voice. "I only want the best for you."

She snorted. "So that means you have to butt into my coffee preparations? You're just bossy, that's all. If I like my coffee light, that's my business."

I didn't have a chance to reply.

"What's the point of drinking coffee with that much milk in it?" Angela said from behind us. "I mean, really, it's just a waste of coffee beans, isn't it?"

She was smiling to take the edge off the comment, and I knew she was just trying to be funny and break the ice. Maren looked up at her and smiled without warmth. I winced. It was one thing for me to make fun of my sister, she expected it from me. But Maren was no longer a shy little girl who let life happen to her, and I could tell she didn't take kindly to Angela mocking her even before anyone had said hello.

I tried to repair the damage by laughing heartily and pulling Angela down into the empty seat next to Maren.

"Angela! You remember my sister, Maren—Maren, you met Angela before, right?"

Maren maintained her frozen smile and reached out to shake Angela's hand just as Angela opened her arms and leaned in for one of those air-cheek kisses some women give. It occurred to me that I hadn't seen Angela with many other women—she didn't have any close girl-friends at Duke that I knew of, so I'd never seen her do this. There was an awkward moment where Angela was forced to reposition herself into handshake mode because Maren made no move to reciprocate the air-kiss.

Once it was over, no one had much to say. I tried again.

"How's your milk?" I thought that keeping the coffee joke going between me and Maren would diffuse things. Why pretend the elephant isn't standing in the middle of the room?

Maren glared at me, then turned to Angela. "So, Angela, where are you from?" My sister gave me another look, as if to tell me that she was going to make an effort and I'd better appreciate it.

"Chicago, actually." Angela's voice was bright, and her smile looked genuine. I couldn't tell if she saw how she'd rubbed Maren the wrong way or not. Angela was very good at hiding her feelings when she wanted to.

"Small world, hmm?"

"How do you like UF?"

After a rough start, they started chatting and Maren's face began to thaw. I released the breath I had been holding and piped up when my opinion was required, but for Angela's entire twenty-minute break, Maren sized up Angela, and I was fairly certain that Angela was doing some evaluation of her own.

Toward the end of their conversation, things started to get prickly again. They were talking about books and Maren mentioned that she had read *Beloved* for a class and loved it.

Angela looked incredulous. "You liked that pretentious novel? God, after Ellison told me how smart you were, I would have thought you would have better taste than that."

Maren titled her head and stared at Angela. "A lot of people in class said they found it hard to get into, and I agree, but once I was in, I thought it was quite well done."

My sister had taken on the tone of a *New York Times* book reviewer, while Angela went in the other direction, say, *National Enquirer*.

"It was a load of crap," Angela declared, waving her hand in the air as if to repel the smell of Toni Morrison's failure.

Maren's cold, tight smile returned. "I don't really think they award the Pulitzer to 'crap.' "

Angela shrugged and looked at her watch. "I've got to get back to work. Maren, it was great meeting you." She flashed a brilliant smile at my sister, who only nodded in reply. Angela turned to me and kissed me, one of those deep, searching kisses that has no place in public. I finally pulled away.

"See you later, baby," she called over her shoulder on the way back into the kitchen. I shook my head. She never called me "baby."

Maren and I got up to leave, and as we walked down the sidewalk, I was afraid to look at her. When I did, she was smirking.

"Is she serious? *Beloved* is crap, I take my coffee the wrong way, and you're 'baby'?"

I held up a hand. "She was probably just nervous to meet you, now that she and I are together. I mean, you're my sister, she knows you were sizing her up."

Maren looked at me in disbelief. "So that's how she tried to win me over—insults and insinuating that I'm an idiot for liking a book?"

I cringed. "I know. But she's actually really sweet. Really."

Maren shook her head. "If you say so, El."

My fantasies run toward the mundane. When I was a kid, all I ever wanted was a mother who stayed home and baked cookies. When my mother died, all I wanted was a father who could understand me and care about something besides himself. When I met Angela, I imagined she was perfect, a princess to be desired from afar until she realized we were meant to be together. And when I kissed her, I thought it was forever.

My mother worked all the time and didn't even buy cookies, let alone bake them. My father cared more about his writing than me. With Angela, it wasn't forever. More like a summer.

"I'm just not looking for a relationship right now," she told me on the telephone just a few days after classes began.

I had called Angela, like I did every day, sometimes twice. Since the fall semester began, she rarely called me, but I thought it was because I never gave her a chance. After nearly two months of sleeping together, I thought it was more than that. I wanted to call Angela my girlfriend. I wanted the world to know that we were together. She had launched into her speech after I told her we should come out, to Jason, to Duke. To whomever cared.

"Wait, what? 'Looking for a relationship?' Aren't we already having a relationship?"

"Ellison, don't make this harder than it has to be."

"How am I making this hard? What is 'this'? You're breaking up with me?"

She sighed. "What we had was a summer thing, not something that can last. El, it's not about you, it's about me. I'm just not ready."

I couldn't believe she'd just pulled "it's not you, it's me." I allowed myself to be angry, because the alternative was to feel the crush of what she was saying.

"At least do me the favor of avoiding the clichés. And I don't believe you. This wasn't just a summer thing."

She was silent for a long time, and I worried that she'd hung up. "Angela?"

"You can't tell me what to feel, Ellison. If I say it was a summer thing, then that's what it was. Just be a man and face it."

Ouch. She meant for that remark to hurt, and it did, even though on some level I truly didn't believe she meant any of this. I just couldn't figure out why she would say it if she didn't mean it.

Part of me just wanted to hang up and try to forget about Angela, about this conversation, about the entire summer. No one really knew about us. I could save face, and I'd be graduating in nine months. But the more convincing part of me didn't want to let go.

"So you don't love me and you never did? That's what you're saying?"

Her reply was almost too quiet for me to hear. "I never told you I loved you."

"That's not an answer."

I could hear her take a deep breath. "Not everything is about you, Ellison. We can't see each other," she added.

I had difficulty swallowing, not as if something was in my throat, but like my throat closed in on itself. My body rejected her words. She sniffed.

"Are you crying?"

"No."

I thought I could hear a slight tremor in her voice, but she wasn't changing her story. Or maybe it wasn't a story. Maybe what I thought was something special between us had just been a way to pass the time for Angela. Maybe I was just a convenience, the poor sucker who had been following her around, wanting her since freshman year. Maybe she was not the person I thought she was.

"Goodbye, Ellison."

"Angela?"

There was a click, and a buzz. Then the insistent quack of the phone line that signals that you haven't hung up yet but the person you were talking to did. The phone accused me of holding on too long. There was no reason that I could see for the disconnection. We had been the only two. Now there was just me.

I called my sister. She was the only person who could make me feel a little less alone. She was just hours from leaving for Gainesville, heading back for her sophomore year at Florida.

"Maren."

"Hey, El." When I didn't say anything else, she knew something was up. "What's wrong? Are you okay?"

My first instinct was to make up some reason for calling, to avoid talking about Angela, to try to escape the pain. But I couldn't think of a story that would convince the person who knew me better than anyone else in the world, so I just started talking.

Maren just listened as I poured out the story.

"Maybe this isn't really about you," Maren said when I finished. "Maybe something's going on with Angela."

I frowned. "How could it not be about me? You know the whole 'it's not you, it's me' routine is bull."

I hated the way I sounded: whiny and desperate.

"Not everything is about you, Ellison."

I couldn't believe it—first Angela, now my sister. Was everyone in the world going to call me a selfish bastard today?

Before I could reply, Maren went on. "You always criticize Dad for being self-involved. But you and he aren't that different, you know."

This hit like a blow to the kidneys. I was not like my father. I wasn't. I wasn't.

"Where did you get that, Intro to Psych? I took it, too, and believe me, you don't want to start psychoanalyzing people."

We both knew I was talking about the whole thing with Chris. Having sex with our half-uncle didn't exactly qualify Maren to point the finger.

It was a mean thing to say, especially since I blamed myself for not seeing the signs and stopping Chris from hurting Maren. It was almost four years ago, and we still hadn't talked about it. I dredged it up to distract my sister from my own weaknesses. I was a selfish bastard.

"Mare, I'm sorry—"

She cut me off. "I have to go now."

"Maren, please."

She hung up. I was two-for-two.

I wandered through the fall of my senior year in a daze. I didn't talk to Jason. I didn't talk to Angela. I didn't talk to anyone I didn't have to. All social contact ceased. I was already doing well in my classes, so I decided to take the MCATs earlier than anyone else I knew. I told myself it would give me a chance to take them again in January if I didn't do well. But I knew I would do well, at least on the biology, physical sciences and verbal reasoning sections. But I spent hours considering the writing sample prompts:

The object of education should be to teach skills, not values.

There are as many versions of history as there are historians.

In advertising, truth is irrelevant.

Violence is sometimes necessary to achieve social change.

When there is a choice between obeying the law and following one's own beliefs, it is best to follow one's beliefs.

Students should be more interested in the process of learning than in the facts learned.

Our belief in an idea only lasts until the introduction of the next idea.

Progress often complicates as much as it simplifies.

I tried to write out possible answers and ideas, to agree or disagree with the statements. The questions were about culture and society, but everything reminded me of Angela. Progress complicates as much as it simplifies.

I moved on to the verbal reasoning practice test:

The expression "This is driving me around the bend" would best support a metaphor that compares madness to:
A) a location
B) a vehicle
C) a road
D) a force

Madness as a location. Or a road? I thought I might have arrived, driven there and stopped. Lost. Was Angela the vehicle? The force? Or was I?

It was when I started filling out my medical school applications that my sense of taste disappeared. I chose ten schools all over the country. Maren was gone now, and even if she chose to return to Durham after college, I knew she could take care of herself. She was certainly more together than I was at the moment. Maren was gracious and sweet when I apologized for taking out my frustrations about Angela on her.

"Ellison, I knew that was the hurt talking. I forgave you in about an hour, even though I didn't speak to you for a week," she had said, laughing.

"How did you turn out to be so reasonable while I'm such a mess?"

"El, you're not a mess. You just had a weird breakup and you're stressed about medical school. I'm goofing off down in Florida—I can afford to be nice."

"I don't deserve you, Mare."

"You deserve all good things, Ellison. You should remember that and try not to be so hard on yourself."

"Easier said than done, sis."

Maren was right—I was feeling sorry for myself, and blaming myself for somehow driving Angela away. I was stumped when I had to write my personal statement. I knew what they wanted: something to make me seem interesting and dedicated, something to make me stand out from the crowd. I spent hours staring at the blank white page, the cursor blinking accusingly, mocking me.

Finally, one night I stayed up drinking coffee and smoking cigarettes I didn't want. I wrote a 2,000-word personal statement and then passed out halfway through editing it. I woke up the next morning with my mouth feeling like cotton and pages of gibberish spread over my chest.

I spent Thanksgiving weekend in the library, preparing for finals and writing my real personal statement. It was full of lies, not about my accomplishments, but about my mental state.

Sunday night, Angela called me.

"Ellison."

I swallowed. I hadn't heard her real voice in so long, though I dreamed it.

"Hi."

There was silence. I opened my mouth to apologize, but I realized I still didn't know what I had done.

"I'm pregnant."

It took me some time to digest her words. As the enormity of what Angela had just said began to settle, I felt light-headed, and I slumped into a chair. I couldn't quite order my thoughts, and they jumped around like ping-pong balls in a lottery box. Pregnant? I had never even considered it as a possibility. Last summer, Angela told me she was taking birth control, and we hadn't spoken in months. This wasn't supposed to happen, not to someone like me. I was only twenty-one years old. We were too young. Was she going to keep the baby? Did I have a say, and if I did, would I want to have a baby? And, oh God, what did I, of all people, know about being a father? It's not like I had a great role model. What if we kept the baby—what about school? How would we support him? Or her. Where would we live? Would Angela and I be together, a couple again? Could this bring us back together?

This last thought was the one that stuck and took over all the others. A small voice whispered that I was being irrational, that a baby never kept a couple together. Look at your own parents, the voice said. They had two kids and it didn't work for them. How different can you be from your own father? Is that what you want to do to another kid, *your own kid?* Shouldn't you be worrying more about how this happened, and do you want to have a family Angela after the way she treated you?

I squeezed my eyes shut to banish the sly murmurs and the panic welling in my gut. In the moment before I spoke, a fantasy flashed across my mind. Angela and I. Married. Kids—three, four. Happy. Together.

"I'm coming to see you." I hung up and left the apartment before she could reply.

My stride was long as I made my way to Angela's dorm room. She was a resident assistant that year, living in a freshman dorm, helping girls adjust to college life. She was taking a senior seminar on Zora Neale Hurston. She brought a sandwich and ate it with her friends in the Bryan Center every Tuesday and Thursday. I didn't think of myself as a stalker because I didn't intend to do anything with all of this information. I never tried to talk to her after she broke up with me. I never approached her or let her see me watching. I convinced myself that this was, if not normal behavior, then acceptable because I was in love.

Once I was on the main quad, the wind swirled around me and I pulled the collar of my jacket close. The sky was overcast, and it was colder than it had been since I'd moved to Durham. My eyes watered and the tip of my nose grew numb. It reminded me of Chicago, of spending months in parkas and boots. As kids, we were used to the cold pain on our ears when we forgot to wear a hat, the feeling of frozen nostrils, the tingling sting of fingertips left bare. I thought of my mother, of Maren. When I was a kid, my life had seemed so complicated. No father, a mother who worked too much, a life that wasn't my idea of perfect. Now, life back in our spacious suburban home in Evanston seemed simple, even idyllic.

As I walked up the stairs to Angela's floor, I practiced the perfect reaction to her news. I was not naïve enough to think that she would view the pregnancy as positive. She had plans, for graduate school, for a career. None of that would be easy with a baby. But I focused on how it could work. Maybe I would have to put off medical school, get a job. But I could do all that. The most important thing was that this could bring Angela back to me. We had a child. We were going to have a child. That would be the most important thing to both of us. Us. I talked myself into believing all this in the fifteen minutes it took me to get to Angela's dorm.

I knocked on her door. It opened, and Jason Davis stood looking at me. I had only seen Jason Davis in passing during the first semester of our senior year. We didn't have any classes together, and when we passed on the quad, one of us pretended not to see the other to avoid an awkward greeting. As for his friends, people I had thought of as my friends in a distant way, none of them ever talked to me either, although most nodded in acknowledgement when our paths crossed. Since I was no longer in that social scene—really, since I was no longer Jason Davis's friend—I no longer existed.

It was hard for me to remember what I liked about Jason. When I watched him strut around campus, he was so different from the guy I met that first day at Duke. He reeked of arrogance and entitlement. He sneered instead of smiling. If I had any energy left after pining for Angela I might have hated him. But she had used me up.

Jason's arms were folded as he stood in the doorway of Angela's room. I couldn't read the look on his face, but his stance claimed that he was the protector and I was an intruder come to threaten what was his. Angela sat on a futon underneath the window, looking out on the parking lot as if the rows of Audis and Hondas held the answers to all her questions. She wouldn't meet my eyes, and even if she had, Jason was like a brick wall blocking most of her from my vision.

The panic I had banished crept back like an intruder. I felt dread, the same kind of dread I felt the night my mother died. Maren and I sat in the dark, watching television. My mother was due home, and then it was past dinner time, past any reasonable excuse for why she hadn't called. I pretended not to be worried, thinking I was protecting Maren from my own fear. The entire time, the gnawing certainty that something was wrong expanded in my chest until I had to take deep, searching breaths just to get a tiny bit of air into my lungs. In the moments before the police arrived, I knew that something was damaged. Something was gone forever.

For a moment, finding out what was gone, what was damaged, was a relief. The anticipation of devastation was almost unbearable, and I longed for that same relief as I stood in the doorway of Angela's room. I stepped inside and Jason moved behind me to shut the door as if he owned the place, as if I couldn't even be trusted to complete even the simplest of tasks. Jason resumed his place between me and Angela. His eyes were narrowed, his lips pursed. I could see from the line of his jaw that his teeth were clenched. The anticipation of devastation swirled inside me. Not again, I thought. Not again.

I wanted someone to speak, to get it all over with. But I didn't know what to say; Angela looked like she'd rather be anywhere else besides here, and Jason was enjoying my discomfort too much to end it quickly.

"Angela wanted you here," he spat at me.

So Jason was mad at her, too. I refused to see this as a sign of hope. Jason and I turned to look at Angela. She dragged her gaze away from the parking lot.

Her eyes were bloodshot, and the skin underneath was swollen. Her cheeks looked fuller than the last time I saw her, as if she had gained weight. The baby. But she couldn't be more than three months pregnant, or so I assumed. Would she have called me before it was too late for an abortion? Why was Jason here?

I tried to slow my thoughts. I was getting ahead of myself without knowing the whole story, without knowing anything, really. With Jason standing here, there must be more to it than I first hoped. I felt like an idiot. I wanted to just run out of the room before anyone spoke another word.

"I'm pregnant."

"Everyone already knows that," Jason snapped. I wondered if he meant everyone in the room. Or had Angela been the subject of campus gossip? I had been so isolated during the fall semester, I wouldn't know what people were saying about anything.

Angela glared at Jason. "I guess I'll get to the point, then."

I wondered at the idea that there was some point other than the baby.

"Jason and I are back together."

Jason smirked at me, as if he had won. I ignored him and watched Angela for a signal, something to make me understand why she was doing this, why she couldn't see that I loved her and Jason was an ass. He didn't care about her, not like I did. She gave no signal, just looked at Jason, who was still watching me.

"For how long?" I didn't know why it mattered, but it did.

"Since July." Jason answered for her.

"And the baby?" I waited for Angela to reply, but she looked away.

I turned to Jason and our eyes locked. Until that moment, I had never considered the fact that it was me against Jason in the fight for Angela. Had this been a part of our friendship since the beginning? I always thought no one knew I had a crush on Angela, but perhaps my feelings weren't as opaque as I thought.

I had considered myself so much better for her, so much more sincere, that I had assumed she saw the same things. Now, I wondered whether I had just been a pawn in her game with Jason. Had she ever really been interested in me? Or was I a way to convince him that he would lose her if he didn't change? How could she do this to me? How could I be so stupid?

"What about the baby?" I didn't even try to keep the bitterness out of my voice.

Jason opened his mouth to speak, but I held up my hand.

"Angela?"

She looked at me. Her eyes pleaded with me, but how could I give her an answer when I didn't know the question? We all waited for her to speak. For a long moment, she seemed on the verge of crying. But the tears didn't come.

"I don't know if it's yours or Jason's. But I'm going to . . . get rid of it. I just thought you should know."

Get rid of it. It? I had no concrete thoughts about abortion. I suppose, if someone had asked me in the abstract, I would have said I was pro-choice. Whenever it was debated on television or in the papers, my mother always said it was a shame for men to tell women what to do with their bodies. I didn't disagree—how could a man know what it felt like to carry an unwanted child? How could we judge?

Angela glanced at Jason, her eyes nervous and unsure, and I realized that this wasn't really her choice. Somehow, Jason had convinced her to do this.

I stepped further into the room, walking around Jason to sit next to Angela. I felt him tense, but he didn't try to stop me.

"Why are you doing this?"

Jason snorted. "Why? She can't take care of a baby. We're too young. It would ruin our lives. *That's why.* Don't be retarded."

I have never wanted to hit someone so much in my life. All the anger I felt toward my father was nothing compared to what I felt at that moment. I could imagine the feel of his cheekbones crushing beneath my fist. I felt the wetness of his blood on my skin. I heard his screams echoing in my head.

I mustered an inhuman amount of restraint and kept my focus on Angela. She looked afraid, and I realized that my fury must be showing on my face.

"You don't have to do this." My voice was low, soothing. "I don't care whose baby it is. I can take care of him. We can take care of him."

Now she cried, fat tears that quickly wet her face. There was no sound to it, just her ragged breathing and the wetness on her face and shirt. She turned back to look out the window, but I didn't think she could see through the tears.

"Please just leave. Both of you." She whispered, but the room was so quiet that her words were clear.

Jason cleared his throat. "I don't think you should be alone right now."

"Get out!" she screamed. Her face was a streaked mask of sorrow.

Jason looked startled and quickly left the room. I waited a beat and then followed him. He was gone by the time I reached the hallway. I thought about going back, but Angela's door was already closed, and I heard her sobs, loud and desperate. I left her there, crying and alone.

Later that week, I received a letter with a Chicago postmark. The only person who ever sent me letters was Maren. My sister was the only person I knew that was old-fashioned enough to prefer real stationary and fancy pens to email. I tore open the letter and read Angela's loopy handwriting. It didn't even fill the page.

"Dear Ellison, please don't hate me. I wish I had your strength, but I don't. I'm not ready to be a mother, and you deserve better than me. Love always, Angela."

After I read the note, I laid on the bed with my arm over my eyes, trying to will myself not to think, not to feel. I listened to Nick Drake's *Pink Moon* CD on repeat, going back to the one-minute instrumental "Horn" over and again. It captured the sadness I felt better than any words could. I had been wrong. This was nothing like losing my mother. I knew what I was losing when my mother died. It was a whole different feeling to lose something you'd never known. I wished I'd never had to experience either feeling.

Calvin on his mother:

I never knew why my father left my mother when I was a small child. I guess I didn't really care much at first, since his absence meant I didn't have to go get a switch for my own beating every day. When you're a child, you care most about your immediate comfort, the nature of day-to-day life. The value of things and the value of people was directly related to how they made me feel. Pop made me feel bad. At first, I was happy when he left.

When I got older, not having a father made me stand out. In our small town, fathers didn't just leave. They took care of their children by working agricultural jobs or selling necessities to those who did. Mothers took care of the home and the children, and sometimes kids felt like they had ten mothers instead of just the one.

It was a scandal when a woman had to work, because it meant her husband wasn't doing his job as a provider, or the money he earned was being spent in ways that didn't sit well with our God-fearing community. Or it meant that the man simply wasn't there, as it was in our case. My mother cleaned the houses of white people who lived in towns miles away. She left early in the mornings, driving the rickety old Ford truck my father left behind. She came home long after it was dark. On Sundays we went to church, but none of the other mothers talked to her much. They said there must be something wrong with Esther—why else would a man abandon his family?

When Momma wasn't home I wasn't allowed to run around the neighborhood with the other kids, so I stayed inside and read books. I read anything I could find, and I wrote stories about the characters, picking up where the written stories left off. We didn't have a farm to tend or a business to run, so I stayed in school. There were only a few of us left in school by high-school graduation, so there wasn't a formal ceremony. We got our diplomas in the mail and Momma took the day off work to pack. She'd found a house in Durham. She'd worked and saved to afford the move to the city where no one would judge her for driving my father away.

—From *Save Me: A Memoir* by Calvin Emory

CHAPTER 13

May 1999

Back in March, I returned from the book tour with Calvin, determined to call Angela. But when I sat down to do it, I couldn't think of anything to say. What did I want from her? She'd cheated on me with Jason, there was the baby that might be mine but no longer existed. Not even I was naïve or romantic enough to think that we could go back to the way things had been last summer. I forgave her, but I didn't know if I loved her anymore. I didn't know if she'd ever loved me. So what would be the point of calling?

Instead, I focused on Calvin's advice at the bookstore in Miami. Finish strong. Focus on my future. Maybe it was time to face the fact that Angela wasn't meant to be a part of that future.

I didn't walk for graduation. Instead, I received my diploma without the pomp and circumstance, in a heavy blue folder that came in the mail one day. I let myself focus only on what was ahead: medical school, years of grueling work and paying dues, and the eventual rewards of all my hard work. Since all I had to do was maintain the grades I had, the end of senior year was all about getting through each day with a minimum of emotion or human contact. I spoke little in my classes, kept my head down when I walked the quad, and I ate my meals alone in my apartment or at off-campus restaurants frequented by locals instead of college kids.

The key was precision. I planned my days down to the minute, because spare time meant time for reflection, and I wanted none of that. Routine was my friend. Routine was my savior. I thought back to those eight months when Angela and I weren't speaking, after she left me for Jason and I spent those strange days with Calvin. I reminded myself how it felt to be numb. I tried to recapture that numbness, tried to ignore the searing melancholy left by Angela's absence, by the loss of a child who had never been. I found that pretending to be numb was almost as effective as the real thing. Almost.

When I received the acceptance letter from the Feinberg School of Medicine at Northwestern University, I didn't even open the other letters. I glanced at the return addresses on the envelopes, most of them thick, full of scholarship offers and housing information. Those schools didn't matter. I was going home. After living in Durham for five years, I was going home to Chicago. When I went to college, I chose Duke because Maren needed me to stay close. I didn't trust my father to take care of her, and even when it turned out that Maren could take care of herself, I never considered moving. But Maren was going to be a junior at Florida next year. She wasn't even in Durham most of the time, and so I didn't need to be, either.

I still felt like I had to make sure Maren would be okay. She was in the middle of finals, but I called her cell phone, hoping she wasn't in the middle of an exam.

I could hear the exhaustion in her voice when she said hello.

"You sound terrible," I greeted her.

"Hello to you, too, El. So what's up? You called me in the middle of exams to insult me?"

I smiled. "I'm fully capable of that, as you know. But no, I have something serious to talk to you about."

Her intake of breath was filled with silent dread. I rushed to reassure her.

"Nothing horrible, Mare. Just about medical school."

She released a long sigh. I felt bad—we had both been through so many horrible things these past few years, I should have known better than to use that phrasing. Something serious was when our mother died, when we moved in with Calvin, when she got tangled up in that ugly business with Chris. This was nothing compared to all that, and putting it into perspective helped me relax a little.

"You got in? Where?" Her voice was excited. She no longer sounded tired. Maren was always rooting for me, and I did the same for her. We had promised that we'd always do that for each other, no matter what.

"Well, I got in to five schools, actually."

She laughed. "And you only applied to eight, right? Ah, so modest. I knew it! You're brilliant—why wouldn't they want you?"

"As much as I would like to hear you go on about my brilliance, the thing is, I want to go to Northwestern." I paused and cleared my throat. "I want to go home."

We both knew that what I was really saying was that I was leaving her. Even though she was at school in Gainesville, our only family was here in Durham, so for practical reasons, this was home. This was where she came back to for breaks. This was where our father lived, and although she had a better relationship with him than I did, I had promised I would be here for her, too. Now, I was breaking that promise, and asking for her permission to do so.

I wouldn't have blamed her if she didn't want me to go. She had two more years left in school, and she was only twenty. I was two years older, but those two years felt like two dozen. I was torn between my desire to protect Maren and my desperate need to get away from all the ugliness I'd experienced in Durham. Going to Northwestern would be a fresh start and a return to a better past, all at the same time.

But I left it up to Maren. She didn't make me wait long.

"Ellison. Of course you should go. I can take care of myself."

"That's just it. I don't want you to have to."

She sighed. "But at some point, you're going to have to trust me."

"It's not you I don't trust."

"I know, El. It's just that, well, you've spent the last few years being my big brother instead of living your own life."

"I have a life," I protested. Right. A life that included mooning after a girl who didn't want me or my baby, no friends to speak of and a lonely apartment I could barely afford. I'd given Maren the abbreviated version of the breakup with Angela, leaving out the part about the pregnancy, but my sister always knew when I was hurting, even if she didn't know all the details.

"But are you happy?" A rhetorical question, we both knew.

I waited, as if I was considering the question. I was tempted to lie. I hadn't told her about the baby, partly because Maren never really liked Angela, and mostly because I was ashamed of the entire thing.

"I'm hanging in. It's the best I can do right now, and I'm feeling better now than I was six months ago."

"Then go to Chicago. Figure out what you want out of life. Not just what you want to do. I know you're going to be a fantastic doctor and save millions of lives and get a house on the lake. But you need to find out who you want to be, and figure out a way to be happy. That's what Mom would want."

I took a deep breath.

"When did you get to be so grown up? You're like Yoda without the speech impediment."

"I've got this really smart big brother who taught me everything I know. That, and the Force."

I smiled. "So I'm going to Chicago."

"I'm happy for you, El. And I love you."

After I hung up, I realized that for the first time in months, I didn't want to pretend to feel numb any more.

I started making plans for my return home. I would look up old friends from high school. I could visit my mother's grave. I could get a proper slice of pizza whenever I wanted. Northwestern was a great school, and they offered me a fellowship and financial aid that paid tuition and some living expenses. I told myself that going to Northwestern made perfect sense for my present and my future.

Before I left Durham, I began looking for apartments near the medical school, and I found a nice one in Streeterville, a couple of miles from my old house and just minutes away from all of my classes. Even with the support from the school, I knew that I couldn't really afford the $1,000 rent on a one-bedroom apartment in Lake Shore Plaza. At least I couldn't afford it for the long-term. But my options were limited and I wanted to be near the neighborhood where I grew up, so I figured I would get a part-time job after the first semester of school, eat ramen noodles and survive, somehow. It was shocking to pay that much for a boxy little square of a place. I'd been living in Durham so long that my big-city instincts were dulled. But even this buoyed me. I looked forward to being in a city again, being the old Ellison, who rode the L and knew the best places to find deep-dish pizza for cheap.

I spent the first weekend scouring thrift stores for used furniture. I decided not to focus too much on style (a luxury for people with a lot more money than I had), and concentrate on comfort. I only had myself to please anyway, and I didn't expect to be spending much time entertaining during medical school. I found the basics— a rectangular dining set made of scarred oak, which would double as a dining and work area, a twin bed, a futon for the living room, a couple of chairs, lamps and kitchen supplies. The only things I bought new were bedding and towels. I had the same television and stereo I'd had since high school, and anything else I might need, I'd get someday when I had more money.

By Sunday night, I was feeling pretty pleased with myself. Next on my agenda was to figure out when I'd run out of money, but that could wait until tomorrow. Instead, I put the Lauryn Hill CD on, and considered the near-empty refrigerator for dinner options. I'd just about settled on cheap takeout when the sound of the door buzzer surprised me. I didn't know anyone in Chicago, and nobody knew I was even here besides Maren, who, as far as I knew, was 800 miles away in North Carolina.

"Yes?" I spoke hesitantly into the intercom.

"Ellison, it's me."

It took me a moment to realize who "me" was. Angela. She now lived in Chicago. It was where she had gone to have the abortion, back to her parents. I had done such a good job of trying to put her out of my mind that I hadn't even thought about her since I moved into my apartment.

"Come on up."

I didn't let myself speculate on why she was here or how she found me. I tamped down the feelings of happy anticipation I had at the idea of seeing her again. I would just have an open mind, no expectations, no desires, no disappointment. I just waited at the door, holding it ajar while I listened for the soft ding of the arriving elevator.

The elevator was across the hall from my door, and when the doors opened, I focused only on her face. Her hair was cut short in a natural style that made her look even prettier than before. She wore no makeup and her eyes looked puffy. In her ears were round diamond earrings I'd never seen her wear. They looked expensive, and I started to wonder when she'd gotten them when she shifted her position. As she walked slowly toward me, my eyes traveled to the rest of her body, and I held my breath while the sound of a rushing waterfall filled my ears. Her belly was large and round, settling low on her abdomen. Its size seemed to overtake her entire petite frame and it was a wonder that she could support it. Finally, my brain allowed the truth to filter through. Angela was still pregnant.

There was no period of frantic questions and tearful answers. I looked at her face, and I knew. She knew. I was the father. It occurred to me that she'd known all along I was the father, that the whole drama with Jason at the dorm room had been a sham. But it was too much to take in, so I left that part of it alone for now.

I somehow ended up sitting on the hardwood floor, looking up at Angela as she sat across from me in an old tweed recliner I'd found at a secondhand shop. Neither of us had said anything yet. There was so much to say. Where to begin? I looked away toward a wall that was made up almost entirely of glass. It seemed I could see all of Chicago through the window. I imagined that Angela had lived here while I lived in Evanston with my mom and Maren, that she could see inside our home, watching the family dramas that seemed so petty and small now.

I tried to decide how I felt. Angry. Sad. Afraid. And underneath all of that, giddiness lurked. I was going to be a father. Our baby was alive.

"When?" I croaked. It was as if my voice had never been used.

Angela placed her palms on the sides of her belly, using a gentle motion as if she didn't want to disturb the baby. I knew from biology classes that babes were hearty and did a lot of bumping around while in utero. It would take more than a hand motion to disturb an unborn baby. But Angela moved delicately, like she carried a set of precious china inside her.

"He's due in three weeks."

I tilted my head to the side. She seemed to understand this silent motion and nodded.

"It's a boy."

I exhaled. A boy. I was going to be the father of a baby boy.

The panic I'd felt when she first told me she was pregnant was a far cry from what I felt at this moment. There were still all the same doubts and fears, but when the baby is a reality instead of a mere possibility, it changes everything. I could see her belly moving as our son shifted around inside her. This baby was definitely real, and he was coming soon. There was no time to panic, no room to let the fear overtake me. There was only room to figure out how we were going to make it all work.

We sat there for a long moment, looking at each other. Then, we smiled at each other.

"Are you hungry?" I asked.

Angela looked down at her belly. "Ellison, I've been hungry for the past nine months."

I laughed. "Well, let's eat. And talk."

"That sounds wonderful."

We kept things light at first, laughing about Angela's enormous appetite and talking about the summer before, when we'd been so happy, and, I thought, in love. I played CDs I knew she liked: Natalie Merchant, D'Angelo, Lauryn Hill, Weezer. Neither of us brought up Jason until we had devoured our sandwiches from the deli across the street and Angela finished both of our chocolate chip cookies for dessert.

"So how did you find me?"

She shook her head. "It wasn't easy. I called all over trying to find out where you were going to med school, but no one at Duke seemed to know much. Then, I finally got the idea to call your sister."

"Maren?" I was horrified at the thought of them talking, since she and Maren hadn't exactly gotten along the last time they spoke.

Angela gave me a crooked smile. "Do you have any other sisters?"

I decided not to say that I was surprised Maren even talked to her. Actually, I wasn't—my sister was too nice not to help someone in need, even someone she disliked.

"She was sweet, although I think I might have offended her by refusing to say why I wanted the number. I told her it was none of her business."

"Oh no. I suppose this was *after* she had already given you the number?"

"Naturally."

Angela sat still for a moment, picking at the crumbs on the table in front of her. She winced and reached back to rub her back.

"Do you mind if I lie on the futon? I can't sit in a straight chair for too long."

I dragged the mattress onto the floor and she lay down on her side facing me while I lay on my back, my head resting on folded arms.

"I need to apologize," she said abruptly.

I didn't look at her when she spoke. "Don't."

"I have to. It wasn't fair, what I did to you."

I focused on a yellow spot on the ceiling. "Can't we just let it go?" I didn't want to go over it all again. I didn't want to remember how I felt when I went to her room and found Jason there, watching the two of them tell me that Angela was pregnant with his baby. I didn't want to remember the loss I felt at that moment.

"Ellison, look at me."

I was slow to turn my head.

"I want to be honest with you. I don't want our baby to be born into a lie."

It wounded strange, the way she phrased it, but I knew what she meant.

"What lie? You just made a mistake. You thought the baby was Jason's, but it wasn't. None of that matters now." I took her hand in mine. "We're going to have a son. That's what matters."

Now she was the one who turned away. But she kept her hand in mine.

"That's what you need to know. It wasn't a mistake. I knew the baby was yours the whole time. I only slept with Jason once after we broke up, and it was after I already knew I was pregnant."

I felt the blood rushing to my head as if I were upside down.

"Why?" I could only manage that one word.

Her voice caught when she spoke. "I loved you too much. That's why I broke up with you and got back together with Jason. I was afraid of how much I wanted you, how good we were together. I was supposed to go to Duke to get a degree, go to graduate school, have a career. Not fall in love and get pregnant."

I finally looked at her. Her cheeks were wet with tears. "I still don't understand. Why pretend the baby was Jason's?"

"Don't you see? I could have an abortion, give up Jason's child. But not yours. Never yours. Ours."

I nodded, slowly. "So you told him the baby was his, knowing he would want you to have an abortion. Pay for it, even."

"And I thought it would all be easier that way."

It didn't make sense, really. But I knew the feeling of wanting the truth to be something different than what it was. And so, as much as I wanted to pull my hand away from hers, to be angry, to blame her for all those months I spent numb and alone, I couldn't. Instead, I pulled her to me, and we hugged, her broad belly pressed against mine, our hands still clasped.

Calvin on death and life:

I'm always suspicious of stories about the ways in which death reveals all kinds of life-affirming wisdom to the people left behind. When Momma died after a series of strokes, she was old and feeble and her death was a relief. I missed her, but I didn't feel wiser or better able to face the world after grieving for her. I just felt more alone, and even though I was already in my forties when she died, I still felt like an orphan. I don't know if my father is dead or alive, but since I haven't seen him since I was a child, it hardly matters. Once my mother was gone, I had no parents, no one who knew me when I was a kid. It's an unsettling feeling, lonely. There's nothing wise about it.

The only other major loss I've had is my ex-wife. When Vanessa died, we hadn't seen each other in at least five years, and even before that, things between us were strained. But her death hit me hard. I still loved her, and I knew what it meant for the kids. But her death also meant my opportunity to be forgiven was gone forever. My heart can be a dark, selfish places sometimes. She was dead and now I could never make up to her all those years of pain that I put her through. I could return triumphantly to Chicago, well-dressed, with a bestseller in my hand, showing her the man I had become. I didn't want her to feel sorry or to see what she'd missed. I just wanted to prove to Vanessa, and to myself, that I was a better person than I'd been when she knew me. I had to be, or else I couldn't see any reason to keep going.

When she died, I had not yet become that man and I didn't know if I ever would. And part of my motivation to change was that image of me showing her how I'd succeeded—some of my drive died with her.

I'll never forget how I heard the news. Vanessa was famous in Chicago, the "next Oprah," people said, and she was gaining popularity around the country. I happened to be watching television that September night in 1994 when her death was noted in a short segment on some entertainment news station. I suppose they covered it because of the way she died—in a car accident—and the fact that her show was syndicated in many smaller markets. The show moved on quickly to other people's tragedies or mishaps, but I sat there stunned and crying. I think my mother came in the room at some point and asked me what I was crying about, but I couldn't tell her right then. She never liked Vanessa and had always blamed my ex-wife for my failure instead of me. I couldn't talk to her about what this might mean for my teenaged children. All I could do is look at an old picture I had of Vanessa, when she was in her twenties, young and unaware of what life would bring us. All I could do was cry.

Maybe I do have some wisdom to offer after all of this. I wished I had tried harder in my marriage. I wished I had fully understood what a precious gift fatherhood was. If I had, I wouldn't have simply left my children and I would have been a better father when they came back to me. If I could tell my children anything, it would be that the plans we make for our lives don't always work out. Make plans, but when God or fate or other people change those plans, figure out how to make your life work. Concentrate on doing the right thing, and the rest will come.

—From *Save Me: A Memoir* by Calvin Emory

Part II
1999–2000

CHAPTER 14

June 1999

As soon as Angela left that night, I called Maren. She was back in Durham for the summer and we'd made plans for her to come visit me in Chicago before going back to Florida for her junior year. I was afraid of her reaction, but I couldn't wait to tell her. I wasn't focused on all the very real reasons why Angela and I could be disasters as parents. I was determined to be positive, to try to will the situation to work as best I could.

"Angela is pregnant." I had meant to lead up to the news, but as soon as we got through our initial greetings, I just blurted out the news.

"Excuse me?"

"I'm having a baby. I mean, we're having a baby. Angela and I."

The silence was so long that the only way I knew she was still on the line is that I could hear her breathing.

"Okay, I must have missed something. Didn't you and Angela break up last Thanksgiving?"

"Yes."

"And you haven't seen her since then."

"Not until tonight."

Maren slowed her words as if she was talking to a toddler. "So how can you two be having a baby?"

I told her the full story of the breakup, this time including the essential part about the pregnancy, Jason and the abortion. When I got to the part about how Angela pretended not to know whose baby it was, Maren stopped me.

"Wait, she knew it was your baby all along, but she didn't tell you? Ellison, that's horrible."

I knew she was right. Somehow I had diminished the enormity of that little tidbit because I was so focused on the actual, living, moving baby.

"I just don't think it matters anymore. There's a child now. That has to be my focus."

"But Ellison, how can you ever trust her? How do you even know it's yours? Does this mean you and Angela are back together?"

She was voicing all the doubts I hadn't let myself think about. She was approaching it logically, rationally. But if anyone should know that families don't work according to logic or rationality, it was us.

"It's mine. He's mine. The baby is a boy. We're not back together. I don't even know if we should be together. And I know everything you're saying is true, but what can I do about the past now? I've got to focus on my son,

who will be here in just three weeks. That's all I know—
I'm about to be a father, and Angela is my son's mother."

"It's a boy?" she said hesitantly. "Well, I always
wanted to be an auntie. I just didn't think it would
happen this soon."

This was Maren's way of telling me that she was going
to put aside her doubts about Angela, for now. I loved her
for it.

"Thanks, Auntie Maren."

She laughed. "That makes me sound like I'm eighty
years old." She paused. "Hey, El, Dad's in the next room.
Want to talk to him? You should tell him, too."

My stomach clenched at the thought of talking to
Calvin at that moment. I didn't really want to deal with
him and his doubts when facing my sister's had already
been exhausting. I knew I should tell him myself, but I
chickened out.

"Maren, I can't do it, not now."

"At some point, you and Dad are going to have to
settle things, you know. This can't go on forever."

"I know, Mare. But please, I can't face it now. My
head is spinning in a million different directions."

She sighed. "Come on, Ellison."

"I just can't. I've got too many other things to worry
about right now, with Angela and the baby. I don't have
it in me to deal with him, too."

"Okay. But don't forget to take care of yourself, too.
Your son needs his father to be in good shape, too."

"I'll take of myself, Maren. Don't worry."

"I always worry about you, big brother."

Angela's parents hated me. They would never say so, of course. They were far too Midwestern and circumspect to expose their raw emotions. Angela never had too many good things to say about her family. When we were close last summer, she'd painted a picture of them as staunchly middle-class and classist, dismissive of people they deemed below their station in life. During her early childhood, her parents didn't have much money and they all lived in a duplex on the south side. Then her father's business took off and they moved to a high rise near the Loop. Her father frowned a lot but said little, and Angela once said her mother's main occupation was trying to act like a white society maven.

It had reminded me of high school in Durham, when my skin color didn't stop my classmates from saying I acted white. I wanted to tell Angela that there were many ways of being a black person in America, but at the time I was too smitten to disagree with anything she said.

The first time I met them, I stood nervously in the lobby while the doorman called their number and stood watching me with a blank expression on his face as we waited for an answer. He was a middle-aged white man, his hair already grayed, his uniform spotless and pressed. I wondered what he thought about black people living here. Chicago, like most other places in the Midwest, was still very segregated, and there weren't many places where whites and blacks lived in harmony. Those harmonious, multi-racial utopias did not include Evanston, where I grew up with mostly all white neighbors, nor did it include this high rise, from what I could see from standing in the lobby for just a few minutes.

After the doorman hung up, he looked at me for a long moment, just long enough to let me know I didn't belong here, but not long enough to be confrontational. He directed me to the elevators and the twenty-first floor.

Angela's father was a large, gruff man who was born and raised in Chicago, the kind of self-made success who couldn't understand why every black man didn't just pull himself up, work hard and fight his way to the top.

"I can't wait until next year when we can finally get that bastard Clinton out of office," he told me the first time we met. He glared at me, ignoring his wife's reprimand.

"Language, John."

I tried not to grimace. My mother had raised us to be staunch Democrats, and I couldn't see how a black man could be a Republican. But I knew better than to argue the point, especially since I was the man who impregnated his daughter. Johnny Michaels outweighed me by at least fifty pounds, and although he wore pressed slacks, a dress shirt and gleaming loafers on almost all occasions, he seemed as if he wouldn't hesitate to pummel me if needed.

Angela's mother, Winifred, was a classic, upwardly mobile member of the black middle class. She wore her hair in a shoulder-length weave and kept it bone straight, never daring to let any hint of kink come through. Her face was a mask of expensive makeup, and her clothes, though expensive, were matronly and brightly-colored.

She smiled often, but it was a false expression, a mere curve of the lips. Her nose was always just a bit crinkled when I was around, as if she smelled something putrid but couldn't quite place the source.

She reminded me of Jason Davis's mother, except without the sense of humor, and without the genuine beauty. Angela's mother was making the most of her natural assets, but she couldn't compete with someone like Mrs. Davis. Winifred was the seventh of twelve children born to her single mother in Macon, Georgia, and she had spent her entire adult life trying to escape her past. Angela told me never to mention her aunts and uncles, most of whom still lived in Macon in the same ramshackle house where they'd all been born.

"My mother hates to talk about all that," she told me one day soon after I found out she was still pregnant. I couldn't blame anyone for not wanting to talk about family, but it didn't make me like Winifred any more.

"She feels like this is all your fault." She gestured toward her swollen belly.

"I know it's not ideal, but we're adults. She's can't spend the rest of our lives blaming me."

Angela looked away.

"Can she?"

She cleared her throat. "My mother is still mad at me for not going to prom with her best friend's son. Ask her about my eighth grade graduation, and she'll complain that my cap was crooked, ruining all of the pictures. In fifth grade I hurt my knee playing soccer, and—"

I held up a hand and laughed. "Okay, I get it. Your mother can hold a grudge. She can hate me. But she won't be able to resist the baby."

But her parents were certainly able to resist my charms. They interrogated me the first time we met, asking for details about my family, my degree from Duke, my plans for the future. Mrs. Michaels did most of the questioning while Mr. Michaels frowned at me.

"So how are you going to take care of your responsibilities?"

It was an old-fashioned way of demanding information about my finances. I didn't have much to offer.

"I have a fellowship that pays for tuition and offers some money for living expenses. That will hold me over for a while, and I planned to get a part-time job in January to supplement." I glanced at Angela for support. She smiled at me and nodded. I risked a look at her father, whose frown had become a glare.

"You can't support a family with a part-time job," he growled. "You need to get a job now."

"Well, I thought of that, sir, but my fellowship and a part-time job will give me more money than any job I could get right now. It makes the most sense for me to stay in school, especially for the future."

He harrumphed but left his wife to continue.

"Mr. Michaels and I have agreed to support Angela and the baby as long as necessary," she said primly. Meaning forever, since I didn't seem to be bringing much to the table.

"It's very generous of you, Mrs. Michaels," I said, trying my best to be respectful, more for my own benefit than theirs. I didn't think they would ever believe I was anything except some lout who had taken advantage of their daughter, but I knew I was more than that.

"We were raised to take care of our own," she said, glancing at her husband, who nodded his approval.

I could take offense at the implication that I wasn't raised right. I could protest, make a snide comment to match hers. I would have been within my rights to tell them off, to point out that a good upbringing didn't include putting down other people, no matter how much you disapproved of them. But I didn't. My mother raised me better than that.

I thought I would be calm watching the birth of my son. I wasn't afraid of the biology of it all, the blood, the pain, the miraculous turning and stretching it took to be born. I had read all about it in textbooks. I knew the parts of the female reproductive system better than Angela. I even calmed her when the obstetrician told us, at Angela's last checkup, that she'd need a C-section because the baby was breech. A scheduled C-section, on average, offers the same recovery time as a normal birth without complication, I told Angela. This will be fine.

Angela and I arrived at the hospital at seven o'clock in the morning. We were both quiet. I had only been back in Chicago three weeks, not enough time to figure out how to be together or what our future was. Our impending parenthood crowded out all other considerations. We spent those three weeks in a flurry of preparation, discussing names, buying diapers, putting together cribs and packing bags for the hospital stay. Angela would stay with her parents for the time being, and they had agreed to support her and the baby until we figured things out for the long-term.

At no time did we discuss what was really important, like how we would raise our son together, and whether we would be parents together or apart. The baby allowed us to ignore the past and the future. So we rode to the hospital in silence. The practical plans for the baby were made, and the only things left to talk about were the other things, the big things.

Once we arrived, Angela was monitored for a while, then her epidural was placed and she lost the feeling in her legs at the same time her mood was considerably brightened by morphine. She became chatty and a little goofy, which was fine with me. My stomach was roiling and I felt disconnected from my movements, as if I were watching someone else bring ice to Angela, check the baby's monitor and develop a slow panic that he was desperate to hide.

I was great at parroting textbooks and studies. What I did not take time to consider was the raw emotion of becoming a father. A C-section is surgery, and when people think of surgery, they think of long, complicated procedures ending in with a perspiring doctor wiping his brow and declaring success. But once things get going, if there are no complications, a C-section baby is born within minutes. I stood next to Angela's head, a pristine sheet shielding us from the gore. I told myself I could have watched, no problem, but I was choosing to hold Angela's hand instead. Five minutes passed, and I wondered how things were going. Then, the doctor looked up and I could see her eyes smiling above her surgical mask.

"It's a boy!"

"Already?" The panic had taken over and my breathing quickened. I wasn't ready yet. I needed more time, more minutes to think about my son's arrival.

There was a screech, a moment of silence, and then the unmistakable cry of a baby. My baby. My son.

The nurse wiped him off, wrapped him a blanket like a tiny burrito, and handed him to Angela. Her hands shook, and I moved closer.

"He is perfect," she said, tears running down her face. Our eyes met and held. I looked down at our child. He was still crying, angry at the lights, the cold, these unfamiliar faces.

I took him from Angela and held him close to my face. He stopped crying and furrowed his brow, as if he was trying to figure me out. I grinned and kissed his pug nose.

My son.

James Morrison Emory. We called him Jamie.

The Michaels came to see Jamie on our last day in the hospital. We dressed him in his going-home outfit, a blue sailor suit that was just a little too big, and probably too hot for that July day. While we waited for their arrival, I walked down to the Au Bon Pain to get a sandwich for Angela, who was ravenous and recovering well from the surgery. When I returned to the room, they were all there. Johnny stood with his arms folded, watching as Winifred rocked Jamie and sang softly to him. Angela was still in bed, beaming at her parents.

In fact, everyone was smiling until I entered the room. Winifred looked up at me, her smile shifting from genuine to forced. The look of peace on Johnny's face morphed into a frown, and Angela looked worried.

"So you met the little guy," I said, trying for levity. The words hung in the air, leaden. I leaned over and smiled down into Jamie's face. I knew he was too young, but I could swear he smiled back.

"He's beautiful," Winifred said. She turned her body away from me, a slight move that was barely noticeable. "He has my grandfather's eyes and Mother's hair, don't you think, John?"

Johnny grunted in reply.

"I had hair like that when I was born, too," I offered. "In fact, if I let mine grow, we'll be like twins."

Winifred looked at my head. "Oh, I think yours is coarser than James's hair. He clearly has a fine grade of hair, just like Mother."

I noted the insult. I hadn't grown up with ideas about good hair and bad, but when I was in high school in Durham, that was one of the things my classmates made fun of. They said I thought I was better than them because I had good hair. Not good enough for Winifred, apparently.

After pronouncing my hair deficient, she turned back to Jamie and continued cooing at him. I looked at Johnny.

"So, Johnny, how does it feel to be a grandfather?"

I glanced at Angela to see her shaking her head. I had said the wrong thing—again.

"Well, Ellison, I wasn't quite ready to be a grandfather so soon, and I'd have preferred to wait a long while. But what's done is done, I suppose, and Jamie is a fine-looking boy. Hope he takes after me," he said, his voice stern. "And, I prefer to be called Mr. Michaels, if you don't mind."

"Of course not. Mr. Michaels." I handed Angela her sub without meeting her eyes, and I took a chair near the window. Jamie had won them over, but it wasn't going to be that easy for me. I didn't care, except for my son's sake. No matter how rude they were, I would endure it if it meant that Jamie would get to know his grandparents. I wanted him to grow up with a strong sense of family, something I'd always wished I had.

At the end of the day, Angela's doctor signed her release papers and we loaded Jamie into his car seat. My BMW was aging but sturdy, and as I tested and retested the car seat straps to make sure they were tight enough to protect my son, I remembered the day my mother bought it for me. Back then, I would never have imagined that just six years later, I would be loading a baby into its backseat.

I drove slowly through the streets, taking turns at a glacial pace. At this rate, it would take forty-five minutes to reach my apartment, but I was in no hurry. Precious cargo required extreme measures.

Angela was silent for much of the ride, but as we passed the turn-off to her parents' house, she turned to me.

"Where are you going?"

I glanced at her. "Home."

"You missed the turn to my parents' house."

"That's because I'm not going to your parents' house. I'm going to my apartment," I said, frowning.

This was just the first of many practical details we had not taken time to consider. In the three weeks since I returned to Chicago, my days had been filled with shopping for inexpensive furniture for my apartment, finding a crib for Jamie, buying books for my medical school classes, and trying to wrap my mind around the fact that I was going to be a father. In fact, Angela and I hadn't spent too much time together after that night at my apartment—she was tired and the doctor recommended bed rest, and I was afraid to break the connection we had made. I saw the pregnancy as a second chance, and it seemed as if too much talking might jinx things. I had assumed there would be plenty of time to talk about the baby after he was born.

"Well, Jamie can't stay at your place," she said. I didn't care for her tone—proprietary, condescending.

"Why not? It's a one-bedroom, but there's plenty of room for a baby."

Angela sighed. "He needs his mother. I'm nursing, remember?"

How could I forget? She seemed to have no qualms about extracting her breast from her shirt anywhere, at any time. I thought she could have at least covered up with a blanket or a towel.

I spoke slowly, since she didn't seem to get it. "I thought you would come, too."

Angela squinted at me. "Just because we have a baby together, that doesn't mean we're getting back together."

Her words hit me like a punch in the stomach. She still saw me as a pushover and believed that everything between us was her choice, not mine.

I kept my eyes trained on the road but I was seething.

"What makes you think I want to be with you?" I said it to hurt her, but I realized it was also true. Angela had already devastated me once, then simply reappeared in my life and turned it upside down once again. I wasn't sorry we had Jamie, but I couldn't quite get past all the things she had said and done.

When I glanced at her, there were tears in her eyes. Good—let her be the one who cries for once.

"You always assume that you're the one who gets to choose whether to be with me. I'm a person, too, and you didn't exactly handle things well last summer."

"I didn't get pregnant by myself," she said, crying quietly.

"But you lied about it."

Her sobs grew more urgent, and I regretted being mean to her. She'd just had a baby, and even though what I said was true, I could have been nicer about it.

"Angela—"

"Never mind. You made your point."

"Just let me say this. My offer has nothing to do with us. It's about Jamie. He needs to be near both his parents."

As if to underscore my point, Jamie let out a wail, which turned into desperate crying.

"Oh, God, he's hungry."

We were just a block from my house. I said nothing, letting Angela make the decision. Jamie's crying became more insistent, pushing her to speak.

"Okay, for tonight we'll go to your place. But we need to talk more about this."

I nodded. Having Jamie stay with me at least one night was a small victory. But I feared the war had just begun.

CHAPTER 15

July/August 1999

I never heard the word *colic* until Jamie was born. By the time Jamie was one month old and in the full throes of an endless crying jag, I decided the word was just a nicer way of describing a baby who cries all day, every day, no matter what. Or at least, that's how it seemed to me as I held him while he screamed.

I went online looking for a list of suggestions for parents, perhaps helpful hints written in a cheerful tone. What I found was a list of things that make colic worse. Certain foods, although it wasn't clear which ones, exactly. Excessive anger, fear or anxiety in the house (which, I would think, is the norm in a house where there's a newborn). Overfeeding in what was referred to as a futile attempt to stop the crying.

Futile, indeed.

Jamie seemed to cry louder when Angela tried to nurse him, so much so that after a few weeks, she gave up. It didn't help that she was suffering from a terrible case of post-partum blues. She didn't want to go out, she ate only because she had to, and nothing I said was right. If things were bad between us before, now they were downright awful. Just the sight of me sometimes made her break into tears. After the night Jamie came home, we agreed to compromise and split the week in half—Jamie would stay with me Sunday to Wednesday, and he go with Angela to her parents' house the rest of the time. In those early days, she left breast milk for me so I could feed Jamie, and those were my favorite times with him. Before the colic struck, he was an alert, peaceful baby, a good eater who looked into my eyes as he drank.

But after a week of crying, Angela claimed she could no longer take it, that she needed a break and would be at her parents' house if I needed her. Winifred and Johnny tried to pitch in, but Winifred said the crying gave her migraines, and Johnny had no interest in changing diapers or getting anywhere near his daughter's breast milk. So Jamie stayed with me most days and nights. I was the only one who could tolerate Jamie's rages. It's not that the crying didn't bother me; I just looked at it as his way of talking to me. I didn't know what he was saying, but it was clear he wasn't happy, and it was up to me—his father—to listen.

Angela provided what seemed like gallons of milk, and I put them in the freezer. I set up his crib next to my bed. School hadn't started, so Jamie and I had our days and nights free for his long crying jags.

"How is he?" Angela didn't come over much, but she called every morning. I couldn't imagine how she could stay away from our son, but I never criticized her. I could tell from the catch in her voice that she felt bad about not being there. I knew better than to voice my doubts about her mothering skills, although I constantly questioned them in my own mind.

"He's good," I told her, my voice loud enough to be heard over Jamie's screams. "I mean, he eats and is gaining weight, so the doctor says he's normal."

"How can all the crying be normal?" Angela whined. I could tell it was getting to her, even over the phone.

"Babies cry. They can't speak in our language, so that's how they communicate." I tried to stay calm. She should know this. I read all the books, so why hadn't she? She'd known she was pregnant for months; I found out three weeks before Jamie was born.

The moment I saw Angela at her door that day, her belly swollen and her face uncertain, my romantic fantasy of our relationship was re-established. I had hoped that we would find our way back to each other, and although I knew things would be hard, I still believed I loved her.

Since Jamie was born, I found myself not only feeling unloving toward Angela, but half the time I didn't even like her. It was hard to remember why I had loved her before. A shared interest in literature and her smile just didn't seem like enough anymore. Now she seemed selfish and spoiled, more interested in her own comfort than what was best for our child. I knew I was being hard on her, so I tried to bury my doubts in the routine of daily life. But when she called to check on Jamie but showed only a perfunctory interest in him, it was hard to hide my feelings.

"Are you coming over tonight? Not to see me, but for Jamie?"

There was a long pause before she answered. "I can't tonight. I think I'm catching a cold."

I wondered if she was worried about Jamie catching it, or if she just didn't feel up to dealing with his colic. I said nothing about the cold, and the call ended soon after. It was how our conversations always went during the time when Jamie cried from morning to night.

Just about the only thing Jamie found calming was a ride in the stroller. He could sleep there for hours, so I spent my August days pushing the stroller around the streets of Chicago. It was a way for me to get reacquainted with my hometown, and I narrated the sights for Jamie.

"That's where we used to go on Friday nights in high school," I told him, pointing to Rocky's Pizza. "Deep dish pizza is the only real pizza."

He snored in reply. "If your eyes were open," I continued, "you would see Lake Michigan right over there. When I was a kid, I thought it was the ocean."

One day, I strapped him into his car seat and we drove past my old house in Evanston where I lived with my mother and Maren. Unlike the stroller, Jamie did not find car rides soothing, so I had to speak up to be heard over his cries.

"That's where I grew up." I looked back at him and pointed to the house. It had been painted, and my throat tightened when I saw that the new owners had changed the landscaping and window treatments.

"It used to be different. But it'll always be home." Jamie stopped crying for a moment, frowning, and I imagined that he knew what I was saying. Then the car filled with the smell of his dirty diaper, and I realized he had more important things on his mind than a trip into the past.

His business done, Jamie resumed his crying, now with an urgent need for a new diaper adding to his misery. But for some reason, I smiled. We drove back to my apartment like that, Jamie irate and me feeling happier than I had any right to be.

In late August, I reported to the medical school for orientation. We were a small group, just 170 students in total. It was one of the reasons I chose Northwestern. I would be able to get to know my professors and classmates in a way that I wouldn't at one of the bigger schools. We gathered in a large conference hall, and as the talk swirled around me, it struck me that I didn't know a soul in the room. I didn't even know if anyone from Duke was here, and if they were, we hadn't known each other there and were unlikely to recognize each other now. I had been so busy the past two months, I hadn't had time to feel nervous about starting medical school. But standing in the room full of my classmates, a wave of self-doubt washed over me. I'd never had any academic problems before, but I'd also never had a baby before. And Angela seemed to be letting Jamie spend more time with me every week. I was happy to be with him, but I didn't know how I would manage once classes started. I hadn't even considered day care options, since I had assumed Angela would take care of the baby when I couldn't. But that assumption, as with the others, was turning out to be misguided.

Before I became paralyzed with worry, I forced myself to stay in the moment, not to think ahead to disasters that hadn't even happened yet. There were bagels and pastries laid out for us to eat before the presentations began, and a series of facts were projected silently on the wall-sized screen at the front of the room. I grabbed a doughnut and some juice and faced the screen, pretending to be engrossed in the slide show. There were ninety-seven men and seventy-three women in our class. We came from forty-one states and fifteen foreign countries. Forty students were Northwestern graduates. The youngest student was eighteen and the oldest was forty-one. Most of us had majored in biology.

"Fascinating stuff."

I turned to see a tall blond guy smiling at me. He had a deep tan and curly red hair that circled his head like an afro. He held out his hand.

"I'm Rob Lee. I don't know anyone here, so I was watching the screen, pretending I care how many people here are from Korea. Nothing against the Koreans, you understand. I looked around and noticed you were the only other person in the room watching, too."

He spoke slowly, with just a hint of nasal drawl. His eyes were round and deep blue, and they seemed to laugh even when his mouth wasn't. I liked him immediately, and I could feel some of the tension leave my shoulders as we stood together.

"Now we both know someone else. I'm Ellison Emory."

"Ellison Emory." He seemed to consider my name carefully. "I like that. We can definitely be friends."

I laughed and nudged him toward the seats. "Well, friend, it looks like the show is about to start."

───※◎───

Orientation was both mesmerizing and overwhelming. Deans, alumni, students and faculty took turns talking about the philosophy of the school, what we should expect from classes, the forms we needed to fill out, where to eat, drink and live, and a host of other things it had never occurred to me to worry about. Some of the speeches were inspirational, like the one from a former surgeon general who went to undergrad and medical school at Northwestern. Others were frightening, like the presentation by a resident whose cheery delivery was belied by the dark circles under her eyes. After several hours, my head swam with too much information and my stomach grumbled with hunger.

At the break, I found Rob near the door. We agreed to head over to a Mexican restaurant around the corner, and we didn't talk much until we had fish tacos, beans and rice on the table.

"So Rob Lee, where are you from?" The moment the words left my mouth, I hoped it didn't sound like I was hitting on him. Rob looked at me with a look of mock horror.

"We're not dating, are we?" I shook my head, laughing.

"Okay, that's a relief. I'm from San Diego. Why did I come all the way to Chicago for medical school instead of matriculating at one of California's fine institutions? Well, I have family here."

At the mention of family, all my worries about Angela and Jamie came flooding back. My expression must have changed.

"Did I say something wrong?"

"No. It's just that family is a sore subject with me these days." I considered this. "Actually, it's always been a sore subject with me."

Rob waited for me to go on, and I debated whether to tell him about the baby. It was personal and I was a private person, but I wasn't ashamed of Jamie.

"I have a son."

I expected Rob to be shocked. I didn't imagine that any of the other first-year med students were in a situation like mine. A few months ago, I couldn't have imagined myself in this situation. I waited for his questions, but instead a slow smile spread across his face.

"Me, too. Mine's five months old. He's why I came to Chicago—his mother, my ex-wife, lives here. His name is also Robert, but I call him R.J."

It was me who was shocked. I had started this day thinking I was all alone, and here was someone who might understand what I was going through.

Rob was one of those people who opened up right away, and he told me the entire story of his marriage, divorce and son's birth over lunch.

"It all started with this guy named Butch."

Rob then proceeded to take several bites of his food, chewing methodically, as if savoring every bite. I waiting for him to continue, but even after swallowing, he took a sip of his soda and savored that as well.

"Intriguing," I prodded. Rob smiled and nodded in agreement but offered no more of the story. I looked at my watch. "Before my imagination runs away with me on the Butch angle, and also before I turn thirty, can you tell me the story?"

Rob wiped his mouth gently. "This story is too good to be rushed." He laughed at the expression on my face.

"But I can see that you're not a man who counts patience among his virtues."

"Do you always talk like you're in a play?"

"Only when I think it might annoy someone. Is it working?"

"Yes."

"Good. So, about Butch."

Rob was right in that the story of his relationship was fascinating. He told it from his ex-wife's perspective, insisting that it could only be fully appreciated if you saw her side of things. He even gave it a title: "Maid of Honor."

"It all started with a sandwich."

I interrupted him. "I thought it all started with Butch."

Rob sighed. "The sandwich and Butch. Without Butch, the sandwich is immaterial. Okay?"

I shrugged. "Okay."

He cleared his throat and went on.

"Or it all ended with the sandwich. Cucumber and cream cheese on nine-grain bread. With chives.

"This was the sandwich Clarissa ordered from the vegetarian café around the corner from MarketingFirst. She shared the sandwich with Butch, who Sasha had begun sleeping with because he liked the Chili Peppers and found the everlasting popularity of the Beatles confounding, as did Sasha. Clarissa, who sat in the cubicle next to Sasha's, offered her a bite of the sandwich. Sasha hated cucumbers, so she claimed she was allergic. Butch worked in tech services and loved cucumbers. By this time, Sasha had been having secretive sex with Butch for three months and she was starting to hate him. His love of cucumbers was just another strike against him. Clarissa gave him half of her sandwich and they spent the rest of lunch raving about its simplicity, its texture, its flavor.

"That was the moment Sasha knew that she and Butch were ending, and Butch and Clarissa were beginning. She hated Butch, she was pretty sure of that.

"But still.

" 'It's too bad you can't eat cucumbers,' Clarissa said.

"She was the type of person who would still be talking about the cucumbers. It was nearly six o'clock and Clarissa and Sasha were the only people left in the office. At MarketingFirst, people set their watches ten minutes fast so when the little hand hit the five and the big hand touched twelve, they knew it was time to wash out the coffee cups, use the bathroom and shut down their computers. By 4:59, Sasha could hear the dead leaves dropping from the branches in the deserted parking lot.

"She'd once left at 4:59 as well. It took her a year of being a senior copywriter to realize that she could get more done after everyone else left. With meetings, emails and disputes with graphic designers, her days were a blur of futile bureaucracy.

"Clarissa had been a junior copywriter for just three months, in which time Sasha had never seen her leave before eight o'clock. In fact, Sasha had no idea how late Clarissa stayed, or why.

" 'Too bad,' Sasha agreed about the cucumbers. Clarissa's breath smelled like chives. It was, as far as Sasha could tell, the woman's only imperfection. Sasha was twenty-nine years old and felt a deep distrust of 23-year-olds with unprofessional curly hair, perfect teeth and perky mannerisms.

"Before the cucumber talk could continue, Butch walked up. Sasha had never seen him stay late before, and he would not meet her eyes. She made up an excuse, gathered her things and left.

"Everybody liked Butch. He'd started at MarketingFirst the same week as Sasha. It didn't take long for him to achieve celebrity status throughout the company. Of the ninety men who worked at MarketingFirst, he was easily the best looking. His competition was limited, but then, popularity is all relative. Of the 180 women who worked with Butch, those who cared about such things declared him hot. It was the highest of compliments at MarketingFirst during the late 1990s.

"Sasha met Butch when her computer monitor died. It was a simple repair, but he lingered while they talked. He was named after Butch Cassidy.

" 'My mom likes Paul Newman. I've never met a black person named Sasha.'

"His British accent made what could have been considered an offense sound charming. That was another thing the MarketingFirst women loved about Butch. His accent was clipped and exotic. It raised his hot quotient.

"Sasha tilted her head to the left. 'My father loved Russian novels.'

"Butch smiled. 'Bit depressing, the Russians.'

" 'So was my father.'

"Sasha and Butch knew each other for three months before they had sex. This was two months and three weeks after Sasha knew she wanted to have sex with Butch, but she let him figure it out at his own pace. She was impressed that it took ninety days.

" 'You are so exotic looking,' he told her. 'I love your hair.'

"Sasha couldn't decide whether to take this as a compliment or as a ridiculous piece of unintentional racism. They had nearly the same skin tone, but to him, she *seemed* darker.

" 'Let's just keep this between us,' he told her the next morning. 'No need to become the latest gossip at the office.'

"He chucked her under the chin and left. She marveled at the fact that he'd *chucked her under the chin*. She was sure that only happened in novels.

"At work, Butch no longer stopped by Sasha's desk to chat. They sometimes ate lunch together, but only if other people were present. For three months, they had sex three, sometimes four, times a week. Butch was still his clever cute self, with the accent. Sasha liked him less each day. She did feel a certain ownership of his public image, and when the women at MarketingFirst wondered who he was seeing, it was an effort not to smirk.

"One day a woman named Carol Smalls leaned into Sasha's cubicle. At that moment, Sasha was singing along to a mindless pop song playing on her computer while looking for a brochure she'd written on home equity loans. Sasha spent most of her days writing junk mail to convince bank customers to mortgage their homes in order to pay for vacations and other trifles. It was a rare moment of peace, so Sasha resented Carol Smalls's interruption and wondered whether Carol Smalls ever considered changing her name to avoid the cruel coincidence of weighing more than 200 pounds.

" 'It's nice to see you happy again after the thing with You-Know-Who,' Carol said.

" 'What thing? Who?'

"Carol Smalls gave her a pitying look. 'Butch. After he broke up with you.'

"Sasha's confusion was genuine, so it showed on her face. She was awful at concealing her true feelings. She could only hide her lies.

"Carol patted her hand twice before Sasha slid hers away.

" 'Oh, we all knew. Once he stopped hanging around your cube, we girls all figured he'd moved on. You should never mope over a man, honey. Even when he's as hot as Butch!'

"There was a note of clairvoyance to the MarketingFirst grapevine, since it anticipated Butch's shift of affections from Sasha to Clarissa. It offended Sasha's sense of melodrama that there was never an actual breakup, since there was never an actual relationship. Clarissa and Butch had sex (the night of the sandwich, Sasha would later learn from Clarissa), and things went from there. Sasha went back to nights alone, waiting out the last months of her sentence writing junk mail at MarketingFirst. Butch was still friendly, and Clarissa was still chatty, and Sasha couldn't complain, mostly because she didn't care enough to bother.

"Sasha quit MarketingFirst on her thirtieth birthday. That same day, Clarissa announced her engagement to Butch, who looked sheepish and pleased with himself.

" 'You *have* to be my maid of honor,' Clarissa gushed. 'If it wasn't for you, I never would have gotten to know Butch.'

"Sasha wondered why Clarissa didn't have any real friends. She wondered how long it would be before Butch pursued a new dalliance, and whether he'd go ahead and marry Clarissa anyway. She wondered if it were possible to come up with a worse idea—asking your fiancé's former lover to be your maid of honor. But Sasha agreed to be Clarissa's maid of honor.

"At the wedding, Sasha met Rob, who knew Butch from high school and had agreed to attend the wedding after running into Butch at Home Depot one afternoon. Rob and Butch had hated each other in high school, but Butch remembered things differently, and before Rob could think of a way to refuse the wedding invitation, Butch had him down on the guest list and vowed he would be devastated if Rob did not attend.

"Sasha had never looked better than at Butch and Clarissa's wedding, since she wanted Butch to see what he was missing. Rob fell in lust with Sasha and they ended up having sex after the reception. Sasha got pregnant, Rob asked her to marry him and she agreed. Six months into the marriage, they realized neither of them wanted to be married to the other, so they got a divorce. R.J. was born, Sasha moved to Chicago to be near her family and Rob followed. The end."

Rob sat back after he finished, grinning with satisfaction over the telling of the story and his meal. I could only marvel that someone else had as strange a story as I did. Actually, his story was much, much stranger.

"You tell that story like you were there, as if you were a secondary character instead of the person's whose life was changed by all of that."

He smiled. "Looking at it all from the outside is the best way I can deal with it all. And Sasha and I talked about it all the time—we have the same sense of humor, which is clearly not enough to keep two people together. Seriously, if she were here, she would tell you the same thing: besides R.J., the story of how we met was the best part of our relationship."

I thought about Angela and wondered if I'd ever be able to laugh about it all.

"I know, it's horrible and sad in its own way, but it is what it is. Either you laugh or you cry, you know?"

I nodded. "I hope I can laugh about my story, someday."

"You will, don't worry. What you need is some emotional distance, and always keep your sense of humor. Just figure out who your Butch is." He glanced at his watch. "Now, let's get back to orientation so we can find out how many of our fellow students are from Texas, Guam and the Balkans."

As we walked back to campus, I had a thought.

"Rob, my son, Jamie, is almost two months old. Do you know anything about colic?"

That night, I went home exhausted at the barrage of information from orientation, panicked at the idea of starting law school with an infant, a depressed ex-girl-friend and no money. I called Maren, but she wasn't at her dorm and her cell phone sent me straight to voice mail. Jamie and Angela were spending the night with Angela's parents at their insistence ("We hardly get to see our grandson," she told me, as if it were me keeping him away instead of Angela), and Rob was visiting his son. I felt like talking, but there was no one to call. Just as I was sinking into sadness, missing Jamie and wishing Maren would leave her cell phone on, my telephone rang.

It was Calvin.

After we said hello, there was silence. I didn't know what to say, where to begin. I knew Maren had told him about Angela and Jamie. And I knew that even though we hadn't spoken since his book tour in March and for years before that, I should have told him myself. But it was so complicated, and there was so much to tell. I hadn't known where to begin. I still didn't.

"Congratulations, son."

If Calvin had ever called me son before, I would have immediately protested. You haven't been much of a father, I would have told him. Don't call me son. I had made a point all these years to call him by his first name.

But now, as I looked at the blown-up photo of Jamie I had put on the wall over my television, everything was different. I now knew what a miracle a son was. No matter what happened from now on, nothing would take that miracle from me.

"Thanks."

"So, how is Jamie? How is your *son*?" The emphasis he put on the word this time said so much. He knew about the miracle, too.

"Jamie is amazing. He cries all the time, I never get any sleep, and he looks like Mom."

I could hear the smile in his voice. "You're in love, aren't you?"

"Completely."

And from there, talking to my father was easy. As long as we didn't talk about ourselves, we were safe. I told him all about Jamie, and he wanted to hear all the details, all the things only another parent understands. The look on Jamie's face when he's almost finished with a bottle and his eyes are half-closed. The feel of his virgin skin against the rough beard I hadn't bothered to shave. The mildly sweet smell of his head as he slept lying on my chest, the deep baby sighs that blew his warm breath against my cheek.

I told him about the differences between Angela's urgency about feedings and diaper-changing, and my desire to just watch Jamie. Once, Angela and I were dozing off in the hospital room after he was just born, and Jamie opened his eyes and let out a squawk. I lifted him from the bassinet, holding him close to my chest.

"I think he's hungry," Angela had said, unbuttoning her top for a feeding.

I had buried my nose in the crook between his neck and shoulder. He was born with a full head of black, curly hair, just like mine if I let it grow out. Just like Calvin's, I conceded.

"He needs milk," Angela had insisted as his crying grew louder.

I took one last deep breath before I handed him over. When I explained it to Calvin, he understood how I could have spent all day basking in the sweet smells of my son.

I told Calvin all of it, and before I knew it, we'd been on the phone for an hour. It was the longest conversation I could remember having with my father.

"I remember when you were born, we always had music playing. Your mother loved Hall and Oates. I think she had a crush on Daryl Hall."

I laughed at the thought of a young version of my mother paired with the shaggy-haired blue-eyed soul singer.

" 'Sara Smile'. She played that over and over. It made you stop crying—you had colic, too, you know."

I hadn't known that. It occurred to me that I didn't know much about what it was like for my parents when I was a baby. They broke up when I was a kid, but things started going bad long before that, and most of what I remembered was tension and sadness.

"Did it drive you crazy, hearing the same song over and over? Especially Hall and Oates, of all things."

"At first, yeah, it drove me crazy. I was more of a funk fan, or the R & B classics, Temptations, Four Tops."

"Supremes?"

"More like Smokey Robinson, Minnie Ripperton. I never forgave Diana Ross for what she did to Florence Ballard and that whole Barry Gordy affair. Anyway, it kept you quiet, and when I listened to it, I realized that 'Sara Smile' is one of those little songs that perfectly captured a feeling. That late-night melancholy, loving someone so much that it almost makes you sad because you don't believe it can last. The way you can look at someone and see the world in her smile. He has that line, almost at the end of the song, a throwaway ad lib: 'Make me feel like a man, now you keeping me crazy, crazy, smile.' I don't even know what it means, but I know how it feels." He took a breath and paused, as if he hadn't meant to say so much.

"You know?"

I knew. It was how I'd felt about Angela, just last summer. It felt like a million years ago. Now we had Jamie, and Angela was like someone I didn't know anymore.

"I felt that way about your mother once. I want you to remember that, Ellison—no matter what happened later, your mother and I were in love once. That kind of wonderful, soul-crushing love that takes over your entire being. We had that once."

I took a deep breath. "It didn't last. Why can't that kind of love last?"

Calvin was silent for a long while. When he finally spoke, his voice was quiet, almost a whisper.

"The thing is, the love lasts, but it changes. You have to let it change, let it grow. Your mother and I were afraid to let it change, so when it did, we didn't know what to do except hurt each other."

He sighed. "Ellison, I know things haven't been great between us. I know it's my fault."

One of the hardest things I've ever done is to swallow my pride with my father and talk to him honestly, without trying to punish or hurt him like I'd been hurt. But right then, I knew it was time to be a man who can admit his own faults, not just to himself, but out loud.

"It wasn't all your fault. I did my part, too. There are things I should apologize for, too."

I paused. Before I could continue, Calvin spoke.

"Maybe apologies are the wrong place to start. We can't undo what's been done. So maybe we should try to move forward. Since Jamie was born and you're starting medical school, I'm feeling like it's a time for fresh starts."

"I think that sounds like a really good idea."

He let out a long breath as if he'd been holding it. "So, when can I come see my grandson?"

Later that evening, I took a walk around my neighborhood as the sun set. Some people might be comforted by the quiet, but I needed the noise of the city to calm my insides. There was a cool breeze as I walked through over to Michigan Avenue, looking in the shop windows at vintage and designer clothing and passing by restaurants with people eating at wrought-iron tables on the sidewalk. The setting sun made the sky glow pink, and cars whizzed by me on the street. I stopped in a small music store called Chico's. A cowbell rang when I opened the door, and the store was cramped and clean, full of racks of vinyl and a select few shelves of CDs. The walls were painted a deep, blood red, and the floor was done in black and white checked linoleum. A woman sat behind the counter, wearing Buddy Holly glasses and a white T-shirt that read "I'm not Chico" on the front in green block lettering. She had an enormous frizz of hair that surrounded her face like a sandy cloud, and she smiled and looked up from a thick textbook when I came in.

I was feeling loose and she seemed nice, so I tried for humor.

"Chico, any chance you have some Hall and Oates in here?"

She raised an eyebrow at me. "Reading is not your strong suit, I see."

I shrugged. "You're asking for it, aren't you?"

She laughed and pointed to the back of the store. "Hall and Oates, in the back, alphabetical order in the 1970s. I assume you are talking about 1970s H & O—things went a bit awry for them in the 80s, for my money."

"I wouldn't know—I'm not a fan, really."

"Right. That's why you came in here looking for Hall and Oates. Don't be ashamed. Nothing wrong with blue-eyed soul."

I laughed and went to the back of the store. When I returned, I glanced at the woman's textbook. It was the book for one of our first units on medical decision-making, which I recognized because I'd just bought a copy at the campus bookstore earlier that day.

"Are you in medical school?"

"Starts next week. Trying to get a head start on the reading, but all it's doing is scaring me to death."

"Northwestern?" She nodded. "Me, too."

She gave a lazy smile. "Small world . . . and your name is?"

"Ellison."

"Well, Ellison, are we going to listen to that, or did you just want to hold it all day? What song does a non-fan want to hear?"

I laughed and handed her the CD. " 'Sara Smile.' "

Her face brightened. "One of their best."

We stopped talking and listened to the song. It was a comfortable silence, and I watched her as she closed her eyes and sang along to the second verse. Her voice was just slightly off-tune, but she didn't care, and her lack of inhibition charmed me.

"You never told me your name," I said after the song ended.

She grinned. "Chico."

We laughed as I paid for the CD.

CHAPTER 16

September–December 1999

Jamie slept through the night for the first time when he was nearly three months old. It was September, the night before med school classes began. Angela had gone to bed early after we argued, this time about whether she should go back to school.

"I only have two credits to go and I can graduate, get my Duke degree." There was a sarcastic twist to her words, but I didn't know why she was bitter about Duke. It wasn't the school's fault that things had gone wrong for Angela, me and Jason Davis.

"But it's so soon. Why not stay home and take care of Jamie while I'm in class? You could go back in January after things settle down." This was perfectly reasonable to me, but I could tell from the way Angela's nose wrinkled that she felt differently.

"Why, because January is more convenient for *you*?"

I took a deep breath, trying not to lose patience. "No, because it's better for our son. He shouldn't have to go to daycare, not this soon, not if he doesn't have to."

"Why do you get to decide? I'm his mother. Don't I have a say?"

"Of course. That's why we're having this discussion."

She sneered. "Oh, thanks for humoring me. So magnanimous of you."

"Angela—"

"Why is *your* education more important than mine?"

I knew better than to respond. After weeks of arguing, I'd learned the folly of addressing rhetorical questions.

"I went to daycare while my mother worked and I turned out fine." She was screaming, her face contorted and ugly.

"You're going to wake up Jamie." He lay in his bassinet just steps away from us. Angela's hands balled into small fists.

"Why am I the only one who doesn't matter around here?" She stalked into the bedroom and slammed the door. I looked into Jamie's bassinet, where he was still sleeping, a smile on his lips. A miracle.

I lay on the sofa next to him, planning to nap until he awoke for his ten o'clock feeding. But Jamie slept the entire night while I lay awake, thinking about medical school and Angela until the sky turned from black to blue to gray, and then it was time to get up.

My first class of the day, of my medical school career, was Human Biology. Here was where we would become intimate with the human body from the inside and out, where any squeamish tendencies would have to be faced and conquered. At least, that's what the professor told us in his opening lecture. He showed gory slides and talked about how we would progress through human anatomy, how we would learn about 8,000 of the 10,000 specialized terms every medical students needs to know. He talked about death and the differences between Hollywood's version of it and reality. I thought about the autopsy I had observed at Duke, the numbness I felt just nine months ago. I was different now. I was a father, a medical student, a Chicagoan. At that autopsy, I hadn't been affected at all by death, and it occurred to me that the professor was wrong, that we should never get to the point where death had no effect on us. What, then, would be the point of trying to save lives if death was not something to be feared?

As the lecture went on, the professor compared ancient mummifying techniques to those used to salt beef and pork. A collective groan rose from the room, along with a few nervous giggles. Of course he was trying to scare us. I looked around and saw Chico by the far wall, sitting slouched in her chair with a wry smile on her face. I caught Rob's eye across the room and I smiled at him, but he looked nauseated. After a bawdy joke about breast implants in cadavers, the professor ended by spelling out his essential message: The Feinberg School of Medicine was not a place for the weak and faint-hearted.

The things that scared me about medical school had nothing to do with the body itself. For the first time in my life, I was scared that I wasn't up for the work, that I wouldn't be able to hack it. When I'd first focused on

SAVE ME

medical school as a goal, I never imagined I'd be a father, living on my own, trying to figure out how to survive on little money and even less sleep. How could I even think this was possible? Maybe Angela's parents were right—I should have gotten a job, some kind of junior executive position at a firm, something to bring in money instead of banking everything on a future that I might not be able to achieve.

I used to walk into a room and feel confident that I was the smartest person there. Now, I looked around and knew I wasn't even close. If I was so smart, how did my life end up being so complicated? Good grades and a fancy degree didn't mean much when I looked at the stack of books I would have to read, when I wondered how in God's name I could remember 10,000 medical terms, when I got exhausted just looking at the exam schedule.

I was petrified, but it was of my own failure, not of blood and guts.

I looked around again, and this time Chico waved and mouthed "Hall and Oates" at me. Suddenly, I felt a release and all my worries just drifted to the background.

My laughter was masked by the shuffling of papers and books as hundreds of first-year medical students prepared for the next class.

"So let's get some lunch later," Chico said after she made her way over to me.

"You can eat after that?" Rob still looked green, but seeing his face cheered me even a bit more. He had a son, and here he was. Maybe we could both get through this.

"Why are you grinning at me like that?" he groused.

"You look ill," Chico informed him. "Didn't you get the message? Toughen up, dude."

"Umm, Rob, this is Chico. Chico, this is Rob." I figured I should introduce them before Chico further questioned his manhood.

"Nice to meet you, Chico. And for the record, I'm very tough. Extremely tough. I was the toughest kid in my sixth grade class, in fact."

"Okay, Tough Rob. Do you tough guys eat lunch?"

He smiled. "I usually eat raw eggs and steak tartar with a couple of shots of Scotch whiskey, but maybe the sandwich place around the corner would be better for a little lady such as yourself."

Chico and Rob grinned at each other. I cleared my throat.

"Does anyone care about me?"

Chico glanced my way. "Sure, Hall. Or do you consider yourself more of an Oates? Hall was sort of the lover-type, the smooth one who attracted all the ladies. But I always imagined that Hall was all style, no substance, and that once you got tired of Hall, a girl would turn to Oates and realize that he had something to offer, even though he was only five feet tall. So which one are you?"

I ignored Rob's quizzical look. "Sandwiches it is, then. Now can you both shut up so I can get to my next class?

We survived the first week full of brutally long lectures, intimidating faculty and residents and terrifying syllabi for our classes. By chance, Chico, Rob and I had most of our classes together, so we scheduled times for study groups and general commiseration. Between sharing Jamie shifts with Angela, who was barely speaking to me, and trying to wrap my head around all the stuff I needed to start learning immediately, I was exhausted by Friday. Still, a celebration was in order, so I invited Rob, R.J. and Chico over for pizza and beer.

"Do you really think it's a good idea to have people over?" Angela hissed the words at me because Jamie had fallen asleep on her shoulder after a feeding. These were the first words she'd said to me all day.

I sighed. "Why wouldn't it be?"

I knew that she meant it wasn't a good time because we weren't getting along, but I didn't feel like playing the game. Being with Rob and Chico was a refreshing change from all the drama of the past few months. It wasn't that they were less complicated or didn't have problems. It just that they were still able to laugh, and Angela seemed to have forgotten how to smile. I needed to laugh sometimes.

"Don't you even care how I feel?" Angela shoved Jamie into my arms and ran out of the room. Jamie opened his eyes for a moment, but then he snuggled into my shoulder and went back to sleep. Angela slammed the door on the way out of the apartment.

I cared. That's what she didn't understand. I cared, but I had no idea what to do to make things better.

⧽◦⧼

When Chico and Rob arrived with R.J., we put the sleeping babies down in Jamie's crib, turned on the baby monitor and ordered pizzas. While we waited for delivery, we sat in the living room drinking ice cold Coronas.

"This hits the spot," Rob said after he took his first long drink.

Chico and I nodded. I turned to her. "So I presume it's not a coincidence that you work at a store called Chico's and your name is also Chico."

She shrugged. "No such thing as coincidence, right? My parents opened the shop twenty years ago and named it after me. When they died, the shop became mine. I just work there part-time, and my uncle manages it."

Rob and I were quiet, not wanting to ask the question.

"Car accident. It was ten years ago."

I cleared my throat. "My mother died in a car accident, too. Five years ago."

Chico gave me a sad smile. "Enough about that. You know how I knew we were all going to be good friends? Neither of you asked me about my name."

Rob and I looked at each other. "So are we friends now?" he asked.

"I just said it, didn't I?"

"Okay then, how'd you get a name like Chico?" I asked. "Remember, we're already friends and you can't take it back."

She shook her head. "I never tell anyone how I got my name."

"Why not? I'm lucky to be Ellison and not Ralph. Rob is Robert Jensen the Fiftieth or something dumb like that."

"Hey!" Rob protested. "Tradition is not dumb. It's . . . noble."

"Right. Noble. Really, Chico, how could your story be worse?"

"You have to promise to not laugh."

"We promise."

"Swear."

"We swear. Come on, tell us."

She took a deep breath. "My parents were both from California, and they met in college. Chico State. It's where I was . . . conceived. In a dorm room their senior year at Chico State University."

I refused to look at Rob, but he was sitting next to me on the sofa, and I could feel his shoulder shaking before he finally lost it. Then we were both laughing, bent over at the waist with tears streaming down our faces. Even Chico had to smile as she complained.

"I can see your word is worth a lot, guys," she grumbled. It just made us laugh harder. Finally, the doorbell rang, which Rob and I could barely hear over our cackling.

"You liars have to buy pizza," Chico shouted at us. "It's the least you can do. Losers."

Even with Chico and Rob's help, the first semester of medical school was a struggle. I often went to class just barely awake after long nights with Jamie, and things with Angela just kept getting worse. We lived in my apartment but we were like roommates who hardly know each other and don't like what little they know. She criticized the way I held Jamie. She claimed I fed him too much, or too little. I dressed him too warmly, or not warmly enough. I knew a little about post-partum depression so I tried to be patient, but I was afraid that what was happening between us had nothing to do with Jamie and everything to do with us.

Of course, my exam courses and coursework suffered. In my Problems-Based Learning class, we began with a series of group projects where we were given a patient's history, symptoms and results from a mock physical examination. Then, we work together to make a diagnosis and explain how we came to our conclusions. The good part about working in groups is that we share the responsibility, so if we misdiagnose the patient, we share the blame, and if we diagnose correctly, we can all point to individual contributions to the success.

But that's not how it works in the real world. Physicians as individuals are responsible for their patients, and so this course required individual projects as well. With all the stress I was under, I dreaded the moment when the fate of the fictitious patient lay in my hands. I hadn't had nearly enough time to study, and worse than that, I had very little confidence in myself. The only good thing about the project was that the patient wasn't real, so at least no one could be hurt by my failure.

My patient was a 52-year-old woman who had been experiencing pain in her legs for the past year. The pain had been intermittent and variable until recently, when it became so bad that she could no longer walk. She also complained of constant exhaustion and suffered from mild arthritis in her knees. She smoked a half-pack of cigarettes a day, was not a drinker, had no glaring health problems. Her legs were swollen and spotted with a rash and bruises—photos were provided.

When I received the assignment, I couldn't believe my luck. I looked around the room, certain I'd gotten the easiest case in the batch. The spots were palpable purpura and they were likely the result of leukemia, since there was no reason to think the patient had Hepatitis C, which can also cause the rash.

Things were turning around, I thought as I presented my written report, backed by extensive research, to the professor. I really could do this, and I chastised myself for doubting my own abilities. One thing I'd always been was smart, I reminded myself. No amount of personal upheaval could take that away.

My smugness remained as I presented my findings to the class. When I was finished, the professor asked questions, as she always did after individual presentations.

"What was your impression of the patient's weight?"

I answered right away. "She looked somewhat thin and unhealthy, but that is likely because of the pain she'd been experiencing."

"What about her diet?"

I had to glance at my notes. "She claimed to have a lot of food allergies, so much so that she had a very limited diet that did not include dairy, fruit or most vegetables."

There was a niggling sense of unease creeping up my back, but I decided to ignore it.

"Did you consider other options besides vasculitis or cancer as the cause of the spotting and swelling in the legs?"

The answer was no, and I could tell that the professor knew. I decided to remain silent, and after a moment, she took mercy on me.

"Anyone else have any ideas of what this might be?" she asked the class. Several hands shot into the air, and the unease I had felt turned into full-blown embarrassment.

"Scurvy?"

"Good. Explain."

As the explanation of how the patient's limited diet had led her to a vitamin C deficiency that caused her symptoms, I wanted to disappear from the room and never return. Unfortunately, I did not possess that particular power, so I stood, enduring the humiliation of my failure.

"Mr. Emory, in a real-life situation, you would have run tests to check for leukemia and hepatitis, and perhaps those negative results would have led you to consider other options," the professor offered. "We can all learn from this—we need to consider all the options, not just the most likely or the most common. In practice, this means taking more time and doing more research, but it's vital to providing the best care possible."

Her eyes were not unkind as she spoke, but I was still mortified. The rest of my first semester wasn't quite as bad, and I scraped by, earning admonishments from my academic advisor. By December, I was so tired that I fell asleep trying to study for finals. The semester ended the week before Christmas, and I decided not to check my grades until after the holiday.

The first snow of the season came just days after Thanksgiving that year, and it snowed consistently every few days so that the snow cover by Christmas was white and fluffy. It was the kind of snow that made kids dive into snow banks without notice, the kind that inspired snowball fights, the kind that every kid wanted to taste.

I was spending Christmas morning at Angela's parents' house, and Angela and Jamie had spent Christmas Eve there. I woke up that morning and looked out the window, remembering my last white Christmas. Back then, my mother was still alive, Maren and I were still innocent, kids who had no idea how our lives would change. We had gone on our annual vacation, that last time to Maui. My mother was as relaxed and beautiful as I'd ever seen her. And it was the first time that I saw the woman my little sister would become. She looked so much like our mother, even though she couldn't see it then. We were a small family, just the three of us. But we were happy.

I thought about that first Christmas after my mother died, how lonely I felt in Durham, living with my father, hating him. I was an outcast at school, adrift without my mother, without my life. I remembered being miserable, and there seemed to be no way out.

Things might not be perfect this year, but I had blessings to count. I was back in Chicago, I had survived my first semester of medical school, and I had Jamie. On my way out, I picked up a bit of snow from a hidden spot next to the building and laid it on my tongue. Just like when I was a child, the snow was just a little bit sweet.

At six months old, Jamie was babbling and shouting, and when I arrived at his grandparents' house, he gave a great yell and raised his arms above his head when he saw me. He was sitting in a high chair, his smiling mouth covered in oatmeal mush. I grabbed him out of his chair and hugged him to my sweater, not caring about the mess.

"Hey, buddy. What's up?"

He answered me with a long string of babble, motioning with his hands as if he was actually saying something.

"Really? And then what?"

Jamie grinned me, wiped his hand over his lips and then smeared oatmeal all over my chin.

"Thanks, buddy. I needed a facial."

I noticed that Angela's mother was frowning at me with a spoon in her hand, so I set my son back in the high chair.

"Finish eating, James. Then we can open some presents."

Angela's mother sniffed. "It's good you got here when you did. We thought we would have to start without you."

I didn't bother to ask why there was a gift-opening schedule in place, nor did I point out that I was actually three minutes earlier than we agreed I would be here.

"Merry Christmas, Winifred," I said pleasantly. During the past six months, I'd discovered that there was nothing I could do to make Angela's parents like me. All I could hope for was civility. John managed this easily, since he said very little to me and therefore had few opportunities to be rude. I could see Winifred fighting the urge to kick me out of her house every time I went there. She and John still blamed me for the pregnancy, and my hopes that Jamie would thaw them were in vain.

"John, Angela?" She called out instead of answering me. "Ellison's finally here. Let's open the gifts."

She turned to Jamie, cooing at him while she wiped his mouth. He tried to avoid the napkin, smiling at me and laughing every time he managed to dodge his grand-mother's hand. I turned my head to hide my own smile at his efforts to resist being cleaned up. I hoped he'd always have that kind of spirit that made him determined to be his own man, no matter what.

I'm certain no six-month-old boy ever got more gifts than Jamie that Christmas. There were stuffed versions of every character from Sesame Street, including the lesser-known characters and, of course, the ubiquitous Elmo. This fuzzy, red ball of cheer hadn't existed when I was a kid, but it was clear that he'd taken over the street. He was supposed to be five years old or so, but he had his own segment on Sesame Street called "Elmo's World," and from the looks of the various incarnations of dolls, he had a lot of jobs and hobbies for such a young Muppet. I'd once seen a book called *Elmo Visits the Dentist* in the bookstore, which I thought was strange since he has no teeth.

"Maybe he was getting dentures."

Angela laughed, he father ignored me and her mother took offense, as she did at most of what I did and said.

"I'm sure it's to help toddlers overcome a fear of the dentist," she said in a patient tone, as if I were the five-year-old. Angela snickered, but with her mother glaring at me for making fun of Elmo, I cut my losses.

"I see," I said seriously. "Well, whatever encourages dental hygiene is a good thing." Even though Elmo doesn't even have teeth, I didn't add.

Naturally, Jamie was more interested in the paper and the boxes, and he threatened to topple the enormous tree at least twice. But there's something about a baby's joy in ripping open a package that relaxes even the most tense situations, so I felt relaxed enough to give a sincere thanks when Winifred handed me a package of handkerchiefs and muttered Christmas greetings as if she wished she didn't have to. John just grunted and nodded at me, as if to acknowledge that my presence was necessary but if he had a choice, he'd just as soon never see me again.

As I watched Angela open a thin envelope, it occurred to me that she was happier than I'd seen her since the summer we spent together at Duke. She wore a snug red cashmere sweater and dark jeans, and she sat in front of the tree with her legs crossed, barefoot.

Her brown skin glowed in the reflection of the colored lights, which Winifred strung not only on the white frosted tree, but wound around each of the windows and the door in the house. The house was awash with decoration, actually, and I tried not to be judgmental when I thought that it looked like a gaudy department store in the Michaels' living room. There was a nativity scene featuring black Mary, Joseph and Jesus figurines (although the wise men were white, which confused and amused me). The star on top of the artificial tree was not only lit, but it turned on an axis. Music tinkled in the background, not the Jackson 5 Christmas album that I'd always loved for its cheesy, retro cheer, but classical renderings of standard carols. All of the Michaels family were wearing red, and even Jamie wore a set of green pajamas and red socks. I looked down at my tan fisherman's sweater and suppressed a sigh.

Angela played at opening the envelope, shaking it and mock-frowning.

"I wonder what it is?" she teased.

"Oh, just open it. You already know what it is."

John smiled smugly and Winifred leaned forward so far in her chair I feared she might fall off. Jamie clapped his hands and shouted. Apparently everyone but me knew what was in the envelope.

It was a check. I couldn't see all the numbers but there were several zeros. Angela jumped up to hug her mother and father, and Jamie continued to clap.

"Thanks so much, Mommy and Daddy. This makes such a huge difference to me."

I cleared my throat and Angela turned to me.

"Ellison, I'm going back to school in January!"

I tried to keep my face blank. She was leaving Jamie? Leaving me?

"You're going back to Duke?"

Her laughter tinkled through the room. "No, silly. I'm going to finish my remaining credits at the University of Chicago, and then in May I can officially graduate."

My relief was quickly tempered by anger. We hadn't talked about this, only argued about it. She'd just made the decision without me, and although we weren't married, we did have a child together, and that counted for something. Who was going to take care of Jamie when I was at school?

"We can hire someone to help with Jamie, right? Part of this money can go toward that. It's a lot of money."

I didn't like the idea of Jamie being with a stranger, but I stayed silent. I wanted Angela to stay home, just like I'd wanted my own mother to be that June Cleaver-type of woman whose life revolved around her children. But I knew that wasn't realistic, and I regretted giving my mom a hard time about her career. I never got a chance to apologize to her, and as I looked over at Angela's expression, I knew that it wasn't fair for me to try to impose an impossible stereotype on the women in my life. This was the first time in months that Angela looked and acted like her old self, and that was what I wanted more than anything, to have the old Angela back.

Angela's father interrupted my thoughts.

"We want to take care of Angela and Jamie. Surely you can understand that?" John's gaze bored into me as he spoke, daring me to contradict him. I knew what he really meant—I couldn't take very good care of them, not on a medical school fellowship. But I wouldn't let him make me feel bad about going to school. Becoming a doctor would be the best thing I could do for Jamie— getting some office job to appease Winifred and John wouldn't help me take care of him in the long run.

And anyway, it wasn't their life, it was mine. And Jamie wasn't their son, he was mine. I knew what was best for him. I had to believe that.

"I'm glad you're going to finish your degree," I said to Angela. Her smile was as infectious as always, and I couldn't help smiling back. "We'll figure out something for Jamie."

Now I was the one she hugged. Before she let go, she whispered "thank you" in my ear. I pushed my anger aside and vowed to try to be more supportive, to try not to think only of myself. I had no idea how hard it must have been for Angela to leave school, to make the decision to keep Jamie. Until then, all I had thought about was what it meant to me to be a father. Being a mother must be an even tougher adjustment.

I squeezed her shoulders and Jamie began to cry. I went to pick him up and held him in my lap, where he proceeded to drool all over the handkerchiefs. Angela sat down next to me, and for the rest of the morning, she held my hand.

After lunch, I brought Jamie back to the apartment with me while Angela stayed another night with her parents.

"They want me to stay, and it's the least I can do, since they gave me the money for school," she'd whispered to me after lunch.

I smiled. "Ever the good daughter, right?"

She snorted. "I got pregnant in my senior year of college, I'm not married, and, let's face it, I haven't been the best mother. Not exactly a model daughter in my parents' eyes."

"You're a fine mother," I argued. "Post-partum depression is a real problem, not something you can control."

She held up a hand. "I know all that. But I also know that I haven't been there for Jamie like I should have. I've been selfish, wallowing around because I knew you were taking such good care of him. But Jamie needs both his parents, and going back to school will help me, I think."

I nodded. "You deserve to finish. I did, and I'm still in school. Why shouldn't you have that opportunity, too?"

"I'm starting fresh in 2000, El. Things are going to be different. Better."

Before I could answer, she leaned in and kissed me softly on the lips. The kiss was brief, but it held promise. It held hope. I couldn't ask for anything more.

Later that night, I called Maren. She was in North Carolina spending the holiday with Calvin, and they were both planning to come up to Chicago for New Year's. I told her all about the day, from Jamie's oatmeal to Angela's plans to return to school.

"The only thing is that we'll have to put Jamie in day care. There are some great ones around school, but I just don't know. I can't imagine leaving him with strangers."

We were both silent for a moment, then Maren blurted, "I could take care of him."

I didn't think she was serious. "Kind of a long commute from Gainesville."

"Seriously. I can take a semester off and come to Chicago to take care of Jamie. I'll be his nanny. Caregiver. Auntie Maren. I mean, he's six months old and he hasn't even met his favorite aunt yet."

"You're his only aunt."

"Still."

"I can't let you take a semester off from school. It's not fair."

She sighed. "Could you for once not be so stubborn and let someone help you for a change? College isn't going anywhere. I can take a semester off and graduate in January 2002 instead of May 2001. What's the difference?"

"I don't know, Mare." I loved the idea of my sister taking care of my son, but I worried it would be selfish for me to let her make such a sacrifice. Also, her history with Angela was rocky at best. I knew that Maren didn't like Angela, and although Angela and I hadn't really talked about her meetings with Maren, I was pretty sure

Angela felt the same. I couldn't imagine either of them getting along for more than ten minutes at a time, let alone caring for a child together.

"What about Angela?" I figured there was no point in avoiding it.

Maren sighed. "I know she and I haven't really . . . connected. But she's Jamie's mother, and that's the most important thing. I'm sure if we get to know each other better, things will be fine."

I wasn't sure about that at all, but I loved my sister for trying.

"And Ellison, I owe you," she added.

"Owe me?" We're family," I argued. "I would do anything for you, Mare, and I don't expect anything in return."

"I know you don't. But you saved me from myself when I was fifteen, and this is my chance to help you. Let me help you, Ellison. Sometimes being strong is about letting people help you."

I smiled. "The wise Yoda comes through, yet again."

"Shut up or else I'll stab you with my light-saber," she laughed. "So I'll take that as yes. Have some champagne ready for New Year's —Yoda likes to toast the New Year with something bubbly."

The panic about the Y2K bug was symbolic of the feeling I had approaching New Year's Eve of 1999. Everything seemed to be changing, although I couldn't pinpoint anything specific that would be different on the day of the actual change to 2000.

Would all of our computers stop working? Would every system that depended, to some degree, on computers be crippled? That would mean pretty much everything—banking, schools, cars, traffic lights, fast food, lighting, gas, telephones, the mail, 911. Were there preparations that I should be making—extra water, canned food, emergency flares, canisters of gasoline, a Mac, tablets of paper, pencils? If I thought enough about it, would disaster be averted?

On a smaller scale, this was how I thought about my life. There were so many questions, about Jamie, Angela, medical school, the future, the past, the present. I felt like I didn't have any answers. I wanted to prepare, to plan, to do things to ensure that Jamie would be a happy, healthy child. But what I had to offer seemed like so little. I knew from experience that his parents might not always be here for him, no matter how much we wanted to be. I wished I could make sure that he'd never have to go through what I did, but no amount of supplies in a basement bunker could make that wish come true.

I was floating in this fog of uncertainty when Maren and my father arrived around noon on December thirty-first. It had snowed heavily the night before, but they'd managed to get a flight out from Raleigh to O'Hare that morning. They took a taxi from the airport to my apartment.

It had been nine months since I'd last seen Maren and my father. Maren, now a junior in college, looked more self-assured and happy than I'd ever seen her. Her cheeks were flushed with the cold, and she danced around the apartment with Jamie in her arms, touching and looking at everything.

"This is so nice," she gushed, waving her free arm around the apartment. "And this baby. God, Ellison. He looks just like you!"

I tried not to grin. I always thought Jamie looked like me, but I didn't want to seem egotistical in saying so. It was a gift to see my face reflected in his tiny one, as if my genetic material repeated in my innocent son meant there was still hope for me.

Jamie took to Maren immediately, cooing at her and laying his head on her chest as if he'd known her forever. Maybe he sensed the connection between us. Maren kissed his furry head and glanced at me just as I was thinking that I loved her almost more than was bearable. The death of our mother had drawn us closer in ways that neither of us had ever articulated. But as she held Jamie, I could feel the unbreakable link between us. Our eyes met, and I knew my sister felt it, too.

"I'm an aunt. Can you believe this, Dad?"

We both turned to Calvin, who sat quietly on the sofa watching us.

"I can believe it. Look at you—you're a natural. I'd be surprised if that boy ever leaves your arms."

As if he knew we were talking about him, Jamie raised his head and looked at me. I've found my Aunt Maren at last, the look said. You won't be needed anymore.

"I think he just dismissed me from the room," I joked. Maren laughed and twirled around the room, eliciting a joyous chortle from my son. But after laughing too hard, he started to hiccup, then cry.

"I think he's hungry," I said, making a move toward the kitchen. Jamie was six months old and ate solid food, but he loved his bottle. Maren waved at me.

"I'll feed him. I should start practicing now so when classes start and I become Nanny Maren, I'll be in good form."

Calvin and I were left alone in the room. I waited to feel that familiar discomfort that had been present during most of our interactions over the last five years, but it was softer and less insistent than it had been in the past. He smiled at me and clapped his hands together.

"So we should talk business."

"Business?"

"Maren and I talked a lot on the way up here, and I ran my proposal by her. She seemed to think it was a good idea, but of course, I need to ask you." While he spoke, he dug into his carry-on bag and drew out a sheaf of papers.

"I have no idea what you're talking about." I couldn't imagine what proposal he might have for me, or why it required legal-looking documents.

My father arranged the papers on his lap and handed me a set of copies. "Why don't you read for yourself, and then we can talk."

I looked down at the paper. It was a loan agreement, which spelled out in formal language my father's intent to loan me enough money to pay the rent on my apartment for the next four years. My mouth hung open.

"But I'm doing okay—I have a fellowship and I'll probably get a job in a lab. Do you even have this kind of money? Why are you doing this?" The words came tumbling out without much forethought. It was an incredibly generous offer—tens of thousands of dollars. Part of me wanted to reject it, because I always rejected anything that felt like a handout.

"It's a *loan*," he said, as if he read my mind. "Not charity. I know you can do it on your own. But I'd like to help. I think it's the least I can do after all that our family has been through." He took a deep breath and spoke before I could argue. "It's for Jamie, really. *Save Me* did really well, and I have a contract for two more books. This is how I'd like to spend the money. On my family."

I closed my eyes for a moment, trying to take it in. I could refuse the money and keep Calvin at arm's length, or I could accept it and start a new chapter in our relationship, and in my life. We had made a start after Jamie was born, when we agreed not to apologize but to move forward. But talking was one thing; taking money from Calvin was quite another. Would he think he had the right to tell me what to do if he gave me the money? I wasn't naive enough to believe that there would be no strings at all. He would want to be a part of my life, of Jamie's life, and once Calvin got close to Jamie, I wouldn't be able to shut him out again—it wouldn't be fair to my son. What if my father disappointed Jamie like he did when I was a kid? Could I forgive him? Should I? It would have been easier in so many ways to just keep Calvin on the periphery of our lives, not to risk being hurt again by a man who'd done it before.

But maybe that wasn't the way to live life, expecting people to let me down. I wanted to believe that people can change—I certainly wanted to believe that I could change, that I had changed since Maren and I had moved to North Carolina to live with Calvin when I was seventeen. Maybe I should give my father the benefit of the doubt. And, it seemed to mean so much to him, not just the money, but the effort of the gesture itself. It would guarantee that Jamie had a comfortable place to live while I was in medical school.

I couldn't say no.

"Please, just tell me the next two books aren't going to be memoirs, too," I said, smiling.

"I need to live some more before I can write any more about myself. The contract is for two novels," he replied. We laughed, and I signed the papers.

At 11:55, I poured three glasses of champagne. My father offered the toast.

"Before we take a drink, I just want to finally tell you both how sorry I am. About everything. I wasn't the father I should have been." He looked at Maren, then at me. "I didn't protect my daughter when she needed it. I wasn't around to be the father that my son needed. I just hope that you'll both forgive me, and that we can go forward from here as a family."

He held up his glass, and, with tears in her eyes, Maren did the same.

"I forgave you a long time ago," Maren said, her voice shaking. "In fact, I never believed you needed to be forgiven."

That was Maren: always sweet and giving. I'd always believed she was too soft on our father. But now was not the time to rehash past grievances. I couldn't relive the past, but I could stop making it the center of my life. I didn't want to be the kind of person who held grudges and lived in the past instead of the present. It had been a sad way to live so far, and I was tired of being sad.

My glass was the last in the air.

"Here's to new beginnings. Happy New Year."

CHAPTER 17

Spring 2000

I felt like a tourist returning to Chicago after so long. Five years might not seem like a long time, but so much had happened to me since I'd last lived in Chicago. Everything in my life was different, especially me. I was older, a father now, without my own mother and sister with me. My whole perspective had changed, and I saw the city with new eyes.

During the second semester of medical school, I had the opportunity to embrace the city in new ways that wouldn't have been possible when I was in high school. On weekends when we had an hour or two between studying, Rob and I took the kids on excursions to my favorite spots.

One February afternoon, we visited the Field Museum of Natural History. We pushed Jamie and R.J. in strollers down through the Loop to the museum district. It was one of those strange Midwestern winter days when it was unseasonably warm and the snow had begun to melt, teasing us into thinking that spring would come early even though we knew better. As we stood in front of the museum, I took a deep breath.

"Can you smell that?"

Rob titled his head and sniffed. "Diesel? Pizza? Lake Michigan?"

I shook my head. "It's the smell of spring. I remember that smell from every year of my childhood. There's just something about the smell of this kind of day that reminds me of throwing off our coats and running around, delirious because the temperature broke forty degrees."

Rob smiled. "In San Diego, spring smells like the ocean and new flip-flops. But I can relate."

We went straight to what had always been my favorite exhibit, the Ancient Americas. When I was in elementary school, the Field Museum was a regular stop on the roster of school field trips. Some kids got bored with seeing the exhibits and didn't care about what the world was like before 1990. But I always loved the replica of the ice age, with its mammoth hunters and crude tools. I was fascinated by the 800-year-old pueblo dwellings and the Aztec empire's ingenuity. The progression of human existence over 13,000 years appealed to my child's desire to find order and purpose in everything.

Rob held R.J. in one arm as he took it all in.

"It puts it all into perspective, doesn't it? We complain about exams and diapers, but these people built empires and created farming from scratch."

I laughed. "So we've become a species of wimps?"

"Definitely." He looked down at R.J., who was chewing on a pacifier and pointing at a spearhead from the ice age. "Not my son, though. Notice he's attracted to weaponry."

I peered into Jamie's stroller. He was asleep. "Well, maybe when my kid wakes up he'll help R.J. build an empire or something."

I also dragged Rob to a mid-season Bulls game with me, claiming that I needed a fix of NBA. It's not that there wasn't basketball in Durham—there was Duke, of course, and nothing rivaled the excitement of seeing the Blue Devils win in Cameron. But there was nothing else quite like watching a Bulls game, even in the post-Jordan years. Bulls fans never abandoned the hope that a miracle like Jordan could happen again. So Chicago fans faithfully crowded into the United Center, tried to get excited about terms like "rebuilding" and "upside potential" while they rooted for Elton Brand and endured a seventeen-win season.

Jordan was no longer there in person, but the ghosts of his six championships swirled around the banners in the rafters, and if you prayed hard enough, maybe Elton Brand would stick around and Ron Artest would turn into the next M.J.

Rob agreed to go while Chico watched the boys, even though he was a Lakers fan who had nothing but contempt for the Bulls. Granted, they were terrible, one of the worst teams in the NBA that year, but Elton Brand was averaging twenty points and ten rebounds a game, so I convinced him that he should attend a game so he could see the future of the league in person.

"Plus, the Lakers are overrated. Shaq and Kobe? Please." I tried to sell this notion, even though we both knew that if the Lakers didn't win the championship that year, something was wrong with the world.

Rob sighed. "This is why people in the rest of the world have no respect for the Bulls anymore. You're delusional."

I tried another tack. "The Staples Center is a dumb name. You haven't won a title since 1988."

"Shaq was the MVP of the All-Star Game this year. We had a sixteen-game winning streak earlier in the season."

"Jordan is the greatest player of all time." It was really all I had left.

"Whatever. Just get us some beer. The least you could do is pay, since you dragged me here."

Rob and I had a solid "guy" bond, but Chico and I had a special connection as well. On the day we met, I had left the record store feeling buoyant and cheerful in a way that felt alien after so much turmoil. As I walked around the streets of downtown Chicago, I found myself spending less time on nostalgia and more time thinking about Chico, the way her smile only lifted one side of her mouth, as if her lips wouldn't commit to a full smile. I actually laughed out loud remembering the things we'd said to each other, drawing quick looks from the people striding by me on the sidewalks. This only made me laugh again—one of the things that people complained about northern cities was the way no one said hi to each other as they passed; when in North Carolina, it was con-sidered rude not to at least nod to those strangers you passed. In Chicago, a lone person laughing to himself could be crazy or simply amused, and the quick look was meant to assess the situation without becoming involved.

Longer eye contact would only be interpreted as encouragement—if engaged, the person might attack, or relay what he'd found so amusing. Neither was an attractive option to the passerby, who had no interest in either option. But I had found a stranger who wasn't afraid to make eye contact, and so maybe people just connected differently here.

Chico. When I finally went home that day, I played my new Hall and Oates CD while I lay on the futon with my eyes closed, a smile still on my face. Flirting. I never flirted, so it took me hours to realize that the feeling I had was the effortless pleasure of connecting with another person on a very basic level. I had always been so serious, about my family, about my relationships, about school, and I seemed to have missed an important part of life. Fun. What a revelation. As Darryl Hall sang about rich girls, I marveled at how this simple concept had eluded me for so long. Chico seemed fun. She was the type of woman I was usually attracted to. She didn't wear makeup, and her only adornment was a row of earrings in one ear (just one in the other ear). She wore that T-shirt that falsely declared she was not Chico, but it wasn't overly tight or meant to draw attention to her body. He jeans were loose and faded, and the beat-up Chuck Taylors on her feet looked like she'd been wearing them since high school.

But more than anything, talking with Chico about a random CD was a relief from everything else in my life, and that element of our friendship didn't change as we got to know each other. I told her about my revelation about fun, and to my surprise, she didn't laugh.

"I think we can learn a lesson from *The Shining* on this topic," she told me one morning in March. We had gotten up early to go over notes for an exam that was coming up the next week. We met at a diner that stayed quiet until the morning commuters rushed through around eight o'clock, and Jamie slept beside us in his stroller.

"The book or the movie?"

"Never read the book. Nicholson has never been better, and even thinking about that scene with the old naked lady in the bathtub still scares the bejesus out of me."

I thought briefly of Angela and smiled. She would never see a movie without reading the book first. How else could we argue about which was better afterward?

"Anyway, what's the lesson? Don't move into a deserted-yet-haunted hotel with your family? Pay more attention to your kid when he starts to go crazy? Lay off the booze?"

"All work and no play makes Jack a dull boy." Chico said this with complete seriousness, as if it were some sage bit of wisdom that was supposed to immediately shed light on the darkness of my soul.

"Chico, everyone knows that you have to have balance in life. It's easier said than done—I mean, look at me," I said, gesturing to my sleeping son. Jamie gave a little snore and shifted, as if to emphasize my words. "I'm dragging a baby out to a diner at five o'clock in the morning to study for a medical school exam."

She shook her head. "Don't be so literal. Remember what happened, how Jack kept trying to write? It wasn't happening, but he couldn't stop doing the same thing over and over? He never stopped to think about changing, maybe trying to leave or just starting a new book. He drove himself crazy trying the same thing and failing, until all he was typing was 'all work and no play make Jack a dull boy' over and over. By the time it came to that, it was too late, he was doomed, Scatman Crothers was his son's role model, and nothing would ever be the same again."

She shrugged, as if the meaning of all of this was obvious and needed no further explanation. She picked up her notebook and started flipping pages.

"Now, can we get back to the Structure and Function notes? I'm really lost."

I was lost too, because I had no idea how I could connect my life to her interpretation of *The Shining*, unless she was telling me not to move to a mountain lodge without at least doing some research. But Chico had moved on, so I motioned to the server for another coffee and opened my own notes.

Later, I finally got what Chico was trying to say. If Plan A isn't working, you have two choices: move on to Plan B, C, or D, or drive yourself insane trying and failing at Plan A. My Plan A had always been to decide what I thought was right, and to fit myself and everyone around me into that mold. Chico was telling me that Plan A might not always be the best choice, and failure was more about refusing to change to a new plan when the first doesn't work.

I didn't know what my Plan B would be, but I promised myself that I'd at least give it a try. All work and no play makes Jack a dull boy.

∼∾⊙

That semester, Angela's break from UIC and my spring break coincided. She had been working hard, taking five classes in order to finish her bachelor's degree, and her parents wanted to reward her with a vacation.

"They want to take me and Jamie on a cruise to Mexico, just for the week," she told me over the phone. "They said they'll watch Jamie while I relax a little. You don't mind, do you?"

I knew I would miss my son, since we hadn't spent a week apart since he was born. But when I thought about it, I realized I could use a break myself.

"Of course not—it sounds like a fun trip. You've been working really hard."

"So have you. Actually, you could use a break, too. I could tell my parents that you have to come, too—we're like a package deal," she blurted.

We both paused, imagining the five of us on vacation together. Angela's parents had shifted from complete dislike to vague tolerance when it came to me. I figured that by the time Jamie went to elementary school, they might have moved all the way up to begrudging acceptance, which was all I really hoped for. So a vacation together seemed a bit ambitious.

"Umm, I think we'd all be happier if I stayed back home," I said diplomatically.

Angela laughed. "You're right. My parents aren't exactly easy to get along with."

"And hey, I can relax right here at home, watch some college basketball, root for our alma mater. Just make sure to bring back my boy—don't let your parents try to keep him in Mexico."

"Oh, don't worry. My father hates Mexicans," she teased. "Happy spring break, El."

Rob went home to San Diego for the week of spring break, so Chico and I were left on our own. It had been a rough winter that year, snowing almost every week until February, when a brutal cold invaded the city. Walking anywhere was out of the question because no matter how much we bundled up, the wind found any exposed skin and froze into solid, making my nose feel as if it was filled with ice.

"I think my eyeballs are actually frozen," Chico called to me over the howl of the wind one day when we ventured out for coffee the first morning of our break. It was a bright, clear Saturday morning, one of those deceptive winter days that looks so appealing from inside. The sky was pure cerulean and the sun reflecting off the fresh snow made air seem crisp and inviting.

Chico had called me, proposing a walk and coffee to celebrate the break, and I had optimistically agreed after looking out my bedroom window. By the time we met at the coffee shop, her corneas were in a deep freeze, and I wondered whether my fingers would ever be functional again. We ordered and didn't dare take off our coats as we leaned over the steaming cups.

"Great idea, this 'morning walk,' " I complained.

Chico waved me off with a mitten-covered hand. "I thought you men were supposed to be tough. Stop being such a pretty boy."

"That was Rob who claimed to be tough. Not me. We pretty boys like to be pampered," I told her. "Where did you get adult-sized mittens?"

She sniffed as if testing to see if her sinuses still worked after the cold's assault. "Why, so you can mock me? These mittens have Gore-Tex in them. It's why my fingers are fine and you look like you have claws."

"No, I asked so I can get some. What kind of a pretty boy has claws? They might take away my membership in P.B.A.—Pretty Boys of America."

"I would laugh at that, but my lips are petrified."

After arguing over who was colder and several more cups of coffee and a plate of pastries, we decided to retreat to the indoors for the rest of the day.

"Your place or mine?"

Chico considered this. "Well, your place is bigger, but my place is closer and there's a video store on the way. We can rent some movies, get some popcorn and red licorice, and we'll be set for the day."

I glanced at my watch. "You know it's only ten o'clock, right? We just ate a bunch of cheese Danish— can you handle licorice and popcorn, too?"

She pulled her knit hat down low on her head, zipped up her parka and stood up. "I can handle anything, pretty boy. The question is, can *you* handle it?"

I made a big show of pulling on my leather gloves and wrapping my scarf around my neck just so. "I can handle it. Just don't tell the P.B.A."

In the video store, Chico was horrified by my ignorance of classic films.

"You've never even seen the obvious ones? *Casablanca*? *Some Like It Hot*? Anything with Fred and Ginger?"

"No, no and no."

She glared at me. I held up my hands. "Sorry."

Chico stomped off and came back with an armful of old movies. "Your ignorance will not stand, Ellison Emory. Not on my watch."

We spent the entire day in a decadent state of laziness, watching *Butch Cassidy and the Sundance Kid*, *Spartacus*, *In Cold Blood* and *Roman Holiday* while stuffing ourselves with junk food. Around three o'clock, Chico paused *Rear Window* to go into the kitchen. I was lying on her over-stuffed sofa and I dozed off for a few seconds. I was jolted awake when Chico kicked at my feet.

"Wake up! I didn't break out the good stuff for you to sleep through it."

I thought she meant the movie until I pried open one eye and saw her holding a bottle of expensive tequila. I sighed and sat up.

"So now this is turning into a real party?"

She did a little dance, holding the bottle over her head. "That's right. You up for it?"

I yawned and pretended to think about it. "I suppose so. I mean, we are celebrating spring break, right?" I took the bottle from her and peered at the label. "Mexican—perfect. We'll bring Cancun right here to Chicago."

Chico nodded. "Now that's the spirit. I'm going in there to make us some margaritas, which I think the P.B.A. would approve of. When I get back, make room for me on the sofa. We're just getting to the good part in the movie, when he notices the invalid wife is missing."

"Thanks for telling me what happens."

"The movie was made in 1954. I can't help that you've been living under a rock your entire life."

It turned out that Chico didn't just have the one bottle stored away in her cabinet. She had an entire stock of fine liquor.

"My uncle gives me liquor as gifts for every birthday and Christmas," she explained after we'd finished the tequila and moved on to vodka sours. We had run out of movies and we were just sitting on the sofa underneath quilts, listening to music that played softly from speakers all over the room. It was only six o'clock in the evening, but it was already dark and with just a lamp on, the atmosphere was dim and cozy.

"Why?"

"He owns a liquor store." This made us both giggle, and then the giggling made us laugh. And then we couldn't stop laughing at the fact that what we were laughing at wasn't all that funny. It was a contagion of laughter, and we fed off each other until we were holding onto each other and Chico spilled her drink onto her quilt, which made us laugh even more.

When it finally subsided, she tossed her wet blanket aside and wiped her eyes.

"Here, share mine," I offered. She snuggled next to me under the quilt, and suddenly the room was still. I was well into a deep, hazy buzz that heightened my senses. I looked around Chico's tiny living room. She lived in an old house that had been converted into oddly shaped apartments. Her personality was evident in every detail of the room, from the Indian rug covering the scratched wood floors to the black and white photos of all things music related that covered the walls. Her stereo was the most expensive thing in the room, and stacks of CDs and albums shared space with books on her shelves.

At that moment, *Purple Rain* was playing and the staccato rhythm of "Darling Nikki" floated around us. I've always thought that was one of the songs that really proved Prince's genius. If you listen to it without seeing the movie, it just sounds like a song of regret because this Nikki won't commit. She's too involved in partying to really settle down, even though the guy in the song wants her more than anything. But then, you see the movie, and it's a taunt, a metaphor for a woman who isn't what you thought she was. It's like he's spitting in her face through music, trying to make her hurt like he's been hurt. And I've never heard a song that sounded, musically, anything like it. It drags you in with some tame notes at the beginning, and by the end he's screaming, begging Nikki to come back. Then, suddenly, he's spent, and on the record there was the creepy backwards singing.

I was thinking all of this, lost in the music washing over me, drunk from too much fine liquor but not caring. Chico's head was on my shoulder, and her hair smelled faintly of coconut. She looked up at me.

"This was the first album I ever owned. I convinced my mother to buy it for me after I heard the big kids playing it at school," she said quietly. "I was the coolest third-grader at my school because I brought the album cover to school. Remember that cover? Prince, with all that long, curly hair, sitting on a motorcycle, smoke all around him?"

"I remember Apollonia standing in the doorway in the background, wearing a cape and hardly anything else. Kind of racy for a seven-year-old kid."

Chico gave me a lazy smile. "My mother didn't know anything about Prince. If she had, she might have thought twice about letting me buy the album."

I smiled back at her, and our eyes held way longer than was necessary. I wasn't thinking of anything except the realization that at that moment, I wanted nothing more than to kiss Chico. She beat me to it, and our lips met, softly. The kiss was long and slow, and when we parted, I opened my eyes to see the question in Chico's gaze.

My head cleared a little, and I considered her question. Another kiss would no doubt lead us further, and part of me wanted that. Maybe this, I thought, would be Plan B—kissing Chico again, seeing where it led us, not worrying about the consequences. But the other part of me always wanted to think about consequences, and even tequila and vodka couldn't completely silence my logical side. That side said that what made Chico so fun was the element of possibility or the unknown. We were attracted to each other, but we were friends. Maybe that's part of what made our relationship fun—we left the possibilities unexplored.

I opened my mouth to say all that, but Chico stopped me. She shifted her body away from me on the sofa and looked away.

"Let's not. Your life is complicated enough. Let's just chalk this up to tequila and keep being friends, okay?"

"Okay. But don't forget about vodka—it deserves at least some of the blame."

For the first time that day, I thought about Angela and Jamie. I didn't know where things would end up with Angela and I, but couldn't deny that I still had feelings for her. And we'd always be Jamie's parents. Chico and I were friends, good friends, and I didn't want to jeopardize that. Adding sex to the mix wouldn't be fair to any of us, no matter how much I wanted to kiss Chico again, to stay under the quilt with her forever, reveling in the feel of lips and the smell of her hair.

I took a deep breath and stood up. "I should go."

She nodded. "But get a cab. I don't want to have to answer to the P.B.A. if you freeze to death."

At the door, I stopped and turned back. "Thanks, Chico."

"For what? Getting you drunk and then kicking you out into the cold?" she joked.

"For being a real friend."

She pushed me out the door, gently. "Don't get all emotional on me. Call me tomorrow. We'll feed our hangovers with brunch, and I'll take you to get some mittens."

It was Chico who introduced both Rob and me to Chicago's tastiest restaurants all that spring. She made a list of her favorites with codes indicating price, location and whether they were baby-friendly or not.

"You're like a human tour book," I told her. I knew she'd done the whole list from memory and personal knowledge.

"Wait, this all isn't from Fodor's?" Rob was incredulous. "I was sitting here wondering why you didn't just give us the book instead of transcribing everything."

Chico sniffed and put on a pious expression. "Fodor's. Please. I am a native. I know Chicago better than those hacks at Fodor's."

"Maybe you should start a line of your own. Call it 'Chico's,' " I suggested. "You could have a little intro explaining how you got your name, give the whole thing a little character."

Rob and I looked at each and laughed, remembering the story of how she got her name.

Chico glared at us. "Maybe I'll do just that. And when I make my millions, you can believe that there are two *little* people that I will definitely leave behind."

We were sitting at a Lithuanian restaurant on the south side eating homemade sausages and trying to decide whether to order mushroom barley soup or something more adventurous. The place was tiny, just a few tables and white walls decorated with oversized, black and white photos of Baltic Sea harbors, Vilnius churches and the Hill of Crosses near Siauliai. The room was warm and disparate fragrances mingled: pork chops, sautéed vegetables, fried steak, pickled herring and something sweet and wheaty Rob and I couldn't identify.

"Beer ice cream," Chico informed us. "Also known as god's greatest invention next to humans."

"What's a kugeli?" Rob asked.

"Don't be such a nerd. Be adventurous and order something without knowing its exact ingredients," Chico demanded, tempering her words with a smile. "Remember, you're Tough Rob."

"Good point, Chiquito. Tough Rob isn't afraid of foreign foods. It's kugelis for me."

The kids were with us, busying themselves with pounding spoons against the tabletop while they sat in twin high chairs. The owners of the restaurant came by periodically to pinch their cheeks, laugh at the noise they were making and coo to them in Lithuanian. I smiled to myself, thinking that five years ago, I never would have imagined sitting in a child-friendly Lithuanian café with these people who had become like family to me.

Kugelis turned out to be a mixture of bacon, egg, cheese, and hash brown, pureed and then fried in a patty. It was served with apple sauce and sour cream, and when Rob's eyes rolled back into his head at the first taste, I worried for his health.

"Your eyes will stay like that if you keep it up. Didn't your mother ever tell you that?" Chico teased.

Rob moaned. "It would be worth it if I could eat these every day for the rest of my life."

He fed a tiny bit to R.J., and we all laughed when his small son made the same face as his father, then demanded more.

I tried the mushroom barley soup and Jamie discovered a love for sauerkraut that surprised us all.

"Are you sure he's not German?" Rob asked, watching Jamie devour spoonfuls of the cabbage mixture. I shrugged and kept feeding Jamie, who grunted loudly when he was ready for another bite.

"Maybe on Angela's side."

While Rob, Chico and I became close, Angela didn't meet many friends in her classes at the University of Illinois at Chicago.

"It's so big," she complained one night. It was a late night in February, and she was staying at my apartment because it was too late to ride the L back to her parents' place. This happened a lot. We often took care of Jamie together at night, taking advantage of the other one's presence to get a little studying done in between marveling at Jamie's every accomplishment. If it got too late, Angela would stay over, sleeping in my bed while I slept on the sofa.

We never talked about the arrangement, never examined it too closely. I don't think either of us wanted to break the spell of happy companionship that was developing between us. She had kissed me on Christmas, but it wasn't a kiss that promised anything. In any case, I wasn't looking for promises. I knew all too well how those could be broken.

Tonight, we sat on my living room floor, staring at the remnants of take-out Chinese food. It was a Friday, and both of us had been too tired even to watch a movie after Jamie fell asleep. We just lounged on large pillows I kept on the floor, listening to Deborah Cox's latest CD. I had been skeptical about her music choice, but Angela insisted that "Nobody's Supposed to Be Here" was the song that perfectly fit her mood.

"There are 25,000 students there. At Duke, it felt like everybody knew each other. At least the black people. I never thought I'd say that there were too many black people at a college, but it just makes it so hard to get to know anyone. They all have these cliques and things, it's impossible to get to know anyone without the whole 'where do you belong' conversation."

I took her hand and held it. "When we moved to Durham after my mother died, something like that happened to me. I went to a private Catholic school with mostly white kids, and I was special there, but I'd known those kids since kindergarten, so I also belonged. When I went to Durham, all the kids were black, and suddenly I wasn't black enough. It's not exactly like what you're describing, but I think the feelings are the same."

This was the most I'd ever told Angela, or anyone, about the time just after my mother died. The only person I had been able to trust before now was Maren. She had been the only other person who understood.

Angela squeezed my hand. "So how did you get over it?"

I looked away. "I didn't. I guess that's why I'm telling you this. You can't worry so much about fitting in, or finding a place. You'll find a place where you belong— maybe at this school, but maybe not. Keep it in perspective—you'll only be here a semester. Then, you'll be off onto something different. Graduate school, a Ph.D., teaching. Whatever you want, you can do. This is just a blip."

I wished someone had told me this when I was seventeen. But there was no one who was close enough to me to talk to me about this kind of thing except my father, and I wouldn't have listened to him even if he had tried.

I could feel Angela's eyes on my face, so I finally turned back to her. I hesitated, not wanting her pity. But when I looked into her eyes, all I saw was caring. Not passion, not lust, just simple affection.

"Thanks, Ellison."

I shrugged. "I only have my own experience—I don't have the answers for anyone else."

She held up her hand. "You helped me, and you opened up to me. So just accept my thanks."

I bowed my head. "You're welcome."

I thought she would change the subject to put us on more comfortable ground. The CD changer was now playing Macy Gray's *On How Life Is*—my choice for the evening.

"It seems like it's been easy for you since you've been back in Chicago. You found Rob and Chico right away," she said. "I've been kind of jealous of the friendship you all share."

I considered this. "We didn't mean to exclude you."

"That's not what I meant. I just meant, I wish it was so easy for me to make friends. I feel like it's always a struggle to find people who really get me."

I nodded. "You know what? I feel the same way. It's just that Chico and Rob were some kid of fluke. We happened to meet and we just clicked." After a pause, I added, "I always thought making friends came easily to you, actually."

We both laughed. "Well, I guess we're learning something new about each other after all we've been through," she said.

There didn't seem to be anything else to say, so we sat quietly, listening to Macy Gray's scratchy voice singing "I Try."

CHAPTER 18

Spring 2000

One of the ways Angela and I reconnected was through cooking. More precisely, I couldn't cook at all, and she taught me.

"How is it possible that you can't cook anything?"

I thought about my mother, who may have known how to cook but chose not to. Maren and I grew up on takeout, first with our mother, then, when she was working so much, on our own. While my father did like to cook, by the time we lived together I spent all my energy avoiding him and anything he liked. When I was a teenager, I would have liked it if he offered to teach me to cook so I could make a snide comment as I turned him down.

"I don't exactly come from a family of cooks who sit around passing on recipes and techniques." And I was happy to keep it that way.

"Well, we're going to change that. What if Jamie wants Thai food, or even a simple bowl of pasta with lemon sauce?"

"Since when do kids like pasta with lemon sauce, or Thai food, outside of Thailand?"

Despite my skepticism, we ended up in a suburban Target one Sunday afternoon in late March, buying sturdy but inexpensive cookware for my apartment. Teaching me to cook had become one of Angela's projects, and when she focused on a project, there was no distracting her.

"I don't think I need a cookie sheet," I told her. "Cookies aren't even good for you. Let's decide right now, Jamie won't ever eat cookies."

She ignored me and put two cookies sheets in the cart. We also bought knives, serving utensils, silverware and a full set of dishes to replace the hodgepodge of single pieces I kept in my kitchen.

"What's wrong with plastic forks? Less to wash, I say," I suggested.

Angela gave me a sour look. "Grow up, Ellison. We're not going to raise our son on disposable utensils."

I tried to goad her as we waited to check out, thinking it might distract her from her mission. "Now you sound like your mother."

She didn't take the bait. "Nice try, insulting me. If I sound like Mother, maybe it's because all your new kitchenware is her treat."

I raised my eyebrows. "Your mother is paying for all this? Why would she do that?"

Angela swiped her mother's credit card and grinned at me. "She wouldn't pay for it if she knew. She gave me the card for emergencies. I think your complete ineptitude in the kitchen qualifies."

Back at my apartment, Angela pulled the thickest cookbook I'd ever seen from her bag.

"*The Joy of Cooking*? Isn't that an oxymoron?"

Angela laid the book down on the table and pressed her palm flat on the cover, almost caressing it as if it was a holy document.

"This is the bible of cooking. Anything you want to know about cooking, you can find it in here. My mother gave this to me when I was twelve years old and she started teaching me to cook."

I wanted to laugh but Angela's face was completely serious. So I put on a solemn look and asked, "What if you don't want to know anything about cooking? Can you just chuck it in the garbage and order Chinese?"

I knew I had gone too far when Angela's glare felt as if it heated the entire room. She stepped close to me in a way that made me want to take two steps backward.

"Ellison, this is important to me, and to our son," she hissed, pointing a small finger at the spot in between my eyes. I wanted to point out that Jamie probably didn't care, since he was only ten months old, but I wisely kept silent. "I'm going to the bathroom. When I get back, you need to have a whole new attitude about this. Or else."

She stomped off. I decided I didn't want to know what "or else" involved, so I picked up *The Joy of Cooking* and thought of a random question about cooking. It didn't take me long to find the answer: sweetbreads are not, in fact, brains, as many people believe; instead, they are the thymus or pancreatic glands of young animals. Good to know.

When Angela returned, I put on my biggest smile, told her what I had learned about sweetbreads, and promised to learn to cook. She looked pleased, and I didn't even flinch when she pulled matching aprons out of her bag and instructed me to put mine on.

"Maybe I'll even make you dinner sometime," I offered.

"Sure—as long as it's not sweetbreads."

My classmates all seemed to have known their specialties since the day they were born. Plastic surgery. Pediatrics. Forensic pathology. Epidemiology. I have no idea what I wanted to specialize in. There was no official pressure to choose yet, but from the moment we stepped on campus, hundreds of other first-year medical students were positioning themselves for research internships, grants and future careers. It hadn't even occurred to me that I needed to be doing this sort of thing, especially not before I'd even taken my first class.

When I finally checked my first-semester grades, I saw that I got two B minuses and two C pluses. Not exactly what I'd been hoping for, but probably better than I deserved. Instead of getting down about the grades, I had adopted Angela's fresh start theory of the year 2000. The old Ellison was still here, but the new Ellison could handle things the old one couldn't. I was a father, I'd survived, if not thrived, in my first semester of medical school, and I'd done it on my own. Now, I wasn't going to be afraid to ask for help to do better, not just for me, but for Jamie.

I didn't want to be left behind, so I decided I should figure out my specialty, too. I checked out a bunch of books from the library, hoping that something would speak to me. On days when I didn't have classes, I kept Jamie home from daycare. I wanted to spend as much time with him as I could, even though it meant getting no sleep and studying in between feedings and changing diapers.

One afternoon, Jamie fell asleep on my lap after I fed him a bottle. I eased back on the sofa and reached with one hand, slowly, so he wouldn't wake, to the pile of books I kept next to the couch. The one on top was *Healing the Mind: A History of Psychiatry from Antiquity to the Present* by Michael H. Stone. It seemed like a perfect way to put myself to sleep alongside Jamie, so I flipped the book open. I read from Chapter 27 on child psychiatry. "A century ago, for example, 25% of the families in the United States consisted of seven or more persons; today, only 3%. Single-parent households are becoming more and more numerous; fewer children get to spend all of their dependent years in a home containing both parents."

I stopped reading and looked down at Jamie. We had that in common, at least. Things were progressing between me and Angela, but slowly. We decided that she should live with her parents instead of at my apartment, and between Angela, her parents, Maren and me, we made sure Jamie was always with someone who loved him.

Not only did she teach me to cook, but we were also talking again, about books, about movies, about classes. We even talked about the things we had avoided for so long, including Jason. We were talking about Duke one day, and she brought up the first time we met.

"Remember that first party freshman year?"

How could I forget? That was the moment I met Angela and my whole life was shifted onto a new track, although I didn't know it then.

"Jason took me. I didn't know anyone."

She shook her head. "Those guys were a bunch of jerks."

"Who, the guys who lived in the apartment, the basketball players?"

"Yeah, them, and Jason."

We both paused and looked at each other for a moment. We'd never really talked about Jason at all. It was a sore subject that I had thought would best be avoided, perhaps forever. Then, to my surprise, Angela laughed.

"Jason was a big jerk. Huge jerk. The worst one of them all."

"You don't even know the half of it. Remember, I lived with him." Angela's giggling was contagious, making me laugh along with her. And then I thought of Rob and Sasha, and the story of how they met. I didn't know why it had taken me this long to figure out that Jason was my Butch.

Angela and I were certainly on good terms, but I wasn't sure what that meant or where it might lead. Chico and I talked about it a lot. I often took Jamie with me to the record store while she was working, and we talked in between customers while Jamie bounced in my lap in rhythm with the music.

"How are things with you and Angela?" Chico was spinning an old CD in the reflection the sunlight made coming in the window, and Jamie was mesmerized by the shadows and streaks of light. His smile always reminded me of his mother at her best.

"We're getting along lately. It's like when we first became friends in college; we can talk and laugh together."

Chico nodded. "Are you in love again?"

I shook my head. "I don't know. I'm not sure what that means anymore. I always thought love was this specific feeling, this excitement. But what about the day-to-day? The kind of thing that I felt the summer we spent together isn't really meant to last."

"That's the fantasy version of love. Maybe what you have now is the real thing."

I thought about it. "I just don't know what would be best for Jamie. Should we be together for him, regardless of whether we're really in love or not?"

Chico frowned. "Maybe you wonder that because your parents didn't stay together and you romanticized the idea of living with both of your parents. But my parents stayed together, and most of the time, it didn't even seem as if they liked each other anymore, forget about love."

She was right. I had this idea that my life would have been better if my parents had stayed together. But it would have been different, not necessarily better. Maybe worse.

"When I was a kid, I couldn't figure out why they bothered to stay married, and once I asked my mother," she continued. "My mother told me that they both loved me, and that was enough."

Jamie yelled out "Bop, bop!" and held his arms open, demanding that Chico pick him up. She laughed and took him into her arms. Then she looked over his head at me.

"But it's not enough. Loving your kid isn't enough of a reason to be together. You have to figure out if there's something that holds you and Angela together as a couple, as a man and a woman, not as parents."

I nodded. "We'll always be parents, no matter what. Now we have to decide if we can be together."

<hr>

As Jamie still slept on my lap, I considered my relationship with Angela. It wasn't like that summer at Duke, but it was nice just the same. The way we were together was changing, but maybe we could weather the changes and end up together instead of apart.

I opened the book again.

"These changes have important consequences for child psychiatry, given the often adverse impact of divorce and paternal absence exerted upon children."

I stopped reading here and closed my eyes. Calvin's absence during my childhood was a problem, but then again, so was his presence during my adolescence. Which was more of a problem, I wasn't sure.

Things were changing between me and Calvin as well. Since I had Jamie, I realized that I maybe needed a father, and Jamie needed a grandfather. There was nothing wrong with needing other people.

Jamie sighed and shifted, squeezing his tiny hand into the space between my arm and chest. I smelled the top of his head, that perfect clean baby smell, and brushed my lips over the fuzz there. He was already nine months old, and I knew that the days of him sleeping on my chest were numbered. He was crawling and was more inter-ested in staying awake to explore the world than cuddling with his father. But that was okay, because he was starting to make sounds that sounded like words, and I was pretty sure that one day, he tried to say "Dad."

All I wanted for Jamie was for him to be happy. I wanted to be the kind of father I'd always yearned for, the kind that was *there*, the kind who helped him become a good man. My entire personal life was devoted to Jamie—why shouldn't my career be as well?

I don't really believe in signs from God or fate, but it seemed like Michael H. Stone had just sent me one. It would mean a longer time in school and more studying, a prospect that seemed exhausting at that moment. But I would consider it. Child psychiatry didn't seem like a bad way to go for me. And for Jamie.

I knew that my own future wasn't the only one I had to consider. Jamie wasn't even one year old yet, but we had to start planning for changes. Maren wouldn't be our nanny forever, and he would need to be in some kind of childcare, then preschool. Where could we send him— what place would be good enough for my son? We figured that Jamie could go to daycare with R.J. between the ages of one and three, and after that we needed to find a good preschool. Rob, Angela and I sat down one afternoon to make a list of all the things we needed to consider in finding a school for the boys. While R.J. and Jamie crawled around on the floor in front of us, we created the list from piles of books, internet sites and magazine articles, and we debated which were the most important factors before we came up with our own list of qualities of a good preschool, in no particular order:

The child is allowed to make choices within a structured environment.

The activities focus on social growth, not just academics.

The atmosphere is fun, relaxed and inviting.

Other parents are active and involved (Angela rewrote Rob's suggestion, which read "The other parents aren't jackasses.")

Children are always active and engaged, not just sitting around doing nothing.

Children have access to various activities throughout the day and should not all be doing the same thing at the same time.

Teachers work with individual children, small groups, and the whole group at different times during the day.

The classroom is decorated with children's original artwork (I included this one after remembering how much I liked seeing my work on the classroom walls when I was a kid.)

Children learn numbers and the alphabet in the context of their everyday experiences (Rob and I didn't know what this meant until Angela explained to us that it meant teaching kids to count using carrots and crackers that they got to eat afterward.)

Children have an opportunity to play outside (Rob wanted to add "every day," but we reminded him that we lived in Chicago, not San Diego.)

Teachers read books to children individually or in small groups throughout the day, not just at group story time.

The school must be clean, bright and well maintained inside and out.

Children and their parents look forward to school.

After we finished the list, we were quite pleased with ourselves, sitting silently for a moment as we imagined our sons developing into geniuses because of the solid foundation they had received in a quality preschool program. Rob was the first one to break the spell.

"So, now all we have to do is find this utopia, which will no doubt be free and populated by kids of all nationalities and backgrounds, right?"

We looked at each and laughed. "Okay, so maybe we are expecting a lot," Angela admitted.

I shrugged. "I'm willing to negotiate on the clean floors. Sometimes kids can get a little messy, I get that."

"Magnanimous of you. My point was really that maybe we should be a bit more realistic going into all this. After all, none of us went to a perfect preschool, and look how we turned out," Rob said.

"Brilliant," I said.

"Extremely well-liked by our peers," Angela added.

"Or at least, we're pretty impressed with ourselves," said Rob. "We could put R.J. and Jamie in a cage with chimps and they'd grow up to cure cancer, broker world peace and other awesome stuff."

We looked down at the boys, who seemed to be having a contest to see who could stuff the most wooden blocks in his mouth. So far, the limit was one, since the blocks were large. After they stuffed a block in, they then chattered at each other until one of them gave up, spit out the block and crawled off, the other following.

"Yup, geniuses in the making."

Angela had also been thinking about the future on her own, which I discovered when she came over one night for dinner. It was a Thursday in April, and we'd gotten into the habit of getting together with Rob and RJ to watch *CSI*. Chico refused to watch on the grounds that America was too obsessed with police procedurals for its own good, and she wouldn't be a part of it. Rob watched for the gory parts where they followed the path of a bullet through someone's intestines, reasoning that it would help desensitize him. I watched because I wanted to keep Rob company.

"And you have a crush on Marg Helgenberger," Angela added.

"Well, she wears those tight shirts and her character used to be a stripper," Rob said.

"Exotic dancer," I corrected him.

Angela shook her head. "Men." She turned to Jamie and RJ, who were busy playing on a rug in the next room. "Boys, don't grow up to be like your fathers, ogling women without shame."

RJ looked up, his head titled to the side as if he was taking this advice under consideration. He had the same blond afro as his father, and always seemed to be in deep thought. Jamie yelled "Da!" and threw a block in our direction.

"I think 'Da' means that Mommy is full of it," I said. She stuck out her tongue at me.

After the show, Rob took RJ home. After she put Jamie to bed, Angela came and sat next to me.

"Can we talk?"

My first instinct was to say "no" and leave the room, the apartment, maybe the city. Nothing good can come of that phrase, and in my experience with Angela, her desire to talk had only ended in:

a) a devastating breakup;

b) the announcement that she was pregnant, I was *not* the father and she intended to have an abortion;

c) the revelation that she was, in fact, still pregnant and I *was* the father

Given the evidence, I felt well within reason to be wary of one of Angela's little talks. At least I knew she wasn't pregnant this time. At least, not by me, since we hadn't had sex since the time Jamie was conceived.

My mind raced through the possibilities. She wanted to move far away and take Jamie. She was getting married to someone else who wanted to adopt Jamie. DNA tests had shown I wasn't Jamie's father after all. I couldn't think of anything important enough for the tone she'd taken except things that involved taking Jamie away from me. There was no way I was going to let that happen, and I started to get angry.

But no, I was being unreasonable. Whatever problems Angela and I had, she knew I was a good father to our son. She wasn't a mean person. She wouldn't try to separate me from Jamie. I took a deep breath and tried unsuccessfully to relax my brow. My jaw was still clenched, but I tried to make a joke.

"Uh-oh. Is this where you tell me it's not working out between us?"

She looked away. "Don't mess around. I'm being serious."

I wanted her to hurry and get it over with. Whatever the bad news was, I wished she would just say it and then I could get on with the aftermath.

"I've been wanting to tell you this for a long time, but I always got scared, or the timing wasn't right. You were angry with me for how I handled things between us, and you had every right to be."

Please just say it. Say it. Say it. I turned away from her. She took a deep breath.

"I don't know if you have forgiven me for what I put you through, but I just need to say this, no matter what. I want to be a better person, a more honest person, and this is one way I can do that. I think . . . no, I know. I love you."

I opened my mouth to speak, but nothing came out.

"And I don't just mean because of Jamie, or because of everything we've been through. Or maybe everything we've been through is part of it. I don't know. I just know that I do love you, and I wanted to say it so you would know, too."

I wanted to be able to say the words back to her, to declare my love, and then we would live happily ever after. But it wasn't that simple, and I didn't want to make a mistake by jumping in too fast again.

"Thank you." We both laughed at how formal I sounded. "I mean, it means a lot to me that you told me that. It was a risk, and it shows that you trust me. But I'm not at all sure how I feel. I just need some time to think about things. Okay?"

Angela look disappointed, but she didn't argue. "I was hoping you would declare your love and we'd ride off into the sunset."

"You know, we're more alike than I ever thought. That romantic streak gets in the way of real life."

She nodded. "I know. We need to be adults, for Jamie's sake. So now what?"

I shrugged. "I don't know. But I think it's a good place to start figuring it all out, don't you?"

CHAPTER 19

July 4, 2000

My sister loved fireworks. Every year, she celebrated Independence Day, "oohing" and "ahhing" over the same circular displays of explosives. Some years they threw in an American flag display that lit up the sky, or they changed the pop-pop-pop rhythm to something unexpected, but really, her fascination with pyrotechnics was beyond me.

By the time I was twenty-three, I was completely uninterested in going to see fireworks, which I made perfectly clear in the month leading up to the Fourth of July. I had successfully fought off Maren's attempts to drag me to Grant Park for the enormous display on the eve of the holiday, but she was persistent.

"I thought we could go down to Navy Pier to watch tonight. We'll bring everyone: Angela, Rob, R.J., Chico. It'll be fun—our last outing for the summer."

My sister was in town for another month before she returned to finish her last three semesters at the University of Florida. She had been working the angle that she wouldn't get to spend much more time with me and Jamie, and she wanted to make the most of it.

"Maren, it's only July. We can go on outings for another month." We were sitting at my dining table in the early morning. Both of us liked to get up before Jamie woke, to have a cup of coffee in peace and discuss the day's plans before I left for my part-time research assistant job and she spent the morning caring for Jamie. Angela took over in the afternoons, which Maren spent reading and preparing to feel nostalgic for a place she hadn't left yet.

"But this will be Jamie's first Fourth of July," she wheedled.

"Not really. He was born in June 1999."

"It's his first fully conscious Fourth of July," she went on, undeterred.

Now I started to tease her. "Who can really say when consciousness begins? And you know he won't remember it. Let's just wait until next year."

She shook her head, her face sad. "You're going to deny your son fireworks? What kind of father are you?"

Guilt, she had discovered, can be a powerful motivator, especially for someone whose main goal in life was to be the best father he could be. She knew very well that because of all the trouble Calvin and I had been through, I was determined to give Jamie everything I had always wanted from my own father. And apparently, my sister wasn't above using my determination to get what she wanted: a night of fireworks.

"Ouch, the trump card. Okay, okay, let's go. I wouldn't want Jamie to be victimized by my reluctance to see fireworks. God knows, he'll probably have enough other issues to deal with in therapy when he gets older," I said, holding up my hands in surrender.

Maren clapped her hands together and wiggled in her chair. "I love fireworks!"

"You're such a child. I thought we were doing this for Jamie."

She shrugged. "And me. Don't you want your sister to be happy?"

I took a sip of my coffee. "Fireworks can't bring you happiness. I'm pretty sure someone wise once said that. Deepak Chopra? Also, if you've seen one fireworks display, you've seen them all. I think that one was from Socrates."

Maren smiled at my grumpiness. "Don't be such a skeptic. Don't you remember, when we were little, Mom and Dad used to take us to the fireworks at Grant Park every year? You loved it."

"I did? I don't remember that at all." It was true—I had no recollection of going to fireworks with our parents. But Maren always remembered those sorts of things when I couldn't. I wondered why something so simple, something I had enjoyed as a child, had disappeared from my memory.

"That's because you spend too much time thinking about all the bad stuff, and not enough time remembering that there were some good times, too." Maren held my gaze, and now we weren't just talking about fireworks anymore. I sighed and took her cup to refill it.

"That's why I need you, Mare. You help me put things back into perspective."

"And don't you forget it."

And so we all met at my place and traveled in a caravan to Navy Pier. Rob and Angela pushed the kids in their strollers, exchanging stories about how many times the boys suffered knots on their heads while they learned to walk. Down in the strollers, Jamie and R.J. chatted in some kind of secret baby language, shouting across the sidewalk far past their eight o'clock bedtime. Chico and Maren walked behind them, gossiping about the celebrity magazines they both loved and ignoring me when I mocked them for caring about Winona Ryder and who won *Survivor*.

After a while, I dropped back a few steps and watched them all walking and talking as if they'd known each other forever instead of having met over the past crazy year. It was an unusually cool night for Chicago in July, and with the breeze from the lake I felt a little chill run through me. As we walked toward the pier, I could smell the sugary fragrance of cotton candy and we passed close enough to a vendor's cart to feel the heat of hot dogs broiling on the grill.

Once we arrived, I heard the boys squeal in joy at the sight of the brightly colored Ferris wheel that seemed to extend right up to heaven. We were early for the display but Navy Pier was packed, as it almost always was during the summer months. Usually the crowds of tourists annoyed me, but I couldn't help but laugh at how Jamie said "hi" to everyone who approached and R.J. supplied the "bye-bye" as they passed. When they were older, we would take them up on the Ferris wheel to see the city from above, and I'd show them the life-sized maze that told all about what came before they were born.

We found a spot and made room for our gang. Jamie and R.J. crowded onto Chico and Maren's laps, because they always picked Chico and Maren when there was a choice to be made. Rob sat next to me where he had a direct view of Maren, and from the way he looked at her, it was obvious that he had more than a little crush on her. He caught me watching him and blushed.

"I can't help it," he whispered. "She's great."

I'd known for months that Rob had a crush on Maren but I hadn't said anything. It wasn't my place to protect her—she was twenty-one and had become quite good at fending for herself. Rob was a nice, funny guy who had become the first man I could honestly call a friend. Maybe it was because we were both fathers at a young age, or maybe it was because we saw each other as support instead of competition. Whatever the reasons for our friendship, I couldn't think of anyone I'd trust more with my sister.

"I know she is." I nudged him to let him know that everything was okay. Just at that moment, R.J. decided that he should eat a chunk of Chico's hair. Chico tried to pull it away while R.J. gave a fake frown and bit down harder, and Jamie squawked with laughter.

I shook my head at Rob. "What's wrong with your son?"

He shrugged. "Probably his mother's DNA. At least he's not laughing like a hyena, unlike your kid."

At thirteen months old, Jamie's personality was very well-developed. He had a mouth full of tiny, square teeth that he flashed whenever he wanted to be charming, which was often. He learned early on that with a grin and a tilt of his head, he could get just about anything he wanted. With his chubby cheeks and a head full of loopy curls, Jamie had me, his mother and everyone who knew him at his beck and call. Some might say he was spoiled, a term I don't really like because it implies a kid is ruined forever; after all I've been through, I believe in the power of change, not just for kids, but also for adults. Anyway, I don't think you can spoil a one-year-old kid. If you can't have what you want when you're one, when can you? The world would try to set all sorts of limits on Jamie soon enough.

He was sweet and gentle, a good listener who understood far more than I thought he should at his age, and maybe that made it easier to let him charm us. He didn't whine when he wanted something, because he seemed to have an intuitive knowledge that a smile would get him much farther than a frown. His grouchy moods were rare enough to seem funny rather than frustrating.

Even the husky sound of his voice and the way he struggled to pronounce words fascinated me. He toyed with "Da-Da" before settling on calling me "Poppy." He could say the names of his favorite foods: cheese ("chee"), blueberries ("bloobs") and Cheerios ("seereeios"), but he wouldn't say goodbye, only "hi." I attributed this to his inner compassion, which made him only willing to welcome people rather than send them away. Further evidence of Jamie's cleverness included a special bottom-wiggling dance he did whenever "Bye Bye Bye" by N'Sync came on the radio. No matter how much I discouraged his love of boy bands, nothing made Jamie laugh and dance like that song. At one, he was already a man who stuck to his convictions.

When we weren't rushing from place to place, I liked to take time to catalogue all the things that made Jamie the most brilliant kid alive. I imagine that every father thinks his child is perfect, especially at this age. Thirteen months old is a magical age of discovery, a time when Jamie began to understand the possibilities of his body and mind, and every new experience was a delight.

Sometimes Rob mentioned something from his own list about his son R.J., and I would nod and smile while thinking that although R.J. was cute, he was no match for Jamie. Of course, this was not something I said aloud to Rob. I'm sure Rob also secretly congratulated himself on not gloating about his own child to me. It was what fathers did.

Jamie taught me a lot during his first year. I had always thought that friendship was a choice people made because they liked to talk to a certain someone, or they had similar interests and values. But Jamie and R.J. had loved each other since the moment they became aware of each other as separate beings, right around four months old. When they learned to roll over, it was only so they could face each other and giggle when we put them in the playpen together. Crawling was a way to get close to each other and exchange pacifiers so that none of us could tell whose was whose. Walking facilitated forays into forbidden territories like cabinets and underneath beds, where R.J. would find something to destroy while Jamie laughed and seemed to egg him on. Angela believed that Jamie's first word was "Mama," and Rob and I agreed not to tell her that he had pointed at R.J. and squealed "Jay-Jay" a week before. R.J. returned the favor and only wanted "Jay-Jay" when he was tired or hungry. It would make for an interesting dilemma when they grew older—who would lay claim to the nickname? Or, the way things seemed to be going, maybe they would share the name the way they shared everything else.

"Umm, is anyone going to help me out here?" Chico whined. Rob and I looked at each other.

"No," we said in unison.

Angela jumped up. "Sorry, Chico. Apparently Rob is raising his son as a cannibal."

After Angela freed Chico from R.J.'s grip, Rob shrugged, took R.J. into his arms and turned to Maren to talk. Angela sat next to me and smiled.

"This is nice."

I nodded. We were still figuring out our relationship and we had decided to take things slowly. But I took her hand in mine.

"I'm glad we're here. Together," she said.

I looked around at the group, all the people who had somehow become a part of one big, unconventional family. Rob, Chico, Maren, R.J., Jamie. We had been through so much: deaths, births, divorce. And none of us was older than twenty-four, so there were bound to be more struggles ahead. I felt as if I had everything, but it was balanced very carefully on a wobbly foundation. I supposed I'd have to build that foundation, make it stronger so that it would hold us up, no matter what. I wished for the ability to see the future, to know what would happen to all of us, to know that we'd all find our way in life, together. But as I looked at the faces around me, I thought that maybe knowing the future would take all of the magic out of life.

I looked back at Angela. Her hair blew around her face and her eyes sparkled with the reflection from the bright lights of Navy Pier. She smiled, and for the first time I noticed that she had a tiny dimple in her right cheek. I reached out and touched it with my fingertip.

"Me, too."

We looked at each other for a long moment and then turned our faces to the sky. The fireworks had begun.

The End

ABOUT THE AUTHOR

Africa Fine published her first Genesis Press novel, *Looking for Lily*, in 2008. She earned a master's degrees in English Literature from Florida Atlantic University and bachelor's degrees from Duke University in Public Policy and African American Studies. She is a writing and literature professor in South Florida.

CHAPTER 1

"You don't have to worry, Lara, I won't take advantage of your friend." Norris Converse smiled brightly at the friend in question. Had he not met the gorgeous Dahlia Sinclair on his own two months earlier, he'd be giving his best friend's wife big thanks for sending Dahlia and her business his way. "I'll see you and Ryan later. Bye."

Norris hung up the phone and approached his lovely companion. "Lara's afraid I'm going to disturb your fragile sensibilities." He laughed. "Little does she know."

"Thanks for not saying anything to her." Dahlia smoothed out her skirt, which was slightly wrinkled from their torrid encounter on his desk. "I don't think she'll understand our arrangement," she said, combing her fingers through her short, dark hair.

"Our arrangement?" He pulled her close to him. Her curvy body fit perfectly against his, and at a couple inches shy of his six feet of height, she was a woman he didn't have to strain his neck to kiss. It was like she was made for him. "You mean hot, guilt-free, no-strings sex? What's not to understand? It's my prescription for a full and happy life."

A hint of rouge toasted Dahlia's rich brown cheek. Norris smiled. She probably thought he wouldn't notice her blushing, but he did. He enjoyed teasing her about their arrangement. He enjoyed everything about Dahlia the dazzling divorcee, a fact he found exciting and unsettling. He didn't get this excited about women. They generally came and went. But not Dahlia. And as much as it scared him, he rather liked it.

Agnes, his trusted assistant and surrogate mother since he'd opened his accountancy firm in downtown Denburg, South Carolina, had announced Dahlia and shown her in more than half an hour before. Less than two minutes later, Dahlia lay atop his desk with her glorious long legs wrapped about his waist, moaning her pleasure.

A very proud and illustrious playboy, Norris had never allowed his extra-curricular activities to cross into his business life. To indulge a woman in his workplace was a staunch no-no. At least it used to be. Thinking of what he and Dahlia had just shared aroused him all over again. He pressed up against her. A deep groan rumbled in his throat.

"Uh, uh, uh." Dahlia took a step back. "We need to move on to other things, Norris. This meeting is about my audit."

"You saying we need to get down to business?" He grinned.

"Yes, real business. I wish you would let me pay you."

"I work pro bono, and I'm more than happy to help you."

"And I appreciate it." She walked over to the leather couch and picked up the portfolio she had set down on her way in. "I think I have everything you need."

Norris stared at her as she rifled through the papers. *If only she knew.* He remembered the night they met. Valentine's evening. A holiday, along with Thanksgiving and Christmas, that comprised his no-women days. Those holidays gave women the wrong impressions, and he wasn't trying to dole out false hope. That night, he and Dahlia had both reached for the last copy of *Shrek* in the video rental store. After some silly bantering over who should get the rental, and realizing they knew some of the same people, they wound up watching it together at her place. And before the movie ended, they were in each other's arms.

He hadn't been with another woman since then, and his fascination with Dahlia gave him no desire to be. Her beautiful heart-shaped face, brown eyes, and full lips kept him transfixed, and her impressive business mind was an aphrodisiac in itself. Thoughts of her filled his days and nights, drawing him dangerously close to a line he never wanted to cross.

Norris shook his head. The singing birds and blossoming flowers of springtime must have gone to his head. He didn't do relationships and Dahlia didn't do them anymore. That's how they both wanted it, and that's why they worked so well.

He buttoned his shirt and moved behind his desk. "I know audit is a scary word, but this is for the year after you sold your four day spas, so we only have your one salon to contend with. This should be a breeze."

"I hope so. The last couple of years have been a bit trying. Which might explain this audit." She handed over the portfolio. "This is everything I have, including the returns from that year. When my accountant retired after I sold the spas, I thought I could handle the books. But an audit . . ."

"Try not to worry. The IRS likes to flex its muscles. More often than not it's minor calculation errors or a simple oversight. I'll take a look at all this, see where we stand, and go from there."

"Thanks for your help, Norris." She flashed her beguiling smile. "If you need anything else, don't hesitate to call."

Sensing a hidden meaning in her statement, Norris met her gaze and approached. "The same applies to you," he said.

Dahlia trailed a scarlet-tipped finger down the buttons of his shirt. "I keep trying to tell myself that if nobody knows about our arrangement, it doesn't make me a skank." Her head dropped. "I should know better. My grandma taught me better." She looked deeply into his eyes. "Why don't I feel ashamed?"

Norris's heart pounded. Was Dahlia asking him or herself that question? Could she feel the change their relationship had taken? It wasn't just feel-good sex. It was so much more. He saw something in her eyes. Something that made him want to open up about feelings he never wanted to feel. "Dahlia, I . . ."

A feathery soft finger touched his lips, silencing him. His breath lodged in his throat. Her touch was his undoing.

"I know what it is," she said. "It's the sexy curls in your jet-black hair, and the devilish twinkle in those sparkling gray eyes that render women helpless. Tall, dark . . . Well, at least as dark as your Greek-Anglo ancestry will allow." She laughed. "And handsome." Her fingers brushed his cheek. "You're irresistible, Norris Converse."

"You're irresistible." Norris softly kissed her lips, all too aware he was heading down a slippery slope with no way of stopping himself. "I'll call you."

As Norris opened the door, he stepped into all-business mode for Agnes, who expertly pretended not to be paying attention. The full-figured older woman with flaming red hair and an accent that rivaled Scarlet O'Hara's thought she'd mastered the technique, but Norris had known her too long to fall for it. He suspected she'd probably had her ear to the door a time or two, grinning like a nosy preteen.

"Thank you for coming in, Ms. Sinclair," Norris said, escorting Dahlia to the elevator.

"Thanks for your time, Mr. Converse."

He smiled. "My pleasure."

"You have a good day, Ms. Sinclair," Agnes called out to Dahlia as the elevator doors opened.

Dahlia smiled. "You, too. Good-bye."

Norris approached the circular reception desk when the elevator doors closed. "Any calls for me, Agnes?"

The woman grinned at him. "That was a long meeting."

"She's a friend of Lara's and being audited. A favor."

"What's that red stuff on your lips?"

Norris brushed his fingers against his mouth.

"Gotcha!" said Agnes, her green eyes dancing with joy.

Norris grunted, annoyed at falling for her trick. Dahlia didn't wear lipstick that smeared.

"Why do you have to be so secretive? That one's really got your nose open."

"She does not have my nose open," he said defensively. "Norris's nose is opened to no one."

Agnes laughed. "If you say so." She handed him a pink message sheet. "You had a call from a Dr. Gail Elders."

"Gail Elders?" He hadn't heard that name in seventeen years, but it was one he'd never forget. She was the beautiful older lady who'd had a hand in creating his legendary persona. Norris smiled as he scanned the message. She wanted him to meet her at the hospital. He could do that. "My calendar is clear for the rest of the day, so I'm going to head out a little early."

"I don't think your Ms. Sinclair will like you meeting up with another woman."

Norris considered those words. *If only.* A part of him wished she would care. Sometimes he thought she did. He frowned at Agnes. "Don't you have some papers to file or something?"

"In fact, I do."

"Then you do that. I'll see you on Monday."

Norris spent the short drive back to his condo trying not to think about Dahlia and the way she made him feel. Ryan had given up preaching the merits of monogamy as a much-appreciated birthday present; now, three months into his thirty-seventh year, the subject of his best friend's sermon had become a constant daydream he wouldn't mind making a reality. Even the idea of a little Norris or two running around excited him. Norris grunted. Ryan and his domestic heaven was killing him.

Norris moved through the living room, shedding his clothes as he made his way through his bedroom and to the shower. The steamy spray pelted his tense muscles. How could he feel so incredibly good after spending quality moments with Dahlia, yet feel like his life was the pits?

He shouldn't be miserable. He had more money than he'd ever be able to spend, he was good looking, and women fell at his feet. For years, those things had been enough. Now he wanted more, and he wanted it with Dahlia.

More? Norris stuck his head under the forceful spray. How the hell did this happen, and what was he going to do about it?

"I'm sorry I'm so late, Reese," Dahlia said to her client when she finally made it to her salon. "Where's Diana?" Reese and her best friend were never far apart.

"She's babysitting for the Andrews tonight, and had to take care of a few things beforehand," Reese said, sliding the book she'd been reading into the backpack settled between her ankles.

Dahlia smiled. Diana's cousin Lara and her husband, Ryan, had dinner plans with Norris. *Norris.* Dahlia willed her heart to stop pounding from memories of their salacious encounter. Five fast minutes in a hot shower had washed away his intoxicating masculine scent, but no amount of soap or water could wash away the indelible mark Norris had made on her.

She could still feel the warmth of his skin against hers, the feel of him as he moved inside her, and the tickle of his breath when he dusted her neck with kisses. Dahlia's face grew warm. Her heart raced faster.

"Dahlia, are you sick?"

Dahlia blinked, shaken from her wanton thoughts. "What?"

"You're flushed. If you're under the weather, I can always re-reschedule," Reese said with a strained whimper.

Dahlia laughed at the well-meaning teen. "Fear not, Reese, you won't have to reschedule. I'm not sick." Lovesick, maybe, but she didn't want to think about that. "I'm a little preoccupied, but I'm up to the challenge of making you more beautiful than you already are."

Dahlia smiled at her young customer. A very sweet girl, and the slightest bit vain, Reese's flawless golden brown skin, light eyes, and flowing curls of coal-black hair made her as striking as she was pleasant. Most of Dahlia's clients would give their eyeteeth to have the "good hair" Reese had, but Reese was chomping at the bit to get it cut.

The two had met a year earlier when Dahlia participated in Career Day at the high school. When Reese learned Dahlia had graduated from Columbia University, a school she had aspirations to attend, they developed a friendly mentor/mentee relationship. Their friendship was made stronger when Dahlia realized her childhood Sunday school teacher was Reese's mother.

"C'mon, let's go back to my chair."

Dahlia ushered Reese to the first booth in a row of seven. She had loved styling hair from the time she was six, spending hours on the flowing manes of her baby dolls. Through the vocational program at her high school, she studied cosmetology and received her license, which she put to work when she started at Columbia. A few hours after class and weekends at Sadie's House of Beauty had generated a hefty savings toward the purchase of her first salon. Now she lived her dream, making women look and feel beautiful, while listening to them talk about everything or nothing. She loved it.

Her parents had conniptions when she'd disclosed her plan to open a beauty salon. "Why waste a Columbia MBA in a beauty shop? Dahlia, this is madness!" her father shrieked. But he said scant little when DBS, Dahlia's Beauty Salon, pulled in six figures after three years in operation. And at age thirty-two, with her original hair and nail salon in Denburg and four flourishing full-service day spas across South Carolina, Dahlia had made her first million. Her studies in entrepreneurship didn't go to waste. Unlike her twelve years as a wife.

The devastating end of her marriage prompted the sale of her day spas and forced Dahlia to face single life at thirty-four. The abrupt change in her world led to a year-long sabbatical in St. Thomas—her time in paradise a journey of self-rediscovery. She returned to Denburg a brand new woman and jumped back into the work she loved in the salon that had started it all. Fourteen months later, things were going well.

"Dahlia, I didn't realize you were back." Marci Jackson, the newest, youngest, and most religious of the shop ladies, exited the shampoo room with a client and directed her to the booth next to Dahlia's. "You had a call earlier," she said. "The message is on your desk."

"Do you know who it was?" Dahlia asked.

"She said her name was Leslie."

In what seemed to be a choreographed move, the necks of the five other stylists in the shop snapped to the right, fixing questioning eyes on Dahlia. They didn't know any specifics of her life, but had no trouble piecing their opinions together to form a truth. Dahlia could only imagine what they'd dreamed up about her. Josie, Mae, Rhea, and Tyra were very hard workers, but tended to slip into high alert when it came to "juice," not unlike the fifth and most vocal member of the crew: Ms. Flo.

"You reckon that's your sister?" asked Ms. Flo, the eldest of the group and the busiest busybody of the bunch. Full-figured, caramel-skinned Ms. Flo was a direct contrast to the petite, mahogany-complexioned Marci who read her Bible and tried new coloring techniques on her mannequin in lieu of dishing the dirt on what got done to whom and why. "You haven't heard from her in what? Two years?"

Dahlia said nothing.

"She still in Atlanta?" continued Ms. Flo.

Ignoring the questions, Dahlia draped Reese and escorted her to the shampoo room, leaving Ms. Flo and the four remaining shop ladies, who fell comfortably between gossip hound and Bible hugger, murmuring in her wake about the call and its ramifications.

"Are you okay?" asked Reese. "You seem a bit flustered."

She had been flustered after being with Norris. Heck, just being around him made her feel flustered in a way she'd never thought she would again. Right now she wasn't flustered. Surprised and a bit steamed, but not flustered. "I'm good, Reese," she said.

"I don't know. I've never seen you anything but together, but today you seem a bit distracted. Is it just this Leslie person or is it someone else? Someone with a Y chromosome?"

Dahlia's cheeks grew warm. Was she that obvious?

"Uh-huh. It is a man." Reese giggled.

"All right, Miss Smarty Pants, enough of that," Dahlia playfully chided. "Lie back."

Reese settled her neck into the rest. "Is he nice?"

"I never said there was a he." Dahlia wet Reese's hair. "Too hot?"

"It's perfect," Reese answered. "You didn't have to say it, your expression said it all. He must be nice. He couldn't make you this giddy if he wasn't."

Dahlia blinked. Was she acting giddy? "Was that a romance novel you were reading when I came in?" she asked. "Your mind seems to be on one track right now."

"*The Great Gatsby*. Required reading."

"A classic." Dahlia squeezed some shampoo into her palm. "You enjoying it?"

"Eh." Reese's hand motioned so-so. "Is Leslie your sister?"

Dahlia laughed as she scrubbed Reese's scalp. "I thought business was your thing. You suddenly want to be a reporter?"

"I'm sorry, am I prying?"

"You don't know the answer to that?" Dahlia quipped.

Reese made a hissing sound. "Sorry."

"Don't sweat it. Lucky for you I like you." Dahlia shampooed and rinsed and repeated the action for the next several quiet minutes. "Leslie is my younger sister," she finally confessed as she turned off the water and squeezed the excess from Reese's hair.

"You're not close?"

"Not anymore." She saturated the damp hair with conditioner and slapped on a styling cap. "Let's sit you under the dryer for a few minutes."

As Reese deep-conditioned, Dahlia slipped into her office. What in the world did her sister want?

Norris ignored the smiling women he passed on his way into Denburg Memorial Hospital. Never short of female admirers, he knew one look in their direction would send them flocking over, and he wasn't interested in fighting off advances.

An attractive blonde at the reception desk pointed him in the direction of Gail's office. A couple of months ago, that honey would have been his lunch. She clearly had a serious hankering for him. The way she smiled and licked her lips as if she'd just finished a serving of her favorite dessert said it all. He thanked the receptionist for her help and headed down the curving corridor to office 110. He knocked on the door.

"Come in," said a voice that took him spiraling back over seventeen years.

Norris cracked the door. The soft scent of jasmine erased the pungent smell of hospital antiseptic. Gail loved jasmine. He remembered she always had the scented candles burning at her home. Norris peeked around the door to find the lady behind her desk looking as beautiful as ever. "Dr. Gail."

"Norris." She approached him with open arms.

He returned her warm embrace. "It's been a long time."

"Too long." Gail took a step back. "Look at you. Just as handsome as ever."

"And you're just as stunning. More." Her flawless dark skin was as supple as ever, and her warm brown eyes still sparkled like two bright diamonds. "You never did share directions to the fountain of youth."

"No directions, just a fact of nature. Good black don't crack." She laughed, returning to her chair.

Norris chuckled with her. She used to always say that. "My first taste of forbidden fruit." He took the seat in front of her desk. "That's what you called yourself."

"I was, wasn't I?"

"Depends on what you call forbidden. I'm aware and have always appreciated the many beautiful hues of the world, but your race didn't make you forbidden. The fact you were thirty-five and I was twenty is a different story."

"The old lady and the stud."

"You weren't old, and I wasn't a stud. At least not until you got finished with me." He smiled. "I had some great times with you. I was a little hurt when you disappeared."

"I thought it was for the best."

"Maybe." He brushed his hands against his thigh. "It's been a lot of years. What prompted the call?"

She tucked a wisp of black hair behind her ear. "I think that can wait a few minutes. I want to hear about you. I know you're an accountant."

"I have my own firm downtown, but you already know that. How long have you been back in Denburg?"

"Just over a year. I missed it here."

"Where did you go?"

"New York. Long Island. I wanted to spend some time with my parents. They were up in age, and both very sick. They died a few months after I moved back."

"I'm sorry to hear that, Gail."

"Thank you. It was very tough for a while. I was their miracle baby. They were from big families and wanted a big family, but had a hard time conceiving. There weren't a lot of options back then, but when all hope was lost, along came me. Mom was forty-three." She expelled a breath. "How did we get on me? I was asking about you. What's new in your life?"

Norris smiled. *What was new? Dahlia, Dahlia, and more Dahlia.* "You know me," he said.

"I do. That's why I'm wondering. You got tired of it yet?"

"It?"

"That playboy lifestyle. Back in the day, I could tell you had a lot of living inside of you dying to be lived. But I also knew that need wouldn't last forever." She clasped her hands together and perched them on her desk. *"Your blond, blue-eyed friend. Your shadow, uhm . . ."* She snapped her fingers.

"Ryan?" Norris offered.

"Yes. Ryan. How is he?"

"Wonderful." Norris laughed, pulling out his wallet and a snapshot of his best friend with his family. "Expecting twins."

Gail gazed wide-eyed at the photo. "His wife's black."

Norris gasped. "She is?" He laughed at Gail's half-hearted scowl. "Ryan lost his first wife eight years ago, but after three years of mourning, he and Justin found Lara, and she's fantastic. They've been happily married over four years."

"What a beautiful little girl they have."

"Sweet Angelica." Norris smiled with thoughts of his precious goddaughter. "She's incredible. A little heart-breaker." He returned the photo to his wallet. "I feel like a proud grandparent pulling out this picture. I don't know what's happening to me."

"It's endearing, Norris. You've changed so much. A good change. Not that you were a bad person before. You've just . . ."

"Grown up?" He shrugged. "It was bound to happen."

"I guess so. You have snaps of your own little ones?"

"Can't take photos of what you don't have. No wife or kids."

"You don't want children?"

"Well . . ." He tilted his head from side to side. "A thought has passed through my mind a time or two. What about you? You ever find the right guy and have kids?"

"Yes and no."

"Sounds like a story."

"It is quite a story. And somewhat involved."

Norris crossed his legs, getting comfortable in the chair. "Let's hear it. I'm not going anywhere."

Gail sighed. "Hmm. I honestly don't know where to start."

"The beginning is always good."

She nodded. "All right, the beginning. When you walked into the ER with your severely sprained wrist, I was at a crossroads in my life. You were young and flirtatious, and I took advantage of you, and I'm sorry."

"You didn't take advantage. I was a willing participant."

"I know, and that's how I took advantage. I wanted something from you, Norris, and when I got it, I left. No good-bye and no explanation."

"We weren't in a relationship. Not a real one. You didn't take anything I didn't give. It was six great weeks. I would have liked a good-bye, but I don't have any regrets. Is that why you called me over? To apologize?"

"No. I'm—I'm not sorry about what we shared. That time with you gave me the biggest thrill of my life."

Norris laughed. "I fancy myself a thrill-giver, so I'm glad to have your joy confirmed. But, honestly, Gail, any thrill I gave you was equaled by the one you gave me. That was an incredible time for me."

"Me, too. And you did give me joy, Norris, so much joy, and that's what I need to tell you about." Gail closed her eyes for a long moment, drawing a deep breath.

Norris watched her closely, curiously. Though it had been years, he couldn't recall ever seeing her at a loss for words. It made him nervous. "Gail, what do you need to tell me?"

"I think it might be easier to show you."

Gail turned the picture frame on her desk in his direction. A beautiful, smiling young woman with flowing curls of dark hair and the golden skin promised by tanning lotion companies stared back at him. Norris held the picture closer. The girl had light eyes. Gray eyes. His heart leapt to his throat. "Gail?"

"I was an only child, Norris. Before I left Denburg, I thought long and hard about how it would feel to be all alone, and I didn't like it. I had my cousins, but it wasn't the same. I wanted my own family, and when you walked into my ER, I saw a way to get it with no ties. You didn't see my seduction coming, but by the time I was done, I had what I wanted. I had your baby, Norris. You have a sixteen-year-old daughter."

2009 Reprint Mass Market Titles

January

I'm Gonna Make You Love Me
Gwyneth Bolton
ISBN-13: 978-1-58571-294-6
$6.99

Shades of Desire
Monica White
ISBN-13: 978-1-58571-292-2
$6.99

February

A Love of Her Own
Cheris Hodges
ISBN-13: 978-1-58571-293-9
$6.99

Color of Trouble
Dyanne Davis
ISBN-13: 978-1-58571-294-6
$6.99

March

Twist of Fate
Beverly Clark
ISBN-13: 978-1-58571-295-3
$6.99

Chances
Pamela Leigh Starr
ISBN-13: 978-1-58571-296-0
$6.99

April

Sinful Intentions
Crystal Rhodes
ISBN-13: 978-1-585712-297-7
$6.99

Rock Star
Roslyn Hardy Holcomb
ISBN-13: 978-1-58571-298-4
$6.99

May

Paths of Fire
T.T. Henderson
ISBN-13: 978-1-58571-343-1
$6.99

Caught Up in the Rapture
Lisa Riley
ISBN-13: 978-1-58571-344-8
$6.99

June

Reckless Surrender
Rochelle Alers
ISBN-13: 978-1-58571-345-5
$6.99

No Ordinary Love
Angela Weaver
ISBN-13: 978-1-58571-346-2
$6.99

2009 Reprint Mass Market Titles (continued)

July

Intentional Mistakes
Michele Sudler
ISBN-13: 978-1-58571-347-9
$6.99

It's In His Kiss
Reon Carter
ISBN-13: 978-1-58571-348-6
$6.99

August

Unfinished Love Affair
Barbara Keaton
ISBN-13: 978-1-58571-349-3
$6.99

A Perfect Place to Pray
I.L Goodwin
ISBN-13: 978-1-58571-299-1
$6.99

September

Love in High Gear
Charlotte Roy
ISBN-13: 978-1-58571-355-4
$6.99

Ebony Eyes
Kei Swanson
ISBN-13: 978-1-58571-356-1
$6.99

October

Midnight Clear, Part I
Leslie Esdale/Carmen Green
ISBN-13: 978-1-58571-357-8
$6.99

Midnight Clear, Part II
Gwynne Forster/Monica
Jackson
ISBN-13: 978-1-58571-358-5
$6.99

November

Midnight Peril
Vicki Andrews
ISBN-13: 978-1-58571-359-2
$6.99

One Day At A Time
Bella McFarland
ISBN-13: 978-1-58571-360-8
$6.99

December

Just An Affair
Eugenia O'Neal
ISBN-13: 978-1-58571-361-5
$6.99

Shades of Brown
Denise Becker
ISBN-13: 978-1-58571-362-2
$6.99

2009 New Mass Market Titles

January

Singing A Song...
Crystal Rhodes
ISBN-13: 978-1-58571-283-0
$6.99

Look Both Ways
Joan Early
ISBN-13: 978-1-58571-284-7
$6.99

February

Six O'Clock
Katrina Spencer
ISBN-13: 978-1-58571-285-4
$6.99

Red Sky
Renee Alexis
ISBN-13: 978-1-58571-286-1
$6.99

March

Anything But Love
Celya Bowers
ISBN-13: 978-1-58571-287-8
$6.99

Tempting Faith
Crystal Hubbard
ISBN-13: 978-1-58571-288-5
$6.99

April

If I Were Your Woman
La Connie Taylor-Jones
ISBN-13: 978-1-58571-289-2
$6.99

Best Of Luck Elsewhere
Trisha Haddad
ISBN-13: 978-1-58571-290-8
$6.99

May

All I'll Ever Need
Mildred Riley
ISBN-13: 978-1-58571-335-6
$6.99

A Place Like Home
Alicia Wiggins
ISBN-13: 978-1-58571-336-3
$6.99

June

Best Foot Forward
Michele Sudler
ISBN-13: 978-1-58571-337-0
$6.99

It's In the Rhythm
Sammie Ward
ISBN-13: 978-1-58571-338-7
$6.99

2009 New Mass Market Titles (continued)

July

Checks and Balances
Elaine Sims
ISBN-13: 978-1-58571-339-4
$6.99

Save Me
Africa Fine
ISBN-13: 978-1-58571-340-0
$6.99

August

When Lightening Strikes
Michele Cameron
ISBN-13: 978-1-58571-369-1
$6.99

Blindsided
Tammy Williams
ISBN-13: 978-1-58571-342-4
$6.99

September

2 Good
Celya Bowers
ISBN-13: 978-1-58571-350-9
$6.99

Waiting for Mr. Darcy
Chamein Canton
ISBN-13: 978-1-58571-351-6
$6.99

October

Fireflies
Joan Early
ISBN-13: 978-1-58571-352-3
$6.99

Frost On My Window
Angela Weaver
ISBN-13: 978-1-58571-353-0
$6.99

November

Waiting in the Shadows
Michele Sudler
ISBN-13: 978-1-58571-364-6
$6.99

Fixin' Tyrone
Keith Walker
ISBN-13: 978-1-58571-365-3
$6.99

December

Dream Keeper
Gail McFarland
ISBN-13: 978-1-58571-366-0
$6.99

Another Memory
Pamela Ridley
ISBN-13: 978-1-58571-367-7
$6.99

Other Genesis Press, Inc. Titles

A Dangerous Deception	J.M. Jeffries	$8.95
A Dangerous Love	J.M. Jeffries	$8.95
A Dangerous Obsession	J.M. Jeffries	$8.95
A Drummer's Beat to Mend	Kei Swanson	$9.95
A Happy Life	Charlotte Harris	$9.95
A Heart's Awakening	Veronica Parker	$9.95
A Lark on the Wing	Phyliss Hamilton	$9.95
A Love of Her Own	Cheris F. Hodges	$9.95
A Love to Cherish	Beverly Clark	$8.95
A Risk of Rain	Dar Tomlinson	$8.95
A Taste of Temptation	Reneé Alexis	$9.95
A Twist of Fate	Beverly Clark	$8.95
A Voice Behind Thunder	Carrie Elizabeth Greene	$6.99
A Will to Love	Angie Daniels	$9.95
Acquisitions	Kimberley White	$8.95
Across	Carol Payne	$12.95
After the Vows	Leslie Esdaile	$10.95
(Summer Anthology)	T.T. Henderson	
	Jacqueline Thomas	
Again My Love	Kayla Perrin	$10.95
Against the Wind	Gwynne Forster	$8.95
All I Ask	Barbara Keaton	$8.95
Always You	Crystal Hubbard	$6.99
Ambrosia	T.T. Henderson	$8.95
An Unfinished Love Affair	Barbara Keaton	$8.95
And Then Came You	Dorothy Elizabeth Love	$8.95
Angel's Paradise	Janice Angelique	$9.95
At Last	Lisa G. Riley	$8.95
Best of Friends	Natalie Dunbar	$8.95
Beyond the Rapture	Beverly Clark	$9.95
Blame It On Paradise	Crystal Hubbard	$6.99
Blaze	Barbara Keaton	$9.95
Bliss, Inc.	Chamein Canton	$6.99
Blood Lust	J. M. Jeffries	$9.95
Blood Seduction	J.M. Jeffries	$9.95

Other Genesis Press, Inc. Titles (continued)

Other Genesis Press, Inc. Titles (continued)

Ebony Angel	Deatri King-Bey	$9.95
Ebony Butterfly II	Delilah Dawson	$14.95
Echoes of Yesterday	Beverly Clark	$9.95
Eden's Garden	Elizabeth Rose	$8.95
Eve's Prescription	Edwina Martin Arnold	$8.95
Everlastin' Love	Gay G. Gunn	$8.95
Everlasting Moments	Dorothy Elizabeth Love	$8.95
Everything and More	Sinclair Lebeau	$8.95
Everything but Love	Natalie Dunbar	$8.95
Falling	Natalie Dunbar	$9.95
Fate	Pamela Leigh Starr	$8.95
Finding Isabella	A.J. Garrotto	$8.95
Forbidden Quest	Dar Tomlinson	$10.95
Forever Love	Wanda Y. Thomas	$8.95
From the Ashes	Kathleen Suzanne	$8.95
	Jeanne Sumerix	
Gentle Yearning	Rochelle Alers	$10.95
Glory of Love	Sinclair LeBeau	$10.95
Go Gentle into that Good Night	Malcom Boyd	$12.95
Goldengroove	Mary Beth Craft	$16.95
Groove, Bang, and Jive	Steve Cannon	$8.99
Hand in Glove	Andrea Jackson	$9.95
Hard to Love	Kimberley White	$9.95
Hart & Soul	Angie Daniels	$8.95
Heart of the Phoenix	A.C. Arthur	$9.95
Heartbeat	Stephanie Bedwell-Grime	$8.95
Hearts Remember	M. Loui Quezada	$8.95
Hidden Memories	Robin Allen	$10.95
Higher Ground	Leah Latimer	$19.95
Hitler, the War, and the Pope	Ronald Rychiak	$26.95
How to Write a Romance	Kathryn Falk	$18.95
I Married a Reclining Chair	Lisa M. Fuhs	$8.95
I'll Be Your Shelter	Giselle Carmichael	$8.95
I'll Paint a Sun	A.J. Garrotto	$9.95

Other Genesis Press, Inc. Titles (continued)

Other Genesis Press, Inc. Titles (continued)

Meant to Be	Jeanne Sumerix	$8.95
Midnight Clear (Anthology)	Leslie Esdaile	$10.95
	Gwynne Forster	
	Carmen Green	
	Monica Jackson	
Midnight Magic	Gwynne Forster	$8.95
Midnight Peril	Vicki Andrews	$10.95
Misconceptions	Pamela Leigh Starr	$9.95
Moments of Clarity	Michele Cameron	$6.99
Montgomery's Children	Richard Perry	$14.95
Mr Fix-It	Crystal Hubbard	$6.99
My Buffalo Soldier	Barbara B. K. Reeves	$8.95
Naked Soul	Gwynne Forster	$8.95
Never Say Never	Michele Cameron	$6.99
Next to Last Chance	Louisa Dixon	$24.95
No Apologies	Seressia Glass	$8.95
No Commitment Required	Seressia Glass	$8.95
No Regrets	Mildred E. Riley	$8.95
Not His Type	Chamein Canton	$6.99
Nowhere to Run	Gay G. Gunn	$10.95
O Bed! O Breakfast!	Rob Kuehnle	$14.95
Object of His Desire	A. C. Arthur	$8.95
Office Policy	A. C. Arthur	$9.95
Once in a Blue Moon	Dorianne Cole	$9.95
One Day at a Time	Bella McFarland	$8.95
One in A Million	Barbara Keaton	$6.99
One of These Days	Michele Sudler	$9.95
Outside Chance	Louisa Dixon	$24.95
Passion	T.T. Henderson	$10.95
Passion's Blood	Cherif Fortin	$22.95
Passion's Furies	AlTonya Washington	$6.99
Passion's Journey	Wanda Y. Thomas	$8.95
Past Promises	Jahmel West	$8.95
Path of Fire	T.T. Henderson	$8.95
Path of Thorns	Annetta P. Lee	$9.95

Other Genesis Press, Inc. Titles (continued)

Peace Be Still	Colette Haywood	$12.95
Picture Perfect	Reon Carter	$8.95
Playing for Keeps	Stephanie Salinas	$8.95
Pride & Joi	Gay G. Gunn	$8.95
Promises Made	Bernice Layton	$6.99
Promises to Keep	Alicia Wiggins	$8.95
Quiet Storm	Donna Hill	$10.95
Reckless Surrender	Rochelle Alers	$6.95
Red Polka Dot in a World of Plaid	Varian Johnson	$12.95
Reluctant Captive	Joyce Jackson	$8.95
Rendezvous with Fate	Jeanne Sumerix	$8.95
Revelations	Cheris F. Hodges	$8.95
Rivers of the Soul	Leslie Esdaile	$8.95
Rocky Mountain Romance	Kathleen Suzanne	$8.95
Rooms of the Heart	Donna Hill	$8.95
Rough on Rats and Tough on Cats	Chris Parker	$12.95
Secret Library Vol. 1	Nina Sheridan	$18.95
Secret Library Vol. 2	Cassandra Colt	$8.95
Secret Thunder	Annetta P. Lee	$9.95
Shades of Brown	Denise Becker	$8.95
Shades of Desire	Monica White	$8.95
Shadows in the Moonlight	Jeanne Sumerix	$8.95
Sin	Crystal Rhodes	$8.95
Small Whispers	Annetta P. Lee	$6.99
So Amazing	Sinclair LeBeau	$8.95
Somebody's Someone	Sinclair LeBeau	$8.95
Someone to Love	Alicia Wiggins	$8.95
Song in the Park	Martin Brant	$15.95
Soul Eyes	Wayne L. Wilson	$12.95
Soul to Soul	Donna Hill	$8.95
Southern Comfort	J.M. Jeffries	$8.95
Southern Fried Standards	S.R. Maddox	$6.99
Still the Storm	Sharon Robinson	$8.95

Other Genesis Press, Inc. Titles (continued)

Still Waters Run Deep	Leslie Esdaile	$8.95
Stolen Kisses	Dominiqua Douglas	$9.95
Stolen Memories	Michele Sudler	$6.99
Stories to Excite You	Anna Forrest/Divine	$14.95
Storm	Pamela Leigh Starr	$6.99
Subtle Secrets	Wanda Y. Thomas	$8.95
Suddenly You	Crystal Hubbard	$9.95
Sweet Repercussions	Kimberley White	$9.95
Sweet Sensations	Gwyneth Bolton	$9.95
Sweet Tomorrows	Kimberly White	$8.95
Taken by You	Dorothy Elizabeth Love	$9.95
Tattooed Tears	T. T. Henderson	$8.95
The Color Line	Lizzette Grayson Carter	$9.95
The Color of Trouble	Dyanne Davis	$8.95
The Disappearance of Allison Jones	Kayla Perrin	$5.95
The Fires Within	Beverly Clark	$9.95
The Foursome	Celya Bowers	$6.99
The Honey Dipper's Legacy	Pannell-Allen	$14.95
The Joker's Love Tune	Sidney Rickman	$15.95
The Little Pretender	Barbara Cartland	$10.95
The Love We Had	Natalie Dunbar	$8.95
The Man Who Could Fly	Bob & Milana Beamon	$18.95
The Missing Link	Charlyne Dickerson	$8.95
The Mission	Pamela Leigh Starr	$6.99
The More Things Change	Chamein Canton	$6.99
The Perfect Frame	Beverly Clark	$9.95
The Price of Love	Sinclair LeBeau	$8.95
The Smoking Life	Ilene Barth	$29.95
The Words of the Pitcher	Kei Swanson	$8.95
Things Forbidden	Maryam Diaab	$6.99
This Life Isn't Perfect Holla	Sandra Foy	$6.99
Three Doors Down	Michele Sudler	$6.99
Three Wishes	Seressia Glass	$8.95
Ties That Bind	Kathleen Suzanne	$8.95

Other Genesis Press, Inc. Titles (continued)

Order Form

Mail to: Genesis Press, Inc.
P.O. Box 101
Columbus, MS 39703

Name _____
Address _____
City/State _____ Zip _____
Telephone _____

Ship to (if different from above)
Name _____
Address _____
City/State _____ Zip _____
Telephone _____

Credit Card Information
Credit Card # _____ ☐ Visa   ☐ Mastercard
Expiration Date (mm/yy) _____ ☐ AmEx   ☐ Discover

Qty.	Author	Title	Price	Total

Use this order

form, or call

1-888-INDIGO-1

Total for books _____
Shipping and handling:
  $5 first two books,
  $1 each additional book _____
Total S & H _____
Total amount enclosed _____

Mississippi residents add 7% sales tax

GENESIS MOVIE NETWORK

The Indigo Collection

J U L Y   2 0 0 9

Starring: Sean Connery, Wesley Snipes
When: July 3 - July 19
Time Period: Noon to 2AM

An ex-investigator (Sean Connery) with expert knowledge of Japanese customs is called in to help a detective (Wesley Snipes) solve a prostitute's murder. Committed during the height of a corporate gala, the crime was captured on video -- but the evidence has been suspiciously altered. As they work together to solve the case, the unlikely partners uncover a chain of corporate corruption that's nearly as gruesome as the victim's death.

Allied Media Partners
1629 K St., NW, Suite 300, Washington, DC 20006
202-349-5785

GENESIS MOVIE NETWORK

The Indigo Collection

AUGUST/SEPTEMBER 2009

Starring: Usher, Forest Whitaker
When: August 22 - September 6
Time Period: Noon to 2AM

Taps meets The Breakfast Club in the inner city in this late 1990s answer to the Brat Pack flicks of the 1980s (with ex-Brat Packer Judd Nelson in attendance). When an incident with a high school security guard (Forest Whitaker) pushes a decent kid (Usher Raymond) past his breaking point, the boy unites a diverse and troubled student body to take the school hostage until they can make their voices heard.

Allied Media Partners
1629 K St., NW, Suite 300, Washington, DC 20006
202-349-5785